I AM THE ONLY ONE OF MY KIND WHO HAS NOT BEEN DRIVEN TO KILL BY THE BLOOD LUST. . . .

Feeling his unnaturally cool skin next to hers, the fact that he had no body odor that she could detect, that the dark centers of his eyes sometimes narrowed to the point where he looked like something not of this earth. . . .

Zero's body began to tremble. She was afraid to look at him, terrified he would know what she was feeling: He could kill her. In a second. Crush her with his supernatural strength. Suck the lifeblood from her body until she was drained dry.

She was about to bolt when, as if reading her mind, he said, "I would never take you against your will. You mean more to me than even the blood."

"Gripping. . . . *NEAR DEATH* delivers everything you could want in a vampire novel—excitement, intrigue, dark and dangerous sensuality, death and beyond-death, and a clever combination of nineteenth-century 'attitude.'"

— Rick Hautala, author of *Twilight Time* and *Ghost Light*

"Nancy Kilpatrick cuts straight to the heart of the story. *NEAR DEATH* is part hard-boiled, part tender, and always tasty."

— Poppy Z. Brite, author of *Lost Soul* and *Drying Blood*

"Kilpatrick invokes the gothic romanticism of Byron with her vampire hero, but *NEAR DEATH* is full of gritty action in a contemporary world filled with street punks and sadistic drug dealers as well as more ancient enemies. Even the Undead are vividly alive in this book."

— Lois Tilton, author of *Vampire Winter* and *Darkness on the Ice*

Near Death

Nancy Kilpatrick

POCKET BOOKS

New York   London   Toronto   Sydney   Tokyo   Singapore

Excerpts from "The Love Song of J. Alfred Prufrock" and "The Hollow Men" in *Collected Poems 1909–1962* by T. S. Eliot, copyright 1936 by Harcourt Brace & Company, copyright © 1964, 1963 by T. S. Eliot, reprinted by permission of the publisher.

An *Original* Publication of POCKET BOOKS

POCKET BOOKS, a division of Simon & Schuster Inc.
1230 Avenue of the Americas, New York, NY 10020

ISBN: 0-671-88090-X

First Pocket Books printing October 1994

10 9 8 7 6 5 4 3 2 1

POCKET and colophon are registered trademarks of Simon & Schuster Inc.

Cover art by Vince Natale

Printed in the U.S.A.

Acknowledgments

Thanks to the many special people who have generously given me technical, emotional, and spiritual support, including: (the late) Edwin Alexander, Naomi Bennett, Rob Brautigam, Charles L. Grant, Bob Hadji, Eileen James, Eric Kauppinen, Steve Kavalles, Claire Lang, Helen Lightbown, Robyn MacGarva, Ricia Mainhardt, Elizabeth Noton, Peter Reid, Giles Schnierle, Karl Schroeder, Caro Soles, Gary Soles, Jack Vecchio, John Went, Jeannie Youngson, and special thanks to Mike "Killer" Kilpatrick and Rebecca Todd.

Part 1

The lunatic, the lover and the poet
Are of imagination all compact. . . .
—William Shakespeare

Chapter 1

THE RENTED VAUXHALL NOVA LURCHED THROUGH THE rusted wrought-iron gates. It sped up the quarter-mile, single-lane road to the circular driveway and turned right— the wrong way to turn in England.

Behind the wheel a jittery blonde cracked bubble gum and stared wide-eyed at the stately home. She was far enough from the city of Manchester that the headlights of her little car produced a beam under the fading sky. She could see that the place was enormous, two stories of stone spread out over a park-like untended lawn. Behind four white pillars stood an impressive double door. Flanking it right and left were windows; she counted sixteen little panes of glass in each. This was her first time across the Atlantic, only her third trip outside New York City, and, except for the governor's mansion they'd driven past when she and forty other girls had been recruited for a private party in Albany, Zero had never seen anything even remotely like this place.

She switched the ignition off and unzipped her leather jacket. Under the front seat was a black calfskin backpack, and she pulled it out. Inside she found a man's handkerchief, a cotton ball, a teaspoon, a lighter, and a clear plastic syringe with a needle already attached. In a side pocket was a sandwich Baggie of pale brown powder, rolled as fat as a cigar.

After dropping a few pinches of powder onto the spoon and adding Coca-Cola from the can she had been sipping from, Zero flicked on the lighter. Within seconds the combination of heat and Coke dissolved the powder. She used the cotton ball and lay the tip of the hypodermic in the liquid, then quickly withdrew the plunger, sucking up the heroin.

Once her upper arm had been tied off with the handkerchief, she probed the inside of her elbow. At first she couldn't get a vein up, but soon a nub of blue reluctantly bulged against the skin. With well-practiced movements the needle penetrated the vein. Liquid fire roared through her body. As always, the blaze scorched her heart first, then her head. She fell back against the seat sighing, waiting for the flames to singe her limbs.

Time slipped past as the welcome numbness finally anesthetized her soul.

His eyes snapped open to the blackness of the cellar. He had listened as tires crushed gravel. Then to the engine die.

There was only one, at least within the range he could sense.

Oddly, it took nearly thirty minutes for the car door to open and then close.

When her energy coalesced enough for action, Zero untied her arm. She shoved the Baggie firmly down the black leather halter she wore as a top, dropped her purse into the backpack, and tossed the works into the glove compartment. Now she was ready.

She stepped out of the car and adjusted the front of a wide leather belt slung across her hips, hooked together by a jewel-eyed silver lizard devouring its own tail. As she grabbed the backpack through the open door, she checked her *Leave It to Beaver* watch. The little hand was aimed at the Beaver's heart and the large one was dividing his balls. Five hours' difference, the stewardess said. That makes it, what? she thought. Seven-thirty here in Manchester? She didn't bother adjusting the time; she wouldn't be staying long.

She peered in one of the dirty front windows. It was dark inside, so she couldn't see much. Just to be on the safe side, she used the rusted knocker shaped like a thorny-stemmed rose to bang on the massive door. When there was no answer, she went around to the back and got in through a storage shed where the lock was busted.

Inside the kitchen she felt along the wall until she touched a light switch and flipped it. Nothing.

"Great!" she mumbled, rooting in the backpack, finally locating the flashlight and a sheet of paper. She used the beam to reread the note. Instruction number 7 said:

> Search the house, every room, no matter how small, starting from the basement up to the attic. Any door that's locked, including closets, try the skeleton keys. If they don't work, use the crowbar. Remember, you must arrive well *after dark*.

She was too blasted to feel anything more than a flutter of nervousness. Still, she thought, if they weren't making me do this, I sure as hell wouldn't be in this stupid place. She found the door to the basement. Although the sun had set, technically it was not dark yet, but she wasn't about to wait.

One invader, her scents pungent: sweet-copper blood; skin slick with sour fear. And what? A bitter odor he could not place.

Of course, he was not afraid. Simply curious. It made no sense. Surely there must be others. There are always others.

But by fine-focusing his senses, he detected only this woman, making her way steadily if slowly toward him. His curiosity was already laced with anticipation. And that, he knew, would be dangerous. For her.

The stairs to the basement were old and creaky, and Zero's foot slipped through the rotting wood on the third step. "Damn!" she yelled, the light careening around the cavernous room as she lost her balance. She scanned the layers of cobwebs and mounds of dust and dirt with her flashlight. The air was dank, mildewy. All of a sudden her arm stopped in mid-sweep and her heart began pounding hard. The center of the floor was taken up by a large stone coffin.

"Gimme a hit!" she whispered, reaching automatically for the heroin. But the idea of being out here alone, with no help in case she OD'd, was scary. And she wasn't really hungry. When she finished what she had come for, she would treat herself.

Snorting's a waste of good dope, she thought, sprinkling a little of the drug onto her fist. As she sniffed the fine powder, the flashlight fell from her hand and bounced down the steps.

There was already so much heroin cruising her bloodstream that she didn't even get a buzz, but within seconds she had convinced herself she felt calmer. When she reached the bottom of the steps, she picked up the light and cautiously approached the box.

She ran the beam across one end. Inscribed in the stone were the words:

DAVID LYLE HARDWICK
1863–1893

***May God Have Mercy
on the Souls of Poets***

Zero forced herself to the side of the casket and placed everything that she was carrying on top, which left the room eerily lit. Bracing her feet, she shoved the lid with all her might, trying to slide the rough stone off. It was heavy and edged across slowly. Pretty soon she was sweating.

When the lid was as far as she needed to move it, she picked up the flashlight and peered in. "Oh God! This is sick!" she whispered. The body of a man dressed in old-fashioned clothing lay on moldy satin. Wavy below-the-shoulders blond hair framed a sculpted ashen face. Delicate pale hands were folded over his chest in a classical death pose. He did not seem to be breathing, but the note had told her that didn't mean much.

Hands shaking, Zero reached into her bag and pulled out a mallet and a wooden stake. "Man, I can't *do* this," she cried. Through her heroin haze the fear she heard in her voice almost reached her, and almost was too close. She decided another morale-booster wouldn't hurt, and had two quick snorts, dulling the terror before it could crowd her further.

But finally she positioned the sharp point of the stake where she thought his heart might be, raised the hammer and swung.

An icy hand sprang from the coffin and grabbed her by the throat.

As the tools hit the concrete floor, she was forced backward, gasping for breath. The hand was followed by the rest of his body lifting out of the coffin. In the dim arc of the flashlight beam, she caught a glimpse of blazing eyes and a face twisted with rage, like something coming to life out of a nightmare.

Dreaming. I must be dreaming, he thought. She's returned.

But within seconds the stark reality before him solidified. This was not Ariel after all. Still, the girl was as pretty as Ariel. A modern Aphrodite, despite the heavy makeup, David thought. Small, delicate, just like Ariel, with probably a lovely figure beneath all that leather. The colors, corn-silk hair and azure eyes, were definitely not the same. They made her appear soft and feminine.

But there was a not-so-sweet aura about her too, a ragged edge that he couldn't put his finger on, something beyond the fact that she had just tried to slam a thick chunk of hawthorn through his heart. Lord Byron's wry words drifted to mind:

> Perfect she was but as perfection is
> Insipid in this naughty world of ours . . .

He hurled her across the room.

She slammed upright, front first into the stone wall, and spun around like a cornered rat to challenge him. "Bastard!"

As he moved toward her, she looked utterly terrified, although her voice disguised it.

"You better watch yourself, man! Hey, look, take it easy, okay? I got dope. We can party, have a time, ya know? I can make you feel good."

This was what he'd sensed. She was hard, brittle. That made her unpredictable, although no real danger to him. He grabbed her arm. His voice sounded raspy to his own ears; it had been a long time since he had spoken. "Who are you?"

She stared at him as if seeing a monster in a horror movie. He gave her a little shake to jolt her back to reality.

"Name's Zero. Hey, look!" She reached between her breasts and eased out a plastic bag, which she jiggled in his face.

"Smack. Almost pure." She gave him a seductive grin, so obviously phony that it was pathetic. He nearly felt sorry for her. "You're kinda cute," she said. "Yeah, I could make you feel real fine."

David snatched the bag out of her hand and pitched it into a dark corner.

"Hey!" she screamed. "You nuts? That's three grams—fifteen hundred bucks' worth! Know how long I gotta work for that shit?" She swung at his face, slicing skin with razor-sharp nails, and would have drawn blood if there had been any to spare.

He shoved her up against the stones, fighting to control a violent urge. "Why did you try to kill me?"

She glared, shaking her head a little from side to side. Suddenly her leg jackknifed. Her knee narrowly missed his groin.

Without thinking, David, who, despite having committed unspeakable acts, had never struck a human being, shocked himself. He heard the sound of flesh meeting flesh ring through the hollow basement, and realized that his palm had made contact with her cheek. She did not look startled, but he was rattled by what he had just done.

"You've a pretty face," he hissed, struggling to get his

emotions under control. "Much more of this and I don't imagine it will be as attractive." He hoped that would be enough to intimidate her. But all the while he was thinking: She's a masochist, bent on luring me to sadism. And I'm participating. Has Ariel altered me this much?

"Forgive me," he said.

Her eyes filled with contempt, and that made him angry again.

"You pricks are all alike. Well, there's nothing you can serve up I can't take. So fuck you!" This time she landed a solid punch to his solar plexus.

He pulled her wrists behind her back and yanked her across the room backward, worrying that she might enjoy being abused. And he understood his own nature enough to see that he could too easily accommodate such dark fantasies. But despite all that he might be, David had never been a brute, and he had no intention of becoming one. He would find another way of dealing with her.

On the way out of the basement he picked up the backpack.

As she was pulled along backward, Zero noticed that the whole house was dusty, unlived in. What a creepy place, she thought, like a haunted house. She knew she should be frightened, but the fear could not break through the solid barrier the drugs had created. And she was grateful. But that wall wouldn't hold for long. And when it crumbled she would be in major trouble.

The second-floor room he brought her into seemed as if no one had been inside it for half a century. A trail of their footprints followed them across the floor.

He tossed her onto a large four-poster bed. A cloud of dust from the dirty quilt sprang into the air. As she watched him bolt the door and light half a dozen candles, Zero touched her cheek, thinking to herself what a bastard he was. That thought dimmed as she looked around.

Old chairs with blackened doilies over the backs and on the arms sat by the stone fireplace. There were wood tables, all sizes and shapes, some with yellowed lace ruffles around the legs. Pictures in oval frames hung on filthy flowered wallpaper.

The hardwood floor had a large braided carpet covering most of it, the wool too soiled to tell the color. What a pigsty, she thought.

While he examined the contents of her backpack, she examined him. He was rumpled but noble-looking, like somebody from another era caught in a time warp. But a real psycho, she thought. Thinks he's Dracula.

His skin was almost white. His clothes hung like he was anorexic. He looked too serious—a worrier. She'd bet he had looked that way when he was a kid too.

When he finished checking everything out, he checked her out with startling hazel eyes.

"Your identification indicates your name is Kathleen Stevens."

"Everybody calls me Zero," she said with hostility.

"You're from New York." He read from her driver's license, his voice surprisingly gentle. "Twenty-five years of age. Single." He dropped her wallet back into the bag. "And a killer."

Zero laughed. "Takes one to know one, right? What're you, a vegetarian vampire?"

"This note, with these instructions. Who gave it to you?"

She took a deep breath and held it. She would never tell him, no matter what he did to her. I wish I had that H, she thought as he walked to the bed. She tensed, ready for him to hit her again.

"Zero, you have a serious problem." He was trying to sound mean but wasn't quite pulling it off. "Are you so high you don't realize where you are? You've waded in far over your head. Whoever you're protecting is hardly worth what can happen to you."

She jutted her chin out, trying to look tough. Men are always more brutal if you let them see you're afraid, she thought.

"Who sent you?" David felt stymied. He knew he sounded like a gangster from an old movie. But he was ill-prepared for so much resistance from a mortal. Ariel had left him unprepared for much of anything.

This girl was too doped-up to hypnotize. He had no idea how to decipher what this was all about—who had sent her—short of thrashing her, and he certainly had no intention of resorting to that. Enough damage had been done.

She's a pretty thing, he thought, much like a small, timid creature of the forest. He laughed suddenly at his own romanticism. Small and timid! A poisonous spider, he realized.

He had tried to ignore her blood scent, but now it threatened to overwhelm him. A week had gone by since he had last fed.

Unable to stop himself, he yanked her to her feet. Around her throat she wore a black band with a silver fox's head attached. The fox's black jeweled eyes matched the eyes of the lizard on her belt. He ripped the choker away and had his teeth at her jugular before she realized what was happening.

He wanted to break the skin. Hot sweet earthiness flowing beneath it called to him. That warmth would coat his mouth and slide down his throat and expand him, reviving the sparks of life. It was a sensation he never forgot, one he wished could last forever. The blood was the promise that kept him going.

A thought crossed his mind: She may be so stoned she won't remember what I'm doing to her. But this blood was tainted with narcotics; he recognized the odor now; the drug, of course, explained such peculiar behavior. His efficient body could separate the nutrients out and expel the poison, but the heroin would temporarily disorient him, and at the moment he could not afford to be out of control. This blood would not satisfy.

More important, he refused to betray all that he believed in. Submitting to his obsession was debasing enough. If he must feed, and he knew he had no choice, it would be when and how and on whom he chose.

Shaking, he stepped back. His teeth ached to the roots, and his jaw went into spasm. She saw his teeth and a look of total disbelief flooded her face, a look he had seen on so many other faces.

"Who sent you?" he demanded, allowing her a good view, hoping the shock would jolt the truth from her.

She put a hand up to her neck, then took it away. Dry fingers did not reassure her. She stared at him with horror.

"Tell me, Kathleen. Why do you wish to suffer?" He felt stronger for his decision. His facial muscles began to relax and the hunger tearing at his gut subsided a bit. She's lovely, he decided, her colors as delicate and ethereal as those in a painting by Reynolds. Mesmerizing. Like a cobra, he reminded himself.

Suddenly her features shifted again, as though what she had just witnessed had been deleted from her memory. She smiled up at him seductively; he detected something beyond the seductiveness but had no idea what it could be.

She toyed with the buttons on his shirt, rocked her hips against him, gazed into his eyes. Hers were glazed. Before he knew it, warm lips pressured his open. Her tongue plunged deep into his mouth, shocking him. He wondered if she was mad.

She pulled her jacket off and unzipped the vest. Her breasts were full and round, the nipples erect fleshy beads. She moved his hands to them, and the warmth and texture of her skin and the throbbing beneath the surface whetted his appetite. His groin felt heavy and the roof of his mouth dry. Perhaps if I show her affection, encourage her to trust me, she'll come round, he reasoned, half aware that he was rationalizing a reaction as completely inappropriate as what she was doing.

She slipped off her leather pants and boots, then lay down and spread her legs wide. She looked both unprotected and at the same time invulnerable. Obviously she's accustomed to doing this, he realized. Remember, she's a killer, a drug addict, he reminded himself sternly. She wants to destroy me.

But then she was pulling him down, running her hands up under his shirt, undoing his pants.

"You'd best tell me what I want to know," he said, his voice husky, the lack of determination in it blaring.

"Maybe I will." She laughed.

He watched her face, hoping to see vulnerability. But the

image flashed to mind of a sponge, and he realized she was sucking up stimulation without really experiencing what was going on. Yet she seemed to be silently begging for more. And he had the uncomfortable notion that in her head she was berating him for being inadequately assertive.

David moved away to lay on the bed beside her, dazed, feeling manipulated, studying her. She looks as though she's just sampled something that might be to her taste but would definitely not be filling, he thought.

"Let's go back to the basement and get the stuff," she said in a cheerful voice, starting to sit up. "Come on! This's really boring. You don't know how to have a good time. If that's as far as you can get with a fuck, you need a fix worse than me."

He pressed her shoulders down, totally baffled by such lack of emotion.

"Boy, I could use some skag." She shivered, but he suspected it was not because she found him intimidating.

"Who sent you?" His tone darkened.

She giggled in his face. "Baby, you're so *serious*. And you ain't gonna get no answers from me no matter what you do. So why don't we just go back downstairs and try to loosen up. Got any needles around here?"

He sucked in his upper lip and stared at her. She's like a creature out of a William Burroughs novel, he thought. But finally he said, "If I give you the drugs, will you tell me?"

"Sure," she said coyly. She reached toward his groin, but he pushed her hand away.

"Man, are all you vampires so tense? Hey, what's it like being dead? Must be great, huh? No more problems. Will you do it to me?"

"Come along." He pulled her up and out the door.

They found the little bag of powder, and he watched her pour some onto her fist and sniff it, hands trembling. Her pupils, small despite the dim beam of the flashlight, contracted even further to pinpoints.

"Want some?" she offered.

"Who sent you? And where are the others?"

She reached out a hand, her movements slow. "Come'ere, baby. Lemme do you."

He grabbed the bag, holding it just out of her reach, although she wasn't sharp enough to get it anyway. "Nothing else seems to frighten you, perhaps this will. I shall play keeper of the drug and we'll see how long you can do without."

She looked frightened. Finally, he thought, an appropriate emotion. It was an emotion that he would see intensify.

Chapter 2

"SON OF A BITCH! BASTARD! DICKHEAD!"

As David entered the bedroom, the string of dark epithets spewed from the bed, where he had left Kathleen tied by the wrists to the bedpost.

"Jerkoff!" she snarled in his direction.

Her entire body was slick with sweat. He had spent the hours since sunset watching her desperation for heroin expand by the minute. The craving reminded him too much of his own. When he could stand her agony no longer, he had driven into Manchester to see what he could find out. And to feed.

He had been lucky. He found the girl sitting cross-legged on a tombstone in a cemetery. Alone. She wore a tight black dress with a high lace collar and heavy black boots similar in style to those worn by construction workers. New Goth was currently in vogue, he knew, a desperate longing by youth to revive romanticism in a cold, dispassionate world. Unfortunately, many of these neo-romantics exhibited a fascination with death. This girl wasn't the first he'd found at the cemetery. She looked depressed.

"May I join you?" he asked.

"Suit yourself, mate." Her tone was dull, her accent thick

and middle class. From the Midlands, he suspected. Probably working as a nanny.

She turned to find him watching her. Her eyes were dark orbs with dark kohl encircling them. She showed barely a flicker of interest, but what there was he latched on to immediately. He was starving.

Within moments the girl had fallen under his hypnotic spell. He lay her back against the stone and unbuttoned the black pearl buttons running down the lace that acted as a barrier protecting her throat. Her neck was long and slim, the vein forced to stand out as he tilted her head at an angle. He bent over her slim body and inhaled her sweet scent.

His own veins felt shriveled, his bones a skeleton of ice holding up a papier-mâché form. His famished body trembled uncontrollably in anticipation. Everything around him disappeared, even the girl herself. The pulsing blue came into sharp focus. He moved to it as if sucked in by a powerful vortex that could not be withstood. And when his teeth pierced her flesh and the hot river of life swirled over his tongue, his thoughts died and he became only flesh. His shriveled veins plumped with vital fluid. His skeleton warmed, and swelling heat radiated through muscle and turned his skin into living tissue.

Refreshed, he rebuttoned the dress and left her to her dreams. And that was how he knew she would remember him. A mysterious stranger—if only he were real—who had taken her to the brink of ecstasy, breaking up an otherwise painfully dull existence.

Once in the city, he learned that the Vauxhall Nova had been leased over the phone two nights ago, for twenty-four hours only, by a woman identifying herself as Ms. Stevens, from New York. The car would be picked up at the airport office. Yesterday an envelope arrived in the mail with more than enough cash to cover the rental plus mileage and petrol. With the money was a typed, one-sentence note: *One day car rental for Kathleen Stevens.* Unsigned. At the Manchester Airport Hertz office, the clerk who had been on the desk when the keys were picked up remembered Kathleen. Nothing unusual took place. At American Airlines the computer could only confirm that a Kathleen Stevens arrived at Manchester Airport on Flight 503 yesterday afternoon and had a return ticket to Kennedy that must be used within seven days.

Either she had arranged all this by herself, which seemed unlikely, or else whoever was behind it was in Manchester, or had help in England. Clearly they were well-organized.

"Are you ready to reveal who sent you?" he asked, perching on the edge of the four-poster.

"Go fuck yourself!" Her eyes were wild, hysterical, tearing, yet she did not appear to be crying.

"You're going to be rather ill soon, Kathleen. I can expunge your misery. Simply tell me what I wish to know."

"You asshole! I wouldn't tell you the time of day."

"You'll tell me. And I can wait. I'm tremendously patient and have more time than you might imagine."

A little white foam had gathered at the left corner of her mouth. He reached over to wipe it away, and she tried to bite his finger.

"You're a hellcat, aren't you?"

"And you're a faggot, if I ever saw one!"

He laughed as he got up to go sit by the fireplace.

Along the way he took a volume of Byron's poems from a bookshelf, blowing dust off the spine. "Care to hear some poetry?"

"Go to hell!"

He hadn't read anything more than a newspaper headline for twenty years. This particular book of Byron's, one that used to be a favorite, he had not even glanced at since returning to England.

The soft ruby leather was worn in places; the impressions fit his hand.

He opened to the ribbon marker and began to read silently.

'Twas thine own genius gave the final blow,
And helped to plant the wound that laid thee low:
So the struck eagle, stretched upon the plain,
No more through rolling clouds to soar again,
Viewed his own feather on the fatal dart,
And winged the shaft that quivered in his heart.

"Please gimme some? Just a little? Be a good guy."

David picked up a letter that had arrived recently and glanced at the return address, etching it into his memory. As he tapped the edge of the envelope on the table, he looked over at Kathleen. Her eyes were soft, hurt, like a wounded fawn's. But her lips had curled into an ugly sneer. He went back to the book.

> What is the worst of woes that wait on age?
> What stamps the wrinkle deeper on the brow?
> To view each loved one blotted from life's page,
> And be alone on earth, as I am now.

By dawn she was groveling.

"Please. I'll do anything. Anything you want. I give good head. I can fuck you till you're crazy. Anything. Just lemme have some."

He lay the book down. "Tell me who sent you."

Her face and lips were pale. She looked even more fragile, vulnerable. Her voice had grown young, like a little girl's. "Please. Don't ask. I can't tell you that. I would if I could."

"And I'd give you the heroin if I could."

"I'm beggin' you!" She started to cry, again without making a sound. Initially those silent tears had almost broken him. But they were always followed by insults and curses. He waited.

"If you gimme a little, I'll tell you everything you wanna know. I don't even got to shoot. Just a sniff."

Large tears rolled down her temples and onto the pillow, already saturated with sweat and vomit.

"Answers first."

Kathleen clenched her jaw and thrashed around. A sound resembling a growl came out of her, and then, "Scumsucker! I hate your guts, you limp-dicked wimp!"

David reshelved the book and walked to the door. "Feel free to make as much noise as you like. We're very isolated and you won't disturb *my* sleep. I'll rejoin you tomorrow evening—in approximately twelve hours."

"Don't leave me!" she cried desperately as he opened the door. "Please. I need it. I'll talk!"

He stopped. Her stomach was moving in and out, concave and convex, with the intensity of the pain, and he felt pity. "Well?" he finally said.

"It was this other vampire."

"Male or female?"

"Male. Female. Both! Two of 'em."

"Why did they send you?"

"I guess they figured I'd have a better chance of killing you than they would."

"And why is that, since my kind are far stronger than mortals?"

"Why? How should I know? They didn't tell me."

"But they instructed you to arrive well after dark? Yet you came before the sky had darkened fully. . . ."

"Yeah. I was early. Can I have some junk now? I told you everything I know. I'm dyin'."

"Why would they tell you to arrive after dark when it's common knowledge, particularly to those like myself, that vampires, as you call us, wake by night and sleep by day?"

"Huh?" She looked confused, hysterical, her chest heaving, body shaking.

"What rubbish!" He laughed. "I wouldn't recommend a career in poetry. You've very little imagination."

She stared at him as though he were speaking Greek.

At sunset he came into the room looking pale and drawn, but Zero didn't care.

For the last God-knows-how-long her legs had been locked into a fetal position in an attempt to keep the discomfort to a minimum. She could only manage shallow breaths. Her body itched unbelievably and she was starting to see things, unearthly shapes and hideous forms emerging from the wallpaper, things that she knew were not there, or at least she hoped weren't.

The day had been sheer agony, but the knot of pain in her gut, the panic in her brain, and the gritty grating feeling racking her nervous system had only increased.

He said something, but at first she couldn't understand him.

Finally she put together the words. ". . . otherwise it will be another long night and day for you."

"Can I . . . have water?"

He left the room and returned with a tumbler of water. He lifted her head gently so she could drink. His hand was icy. She found it difficult to swallow; her tongue felt fat and swollen, and most of the liquid rolled back out of her mouth.

"Are you ready to answer my questions, Kathleen?"

Zero knew that she couldn't go on. She could hardly speak. She nodded, letting him know she had given up.

He sat by the bed, waiting.

"A guy. Came up to me in a bar."

"Where?"

"Alphabet City."

"And where is that?"

"Lower East Side. Near East Houston."

"His name?"

"Dennis. I heard somebody call him Dennis." Another excruciating ache cracked through her. Zero gathered her knees up even closer to her chest, crying silently, groaning and shaking until the cold finger of death no longer stroked her backbone.

"Please. Gimme just a taste," she begged in a small voice.

"Talk first."

She moaned and felt her lips tremble. But finally she said, "He told me I had to come here. Gave me the plane ticket, money and instructions, and said the car would be waitin'. The backpack was in it."

"Why did he do that, Kathleen?"

"Don't know."

He started to get up.

"Please! I'm not lying." She couldn't tell whether or not he believed her.

"Then what?"

"I came here. You know the rest."

"What else did he give you?"

Suddenly her entire body convulsed. Now she had diarrhea too. The brief spasm left her panting. He's starting to look funny, scary, like something that shouldn't be in this world, she thought. And the very thought increased her panic. She trembled violently.

"What else did he give you, Kathleen?"

"What else? Nothing."

"Didn't he give you the heroin?"

"Yeah. That."

"And who is this Dennis?"

"I seen him around but I never met him. He just came up to me. He knew my name."

As she watched David, she now realized that he was pale and hungry-looking, and for the first time the idea that he could actually be what he claimed to be scared her more than the hallucinations. "Can I have more water?"

He gave her some and then said, "You've answered adequately except for why he wants me extinguished."

"Look, I don't *know* why. He didn't say."

"But you do know why you did as he told you."

Zero prayed for the ceiling to just cave in and crush her to death. But she'd wished for death more than once during the long day, and knew from a lifetime of experience that she was not the type who was likely to be on the receiving end of a miracle.

"Please. Just a hit. Just one. I can't take no more."

Tears fell helplessly from her eyes; she was not surprised that they didn't move him.

"There's more to this than the drugs. You could have simply kept them. How did he persuade you to come here? To kill?"

"You're hard," she said bitterly. "You look like a noodle, but got balls like a diesel driver."

He smiled a little. "Refreshing similes. Perhaps you might be a poet after all."

Her body jerked again, and he waited it out. But as soon as the convulsing subsided, he asked, "How is he blackmailing you?"

"Oh God!" she wailed. Tears gushed from her eyes. "Please! He said he'd kill him if I tell. Don't make me tell!"

But finally a strange calm of self-preservation settled over Zero and she knew beyond any doubt that she was going to tell him everything; she couldn't make it through another hour. And maybe it doesn't matter anymore, she thought, trying to justify the betrayal.

"He's got my kid brother. He said if I didn't come here and stake you, Bobby'd die. That's it. It's all I know. Please! Gimme some skag."

David saw in her eyes that she spoke the truth, as much of the truth as could be expected from the twisted mind of a desperate junkie.

He paced the room. It simply did not make sense. Who would want to kill him? His own kind knew it was impossible, at least the way this had been arranged. And why send a mortal woman? An unreliable addict? And the instructions *after dark?* Those aware that this was his home he had called friend; he could not believe any of them would try to harm him. Who was this Dennis, who knew what he was, where to find him, and yet was so inept?

"Where's the dope? You promised!" she whined.

She's far too pretty to be a dope fiend, he concluded. "I shall do you a tremendous favor. I'm prepared to help you kick your habit, if my recall of the terminology is correct."

Her eyes grew large and round. The capillaries in her face filled, reddening the skin just before she screamed. Her words ran together into gibberish. She thrashed her legs and white foam frothed from between her teeth.

He went to the bed and laid a comforting hand on her contorted, writhing body and another on her forehead. A pink rash peppered her stomach and chest during the ten minutes the convulsion lasted. And when she calmed enough to speak, she screeched, "Asshole! Lying, cocksucking asshole! You promised!"

"No, Kathleen, I never promised I'd give you the drug. I promised I would end your misery. There are only two ways I can accomplish that. I can drain all your blood and you'll die, or I can wait this out with you. I'm going to help you because I'm taking you to New York with me to find this

Dennis, and I want you clear-minded for that. And also because I'm a humanitarian. At least that was the case before I was forced to become a predator."

Wet hairs matted to her forehead. Her glassy eyes looked crazed. The sweat on her body was at the same time slick and gritty. She was pale, weak, vulnerable; pathetic. Near death, even. He was reminded of Byron's painful words, "And if I laugh at any mortal thing/'Tis that I may not weep."

But despite her frailty, still she managed to rouse herself enough to shriek out a robust, "Don't kid yourself about being human, buddy! You're the goddamned son of some sorry bitch goddess!"

Chapter 3

TWO NIGHTS LATER, AFTER HORRIFYING, NIGHTMARISH HALLU-cinations, delirium tremens, hysteria, and agonies that she could hardly believe she had lived through, once the exhausted sun collapsed below the horizon, David finally let her up from the bed. The sheets were encrusted with everything that had recently been inside her.

"I've put two pails of well water in the lavatory," Zero heard him say. "If you like, you may build a fire and heat it. The plumbing's been shut a decade ago."

Her head reeled. She staggered across the room but collapsed before she reached the bathroom door. He picked her up around the waist as if she were light as cotton candy and sat her on the edge of the tub. Dried vomit, urine, and feces caked her skin. She wondered how he could stand the smell when she barely could.

He wedged a cloth into one of her hands, which dangled limply at her side. Her shoulders caved inward and her head hung low. She felt boneless, a lifesize Raggedy Ann, and knew she looked like one too.

After a few minutes she sighed and leaned forward, finding just enough energy to dip the cloth into the cold water. The iciness shocked her and she inhaled sharply. She pressed the cloth to her face and neck and kept repeating the procedure and soon was as clean as possible, under the circumstances. After she rinsed her mouth and squeezed water over her head, she felt a little more alive but not necessarily better. She looked up. He was standing in the doorway, unmoving. She shivered.

"Please dress yourself." He handed her a towel.

When she was dry, she put on her clothes and let him half lead, half carry her to the car. He seat-belted her in as if she were a small child, and she sat stunned while he drove into Manchester. The night looked flat and black to Zero, the sky a mural of dark cardboard flecked with white dots and a not quite round colored-in circle. Just outside the city limits he pulled off onto a well-hidden dirt road. After he tied and gagged her, he locked her in the trunk of the car.

Zero felt nothing. She lay in the darkness dazed, in a mindless, timeless state. Her thoughts were snippets strung together, apparently meaningless. Images superimposed on one another: Bobby, her father, a nameless john she had picked up, David. Each took on the quality of a dream, and she, the dreamer, was ignorant of any connection between the images.

She had no idea how long he had been gone—a minute or a day—but when he returned, his face was flushed and he did not look so gaunt. It was reassuring. What was not reassuring were the flecks of red down the front of his shirt. She struggled to get her mind around what was obviously blood because the idea that he really was a vampire just would not play.

"Behave yourself. I have no desire to harm you," he told her ten minutes later as they entered the car rental office.

She was too deflated from depression and exhaustion to cause trouble. She sat quietly while he returned the car keys and paid for the extra days. She wondered what would happen when they got to New York, if they would find Dennis. She thought about Bobby and felt really sad. And then she thought about how she could score some H. Fast.

At a travel agency down the street David purchased a

one-way ticket to Kennedy for himself and confirmed her seat.

"The airplane departs in two hours. We've time to do some shopping and for you to eat," he said.

"I ain't hungry."

"You'll eat anyway. You haven't had a thing but water for at least four days. Probably longer."

They stopped in a McDonald's and he bought her a Big Mac, a salad, and two drinks. She was dehydrated and sucked all the liquid from one cup immediately, but didn't even unwrap the burger or open the salad container. He nodded at the food.

"Don't want it."

"Come along, then," he said, as though coaxing a stubborn child. "There's a cemetery across the road which is always deserted, at least by the living. I'll feed you by hand, although you may not find eating amidst the dead appetizing. Still, no one will hear you protest."

He stood.

"No, wait! I'll eat. Just gimme time."

He sat down again.

While she choked down a bite of the hamburger and her stomach made a major decision about accepting it, Zero watched him. He was looking around the restaurant as if he had never seen the inside of a McDonald's before. He wore the same shirt, a blousy high-necked number, not too clean, especially with the added crimson stains, blue wool tapered pants, a vest, and old-fashioned shoes with buckles. The double-breasted jacket with the velvet shawl collar had been overdoing it, and she was glad he'd left that behind. His fair hair was washed and neatly combed behind his ears, but it hung well below his broad shoulders. He still looks like somebody out of an old photograph, she thought. Boring.

"How come you think you're a vampire?" He looked back at her, so directly and with such emotion-packed eyes that she felt uncomfortable. She was the one usually giving the direct looks.

"Many people cement reality into place before their first

decade of life. Accepting anything outside a preconceived notion appears difficult, if not impossible."

"What's that mean?"

"I mean that I am what I am, and I exist." He paused, as if searching for the right words to make her understand. "Obviously I am not dead in the usual sense of the word. Crosses and garlic do not repel me. I can see my reflection in mirrors. But my skin and eyes are photosensitive and I require liquids—blood—to survive. The Dracula stories and other vampire myths are largely rubbish. The line dividing fantasy and fact is often a mere wrinkle. It would be best to think of me as belonging to a *Homo sapiens*-like species."

"You been alive since 1860-something?" she asked, sipping the second drink, half trying to make sense out of this information, half humoring him so she could set him up and escape. But she watched him closely. She'd met nut cases before.

His golden-brown eyes softened further. With less of a jaw he could have been a girl. In fact he seemed generally sensitive. But she sensed that, whatever he was, or thought he was, he could be tough.

"I was born in 1863. The first thirty years of my life followed a relatively normal course for one of my class. And predictable. I came down at Cambridge with a first. My parents seemed reasonably pleased with their only offspring. I aspired to be a poet and did publish the odd sonnet, although I suspect, careerwise, a chair on the faculty of a noted university would have been my destiny. But fate, cruel as she can be, intervened."

"How'd you get, you know, like you are?"

He shifted a little, but she noticed. "One evening, while in London, on my return to my hotel from a bout of drinking with an old school chum, I stumbled onto the wrong street at the wrong moment. I was attacked. The creature—fanged, hideous, inhumanly strong—pinned me to the cobblestones. He drew much of my blood before I could begin to utter a cry for help. His face was shrouded in shadow but I shall never forget him. The violence. The madness-streaked features. He could have killed me, should have really, but something perverse in his nature inspired him to force me to consume his blood. For what purpose, I have yet to understand. I, naturally, was overwhelmed by fear and impotent rage. I could do nothing but submit. When I awoke the following night, I was alone and in agonizing pain."

He's definitely la-la, she thought, but asked, "You know this guy?"

"I'd not seen him before nor have I since. I've been as I am now since the year 1893."

"That outfit from then?"

He looked down at his shirt and smiled. She got the feeling he was relieved to change the subject. "This is attire Lord Byron himself would have likely worn—circa the early 1800s. But I purchased it twenty years ago. It was a theatrical costume, but fit well with the 1960s, just as it suited me."

"How come you still wear it? You an ex-hippie or something?" She had managed to swallow three bites of the hamburger and none of the salad. She lay the rest of the Big Mac down and shoved it across the table.

"Eat at least half of that or we dine on the grave of a nineteenth-century painter."

She picked up the burger and examined it. The thought of eating any more made her want to puke, but the fear of eating in a cemetery overcame that urge. She sighed before taking a little bite, chewing it to mush. "So whydaya dress like that?"

"I do not venture out often anymore," he said. "Not for the last few decades. It amuses me to sleep in a coffin and act the role of the Nosferatu. I have quite a romantic streak."

"Sounds perverted," she said, taking another small bite.

He laughed. "Probably." She caught a glimpse of two pointed teeth and blinked in disbelief. I'm still hallucinating, she thought.

When what she ate seemed to satisfy him, they left and caught a taxi. "I require your help," he told her. "As I said, I've been largely disconnected from the world. I need to appear current. Perhaps you will instruct me as to what clothing is in vogue?"

They went into several shops and she helped him pick out two pairs of black leather pants, several black T-shirts, black boots, and a black leather jacket. He examined everything as though he'd rarely been shopping. "You got money for all this?" she asked.

"I've plenty of money."

"Yeah? Like how much?"

"Fifty thousand pounds with me."

"Not in cash?"

"Yes."

"Ain't you never heard of banking machines? Man, you could get mugged."

He laughed, adjusting the short jacket.

He's definitely weird, she decided. *Really* weird. She had never met a guy like him. But then she'd never met a vampire before either. Of course, she didn't believe he *was* a vampire—she'd met a lot of guys who said they were something they weren't. Hell, she'd even met a guy in the Village once who said he changed into a werewolf every full moon; well, he was hairy enough! Besides, David was breathing, so he was alive, just a little pale and old-fashioned. But the new clothes were helping. She realized she wasn't afraid of him anymore. In fact, she felt excited. The whole thing was taking on the feel of an adventure. He's starting to look okay, she decided, even kinda cute.

"Ever wore leather before?" she asked, fingering a peaked leather cap with a silver chain across the brim. "Here!" She tossed him the hat.

He caught it and angled the cap carefully on his head. Then he looked in the mirror. She had no trouble seeing his reflection. "This is similar to my attire of the 1960s, when I owned a Harley-Davidson motorcycle and explored North America."

"*You* had a Hog? I don't believe it."

He curled his lips into an Elvis Presley sneer and she giggled.

"Does everyone in New York wear black leather now?"

"Everybody I know. You oughta shave your head or get a spiked cut. If you wanna find Dennis, you gotta look like you belong to some crowd. And you gotta look tough. You wanna blend in, right? But don't worry. By the time I'm through, you will. Get these too." She handed him mirrored sunglasses and picked out a pair for herself.

She convinced him to cut his hair, and had the airport barber snip the sides short with pointed sideburns. The back was clipped about mid-neck length, and the front so that with gel it spiked a little. Looks more like a guy now, she thought. Tougher.

While they waited in the boarding lounge for the overnight flight, she asked, "What are you gonna do to Dennis?"

"That depends on the extent to which he cooperates. And why he's out to destroy me."

Kathleen looked down at her hands. "And where he's got my brother. You oughta see Bobby. Wait! I got pictures."

She pulled two well-handled black and white snapshots from her wallet, one the blurred image of a little boy and the other showing a younger Kathy holding a child. David flipped the second one over. On the back was written *Bobby and Me* and a date several years ago.

"You can't tell there," she said brightly, "but he's got light brown hair, and eyes like mine. He loves the water. I take him for walks by the river all the time. And is he ever smart! He's only eight but he's already in the fifth grade—they skipped him."

David ran the back of his index finger along the warm, smooth skin of her cheek. He felt hot blood race beneath her skin, which he struggled to ignore. She's holding up fairly well, considering all she's been through, he thought. And she's gone through a lot. There had been moments, dozens of them, when he had almost given her the drug, just because it had been so painful to watch her suffering. But he knew that in the long run it was better for her to be clean. And he would need her help to find Dennis.

And as the withdrawal symptoms had subsided, she was not just looking better, but seemed interesting to him, neither crusty nor breakable, more cemented together.

She stared, large blue eyes wide, reflecting an innocence

that touched his heart. "This guy, Dennis. I don't know him, but I seen him around," she said. "He's tough. He'll try to hurt you."

"Don't concern yourself. I can protect both myself and you."

"He's a big guy. Big muscles."

"My body is structured somewhat differently than a mortal's. I'm far stronger than I appear. And relatively intelligent."

"You look intelligent. I wish I was," she said, her eyes sad. "I tried to finish school, but things came up. I just couldn't do it. I worked for a while, jobs, you know, waitress, salesgirl at Bloomingdale's, cabdriver. But now I got a habit to support. Most of the time I hook." Her eyes showed that she was used to rejection and expected it from him.

"Had a habit," he corrected.

"Yeah, sure." She turned away.

The announcement was made and they boarded. "Don't make me sit by the window," she pleaded.

He ushered her into the window seat anyway.

"Please! I'm scared of planes."

He reached across her and pulled the shade down so that she couldn't see out.

"Won't help. Lemme on the outside. Or at least the middle. I ain't gonna try nothin', I promise."

"Turn toward me," he said. "Look at my eyes."

"Why? You gonna hypnotize me or something? It won't work. Some guy in a show tried it once. He wanted me to bark like a dog but I wouldn't."

She's gone through enough trauma, he thought. Why make her confront another fear? Using the power of suggestion, he verbally fed her calming thoughts that would help her cope with the takeoff and landing. Within half a minute he noticed her shoulders relax and her breathing slow.

A meal with wine was served, which David declined. She tried to pass on hers too, but he insisted she accept the tray.

While she ate, he thought about all the changes that had taken place since the last time he had flown. The planes were larger, faster, and far more comfortable. The meals looked appetizing, although he had never tasted one. He wondered what New York would be like now. It was what, he thought, 1963 when I left?

David remembered vividly those years with André and Karl. His friends had connected him with the modern world, forced him to come to terms with the twentieth century. And with his state.

The three had been so close. From different eras and separate cultures, along with the fact that they had all undergone the change—those things should have kept them at odds. But each had a predilection for beauty and art, and, amazingly, aesthetics had been enough to bind them. That and being committed to truth. They shared the same taste in many of the things that proved important. And for a time they had even shared Ariel.

André was the physical one. He loved sports, was keen on movement. He also understood how to get the most pleasure from the blood. And from a woman. It had been David who nicknamed him "La Corps." Karl, on the other hand, he dubbed "Der Verstand," because he thought clearly and had a passion for precise reasoning. Some of that inclination toward logic had rubbed off on David, for whom thinking had always functioned along more intuitive lines.

And they had affectionately called him "Soul," because he read and wrote poetry, and, he knew, because he exuded strong emotions, often somber. But he was not hated for his sensitive nature. They loved him. And he them. It was a word without sexuality attached to it, which only males from another era seemed capable of understanding.

But we all changed, David thought, and not necessarily for the better. Our strengths became our greatest weaknesses.

André suffered loneliness in a physical way and it tortured him to the point of alienation and brutality. Karl's intellect forced him home to Germany, to his roots. He, like André, longed for another kind of intimacy, if only, in Karl's case, to counter a mind so quick that it began strangling all else within him. And me? David wondered. As usual, it was Byron who best expressed his feelings:

I live not in myself, but I become
Portion of that around me: and to me
High mountains are a feeling, but the hum
Of human cities torture....

I have not loved the world, nor the world me;
I have not flattered its rank breath, nor bowed
To its idolatries a patient knee....
... I stood
Among them, but not of them—in a shroud
Of thoughts which were not their thoughts....

Kathleen broke his gloomy reverie. She pushed up the armrest separating them and curled into a ball, her head in his lap. He moved to the outside seat so she had more room to stretch out. The stewardess had given her a blanket, and she covered her chest and head with it. Within seconds he felt his pants unzip and warm fingers reach inside. David glanced around. The old couple with the Blackpool accents across the aisle were sleeping, as were the people in front of and behind them.

Wet lips slid over him and soon all of his attention was directed to what was happening beneath the blanket. She used her mouth in a way that suggested she had done this often.

Within a minute she had him so stimulated he was forced to act. He reached under and pushed her back, zipping himself up. She looked up with those large, questioning eyes.

"Come along," he said, bringing her to her feet, his voice noticeably deeper. He held her hand, leading her up the aisle past row after row of dozing travelers. No one was waiting, and he motioned her into a washroom, locking the door behind them.

Grinning from ear to ear, she undid his pants and lowered them to his thighs.

"Remove your clothing," he told her.

"There ain't enough room."

Instead of more words, he unsnapped and unzipped her pants and pushed them down. As she slipped her clothes

33

and boots off, she shrieked, "I thought vampires couldn't do it! We're gonna be in the Mile High Club."

He braced himself against the swaying of the aircraft and picked her up, forearms under her bottom. But the confused, even frightened look now on her face forced him to set her down again.

"Kiss me," he said. She kissed him like an obedient child, her mouth warm and slippery but passionless.

He licked her nipples and touched her gently with his fingertips, trying to stimulate her, but she was impossibly tight and dry.

Nothing he did seemed to arouse her. He wondered why she had begun this. But her hands had been busy and he was getting beyond the point where he cared about these mixed messages. She whispered things in his ear, rude and encouraging things.

He held her tight, thrusting against her stomach, energy concentrated on the powerful electricity coursing through his genitals. And then he felt himself lose control.

Release flooded him, and with it the familiar depletion. Emptiness. Desperation. The all-consuming need for blood.

She collapsed into his arms, clutching onto him like a child, crying soundlessly. Startled, he held her without understanding what was going on. She seemed beyond consolation, and he found that disturbing. But intuition assured him that he had just learned something about her, something important. If only, he thought, I could make sense of this girl.

Chapter 4

"YOUSE KIDS HONEYMOONERS?" THE CABBIE ASKED. A BLAST of cigarette smoke clouded the windshield for a moment and then evaporated. Even though a thick sheet of Plexiglas separated the front from the rear seat, the acrid smell of burning tobacco filtered back. David wondered how anyone could mistake him and Kathleen, both covered almost head to toe in sinister black cowhide, for newlyweds.

"Kind of," Kathleen told the driver. She slid closer to David. In the gray light she smiled, her eyes so round, so water-blue and sincere, that a description of Venice popped into his head: " 'She looks a sea Cybele, fresh from ocean/ A ruler of the waters and their powers.' "

"Zip us through Times Square first, willya?" Kathleen said. "I want to show my man."

David stared with disbelief at the metropolis he had once, briefly, called home. Vital and throbbing like a healthy pulse, New York had turned hyper, a taller, denser, and more frenetic city than he would have believed possible. The unseasonably cool summer's evening had enticed two extremes onto the streets in numbers that stunned him—well-heeled men and women stepped smartly around the seemingly endless numbers of human beings wrapped in rags and filthy blankets spread out across the fabled sidewalks of gold. Dickens revived, and here, he thought grimly.

Times Square had changed and yet remained the same. A profusion of shops still sold sex in any flavor, but now straighter money dominated. Expensive restaurants condescended to share the sidewalk with greasy spoons. Glass and steel high-rise hotels rubbed shoulders with the depression-architecture dumps that temporarily housed cheap tourists and local losers. David had the uncomfortable feeling that Chronos, the god of time, had swallowed this child, Manhattan, and regurgitated her. She looked pretty much the same yet had clearly been altered, possibly irrevocably, by the experience.

Eventually the driver stopped in front of the Alexander, a seedy Lower East Side hotel on Delancey Street.

"Is this where you live?" David asked.

"I'm kinda between places right now."

She had made sure that he changed enough money, and with her help, he counted out the fare and slid it into the tray.

"Too much!" She snatched back a twenty-dollar tip. The cabbie scowled at her in his rearview.

"You'll get a rep." She replaced the bill with a ten.

The sidewalk in front of the hotel's entrance was littered with half a dozen kids, late teens, a racially mixed group. Staccato music accompanied by harsh words blared from an enormous fur-covered ghetto blaster, shattering the pre-dawn stillness.

"Hey, Zero, baby. What's goin' down? You?" a chubby boy with red hair yelled. He wore a Yankees baseball cap with the peak at the back. The others laughed.

She took David's arm to lead him through the small crowd, which he figured were the members of a local gang, because of the red and blue scarves rolled and tied around their heads in a stylized way. It had been the same when he'd lived in the city—kids from lower-class homes, the disenfranchised, with no future but too much time in the present, devoted to money and sex and perhaps even a fight. And drugs.

"Zero's got a new toy. So who's the pretty boy?" a solid-looking youth of about eighteen with tight curly brown hair and olive skin wanted to know. He wore a self-satisfied grin on his broad face. When he turned slightly, David saw that the hair at the back of his head had been shaved to form the letter *F*. The boy's eyes were glassy.

"My trick. What's he look like?" Kathleen told him acidly, trying to shove past, but the boy blocked her way.

"Looks like a rich trick. Twenty-four-karat dick." He flipped the collar on David's jacket. "Good threads. New treads. Prices goin' up, Homes, time for a bank loan."

"Cut it out, Frankie. Let us by. I gotta make a living, you know," Kathleen said.

"C'mere, baby," the fat redheaded kid called out. "I got a quarter. We'll take a walk."

The other youths laughed.

"Red, I wouldn't take your scum cum for a grand." Kathleen stood, fists on hips, and David stared at her, astonished. She was hard again, the way she'd been when high. Deadly, he thought.

"Come on, Frankie, fuckin' butt out," she ordered the obvious leader. "I gotta take care of business."

"With a fairy?" Red yelled. The others laughed again.

"He's no fag." She stepped between David and Frankie, trying to elbow Frankie out of the way. "He could rip your throat out," she said. "He's a—"

David jerked her arm to keep her from betraying him. But she said the word *poet,* as if that would explain something.

But it only made them howl.

One of the girls yelled, "Hey, watch ya self, Frankie. He might hitcha wit' a couple hard words."

Fascinated as David was by this slice of street life, he was also becoming irritated. He moved Kathleen aside. "Step out of our way, please."

"Whoaaaa!" Frankie wiggled his hips, bent a wrist, and said with a lisp, "Step outta our way, *pul-eeze!*"

"Hey, Frankie, ya bedda be scared." The redheaded boy laughed.

"Call the rim squad, why doncha," a black girl threw in.

David put his hand on Frankie's chest.

"Take your fuckin' yuppie fingers offa me."

David pressed with enough force to send Frankie out to the curb. A pole kept the boy from landing in the gutter.

"What the hell is this?" Kathleen yelled. "I can't bring a john to my own neighborhood without you punks acting brain dead?"

She grabbed David and yanked him through the door. As it shut, he heard Frankie threaten, "Mutherfucker, when you come out, I'll be waitin'. You're roadkill. Believe it!"

"Hey, Zero, long time," the desk clerk said.

"Yeah. How's it hanging, Louie?"

He laughed. "Like always. The wife says low, the girlfriend says high."

"How's about a room for me and my friend?"

"Half hour?" Louie took a key from a rack behind him.

"The night."

"Cost ya fifty," he told David.

David pulled out some bills, but Kathleen stopped him from handing any over. "Twenty," she said to the clerk.

"For you, Zero, I'll make it forty."

"For you, Louie, I'll make it twenty-five."

"I gotta make a buck."

"Honey, after you feed the fleas, it's all profit."

"Thirty-five. That's it."

Kathleen took three tens from David and plunked them onto the desk. Before Louie could reject them, she snatched the key from his hand.

Their room was on the second floor at the front; dingy, old yellowed wallpaper, scarred veneered furniture, a rickety bed, and even a cockroach on the wall. "Colorful," David said. He checked the closet to make certain it was long enough; he needed to sleep in complete darkness.

Kathleen tossed the key onto the dresser. She seemed deflated now, as if these encounters had taken all the steam out of her. And she's still weak, he realized. "Hungry?" he asked her.

She grimaced. "No more food! I ate enough to last me a year."

"You're too thin." He looked her over. She's like a waif, he thought. A matchgirl who resembles the matchsticks she sells.

"You want me fat?"

"Not fat. Filled out a bit, perhaps."

"Barefoot in the winter, pregnant in the summer, right? You guys are all alike."

He went into the bathroom. Dirt that looked permanently embedded ringed the tub. The hot water faucet in the sink refused to shut off. Under the constant flow, the enamel had worn away, leaving a rust trail. He wet his face and dried it on a towel barely holding itself together.

He felt shocked by all that he'd witnessed since their arrival. This was definitely not the postwar New York that he, André, and Karl had shared, nor the New York he had abandoned in the 1960s to explore North America. And Kathleen, despite her vulnerable face, was like a lion cub; she looked cute and cuddly but was in actuality a dangerously unpredictable animal, more so because she had probably been deeply scarred by this jungle she called home. The crudeness upset him, but crudeness always had. One of the things that disturbed David most when he had undergone the change was that he was even more affected by the callous way people treat one another and the way they torture themselves. But I torture myself too, he thought. They bleed and I feel the pain.

"Are there shops open at this hour?" he asked when he came back into the room. She was lounging across the bed on her stomach, knees bent, feet in the air like a teenager, picking the polish off her fingernails.

"Lots. Whatdaya wanna buy, rubber boots?" She laughed a little and then, noticing his befuddlement, explained, "You know, rubbers. Condoms."

"I want to make several purchases. And by the way," he said, closing the door after them, "I've lots of money. There's no need to bargain for everything."

"Habit." She took his arm and pulled him right instead

of left. "We'll go down the fire escape. That why we don't hafta see Frankie-and-the-slimes."

"You really don't believe I can defend myself, do you?"

"Well, you look kinda, I don't know . . ."

"Weak?" he supplied.

"Nah. Just, sensitive, or something. Everybody here's tough. You gotta be to survive. You look like the kinda guy that if somebody made a face at you, you'd bawl your eyes out."

He shook his head and laughed. "I am sensitive, Kathleen. Probably overly so. But I'm not weak. And I'm not afraid to fight, even my own, who are as strong as I, although I believe there are far better ways to settle disputes than through violence. Are you frightened for me or yourself?"

She glared up at him, azure eyes flashing. "I can take care of myself. Always have."

They found a drug/convenience store open on Delancey Street, and David bought, among other things, a razor, soap, comb and brush, a blow dryer, two toothbrushes—which astonished Zero so much that she blurted out, "Vampires brush their teeth?"—several locks and a screwdriver, a clothesline, and a dusty book of poetry that had probably been hiding on the rack for twenty years. The bill came to almost eighty dollars.

"Man, if you keep spending money like water, you'll be dried out by the end of the week," Zero assured him. She picked up one of the white plastic bags and he took the other two.

As they neared the hotel, she saw Frankie leaning up against a car, kissing a girl.

"Hurry up," she told David, "I gotta pee."

He looked at her. "I'm not afraid of him, Kathleen."

"Well, you oughta be. He carries a blade."

David laughed and she shook her head. This guy's a loony, she thought. Too stupid to know how dumb he is, but then what can you expect from a guy thinks he's Gary Oldman.

They entered the hotel without a hassle and made their

way to the room. While he unpacked the things, she pulled the blanket off the bed. The ordeal of kicking, worry about Bobby, the flight, all of it was catching up with her. More than ever she needed a hit of smack. But she knew he'd never let her have it, and she wouldn't be able to get away from him tonight—maybe after he fell asleep.

Sleep's about all I got to look forward to, she thought.

She watched him install two locks on the room door and one on the closet door. When he finished, he tacked the curtains against the window frame. "How come you're doin' that?" she asked. "To block out the neon?"

"To block the sun, which will break the horizon within the hour."

He walked to the bed and looked down at her. Something about his eyes made her nervous. Maybe he was psychotic. She'd been with a couple guys who had gone over the edge and left it far behind. But she didn't get the feeling he was violent, just too damned direct, penetrating. She didn't want him to look at her that closely, and she didn't want to look at him either.

He sat next to her and she began to panic. I better do something before he comes on to me, she thought.

She pushed him back and straddled his hips. He smiled that small sad smile of a guy in perpetual pain. She took off his pants and went to work with her mouth, as she had with so many other men. His body was nearly hairless and his skin cool and a little waxy. Long ago she'd learned how to think about other things when doing business.

He tried to undress her too, but she resisted. But he was so determined that finally she slammed on the brake.

"Hey, look, lemme just do you. I ain't in the mood, okay? I'm getting my period and I'm kinda crampy." She hoped the reference to blood wouldn't set him off with the vampire thing again.

"We don't have to make love," he said. She didn't know why, but sometimes his gentleness irritated her. This was one of those times.

He lay back and let her do her job. But just before he came, he shoved her away, so hard she fell on the floor.

"Why'd you do that?" She crawled back up onto the bed. On his stomach was a stream of red-tinged liquid. She didn't want to believe her eyes.

"I'm sorry. I didn't mean to push you so hard."

"Forget it." She plunked down beside him, unnerved. Whatever had come out of him wasn't normal. Maybe he had a disease or something. "Hey, you're not like terminal or anything, are you? I mean, can I catch what you got?"

"If you ingest any of my fluids, you'll become as I am. I was trying to protect you."

Too many things didn't make sense. The blood on his shirt. His teeth. His unnatural strength. And now this. Maybe he really was Dracula.

But before that thought could blossom into fear and get a firm grip on her, he pulled her to him. Staring at his face now, he looked pretty much like any guy, although his skin was cool. He was sensual and she liked kissing him, even though she refused to let herself get excited. She wasn't used to considerate lovers, and found David too gentle, even if he *had* just shoved her across the room. She didn't know how to react to him.

While he was in the bathroom, she got undressed. As she was stuffing her jewelry into her purse, she noticed the pictures of Bobby and took them out. She held them under the bedside lamp and close to her face, as if studying the fading snapshots would reveal some secret about where he was. Funny how whenever she thought of Bobby, it was this picture that came to mind. And a warm feeling. And right behind that, pain.

To distract herself, she went to the dresser and sorted through the things David had bought, finally picking up the book called *Poetic Greats, Volume II—Byron to Eliot*. She yawned.

When he came back in the room, she said, "Hey, you can read me this if you want."

She was rubbing her eye with a balled-up fist, just the way a child would. He found it endearing. "The entire book?"

"Some."

"Come here, then." He sat on the bed against the headboard and she crawled between his legs. He moved her around so that he held her as if she were a baby. She's soft and adorable, a kitten, he thought, hugging her. "Which poem would you like to hear?"

She glanced at the index and pointed. "That one. I can't say it so it's probably deep, huh?"

He laughed and kissed her on the forehead. "My Eliza Doolittle."

"That ain't it! It's about love. I can read, you know."

"Eliza Doolittle is a reference. To a character in a play."

"I knew that."

As she snuggled in his arms, head resting against his chest, David turned the pages to Eliot's "The Love Song of J. Alfred Prufrock." The last time he'd read this poem had been here in New York, in 1957. He remembered clearly. It had been winter; there was a snowstorm. Ariel had left the previous fall. By the next spring Karl would be gone.

Kathleen's breathing became slow and steady. She was nodding off. But he read to her anyway. And as he read, he remembered:

> "Let us go then, you and I,
> When the evening is spread out against the sky
> Like a patient etherized upon a table. . . ."

Chapter 5

"... I have heard the mermaids singing,
each to each.

I do not think that they will sing to me.

I have seen them riding seaward on the waves
Combing the white hair of the waves blown back
When the wind blows the water white and black.

We have lingered in the chambers of the sea
By sea-girls wreathed with seaweed red and brown
Till human voices wake us, and we drown."

DAVID CLOSED THE BOOK. THE SILENCE IN THE ROOM HAD AT
once a dense and empty feel. André lay stretched on the
floor before the fireplace, hands linked behind his head, long
legs crossed at the ankles, gray eyes closed. His body, that
of a thirty-seven-year-old man, was in peak condition, dis-
guising just over one hundred years of existence. Karl, born
in 1820, the oldest of the three, looked the youngest, no
more than twenty-five. He sat motionless, directly across
from David in a wing-backed chair, his sharp Teutonic features ravaged. There was a hint of moisture at the inner
corners of his brown eyes. It's the way with us, David
thought. Pain that leads to nothing but further pain.

Suddenly André shifted. He glanced first at Karl and then
David. "It loses in the translation."

"Translation?" David asked.

"From mortal to immortal."

"Not for me." Karl pulled out a white handkerchief.
"I'm drowning."

"It's Ariel, isn't it?" David asked, a bit too harshly, regretting his tone immediately.

"Don't be ridiculous!" André told him.

"No, he's right. In a way." Karl stuffed the handkerchief back into his pocket and crossed an ankle over a knee. "Not so much Ariel but what she represents."

"What? A controlling cunt?" André sat up abruptly. "You're both lucky to have survived, balls intact."

David felt his back tense. André's look challenged him. He knows how I feel, David thought, but can't let a mention of her pass without a caustic remark.

"She wasn't only that," Karl said softly. "Not to me. But I need a woman."

"Merde!" André laughed bitterly. "Well, get over it. And you too!" His cynicism radiated beams of black energy throughout the dim room. "You're both dreamers, you tangled up in ideas, and you caught by fantasy." He stood. "Accept it. We are alone and this is our destiny. *Moi je le sais!*" He opened the screen and tossed another log onto the fire. Outside, the wind howled a protest. The bark was damp and the flames made it hiss. There was too much smoke.

David went on the defensive. "Perhaps we are dreamers, but for Karl and me it's different. We did not wish for this life as you did. We're not hardened to our fate."

"Then chain yourself out in the sunlight, if it's so fucking painful. Or is your strength only in self-pity?" Even as he spoke, André's voice faltered, and David noticed. He knew the failures André had suffered, his fears of the weakness he believed he'd inherited. Knowing all this evoked David's sympathy, which André needed but could barely tolerate. But he's right, David thought.

"I am weak," he said quietly. "It's my nature. That's how Ariel reached me." But even as he said the words, he felt no bitterness, only an intense longing that terrified him.

"The weather depresses me." André ran his hands through his hair at the temples where the black was streaked with silver, and sat down on the floor again. The room filled with a sound, like the wind sighing. "It's just that wanting what's impossible is self-flagellation. What's the point, unless you enjoy the pain?"

"I don't enjoy the pain," David said. "But I cannot simply dismiss her from my memory."

André stared at him with eyes the same color as the smoke in the fireplace. They grew soft with empathy.

"I've been thinking of leaving," Karl announced suddenly. "Soon. There's nothing here for me. I'll return to Germany. I don't expect to find anything, anyone, back there, but I can't stay. I need to be alone."

André did not reply. For David, there was nothing to say. He knew how Karl felt and was not surprised. And he understood that André understood also, even if he was incapable of admitting it. They had been lucky to find one another, but nothing lasts forever unchanged. Now their relationship showed signs of toxicity. I've altered, David thought. Fragmented inside. Will the pieces ever come back together? And if they do, who will I be? As it is, I'm an empty shell. All of us are only empty shells.

Karl, who felt an affinity with Eliot, said, "Read one more." He turned toward the window to watch the freezing white dawn encroaching. His erect posture, the way his shoulders squared, his head poised just so, all of it presented a portrait of quiet loneliness that seemed impenetrable. As David studied Karl, and then André, removed, remote, entranced by the flames in the fireplace, he quoted Eliot from memory.

> "We are the hollow men
> We are the stuffed men
> Leaning together
> Headpiece filled with straw. Alas!
> Our dried voices, when
> We whisper together
> Are quiet and meaningless
> As wind in dry grass
> Or rats' feet over broken glass
> In our dry cellar."

Chapter 6

ZERO WAS SO EXHAUSTED FROM THE EVENTS OF THE PREVIOUS week that she slept all day and late into the afternoon. When she woke, she found herself in bed alone, gagged and bound securely to the headboard. No matter what she did, she couldn't get free.

With so much time on her hands and a clearer head, she was forced to think about things. Bobby, for instance, and whether she'd ever find him. And if he was okay. A dismal feeling caught up with her, and she could not shake a growing sense of foreboding. And then there was David. She didn't know what to think. She struggled to avoid coming to the conclusion she was hurtling toward: maybe he was what he said he was. All of these feelings scared her. She felt desperate for some substance that would dim the expanding terror.

After the sun set, David emerged from the closet; not a minute too soon, from her point of view.

He looked thin, pale, and hungry. His bones seemed to press out on his skin. He freed her mouth only, and she demanded, "Hey! What's the idea tying me up?"

"Simply to ensure you wouldn't wander off."

She heard him showering. When he returned, he released her.

She too had a shower, dried her hair, brushed her teeth, and then applied fresh makeup and dressed. She was surprised by how good she felt. *Especially compared to the hell I been through lately,* she thought.

When she was ready to go, he told her, "First you'll eat something, and then we'll look for Dennis."

"Ain't hungry." In fact, food was the furthest thing from her mind. David's cadaverous look was close. Bobby was closer. Junk was the closest.

He took her outside, by the main door. Neither Frankie nor any of the others were waiting, and she felt relieved.

"Is there a restaurant you like in the vicinity?" he asked.

"Mae's Fine Foods. Mae runs it. She's a friend of mine."

When they entered the small diner, an older woman with salt hair flecked with pepper rushed over.

"Kathy! Where you been? I was afraid you was arrested again."

Zero hugged the woman whose fleshy arms enfolding her always felt so comforting, today even more: they brought her back to the realm of being human. "I been outta town but I'm back now. Mae, this's David."

Mae looked him over. "Nice to meet ya," she said, but Zero could tell she was reserving judgment.

"He's from England."

"Where ya know each other from?" Mae asked, her voice laced with suspicion.

David answered. "Kathleen and I met when she was in Manchester recently."

"You was in England?" Mae's face reflected astonishment.

"I had a little business," Zero said casually. She walked toward one of the booths at the back, just to get away from Mae's questions. She loved her dearly and knew that Mae loved her too, like a daughter. But Mae could be nosy as hell.

When she and David were seated, with Mae leaning against the edge of the table, Zero plucked the menu from its holder.

Immediately Mae snatched it from her hands and eased it back into the tight metal fingers.

"She's been comin' in here since she was five years old," Mae told David, shaking her head. To Zero she added, "If ya don't know what I serve by now, ya never will."

"Hey, Mae! Gimme a refill, willya?" a customer shouted.

"Hold your horses, Al." Mae turned back to Zero and David. "So how'd you get to England?"

Zero looked down at the Formica tabletop. She pulled the sugar container in front of her and slid it back and forth between her hands quickly. "Somebody I know had a ticket they couldn't use, so they gave it to me. I was just there a couple days. It was real nice."

"Yeah? So who gave you the ticket?"

Zero looked up. "Mae, I'm starvin'! Can I get some chili? And toast? Without the crusts?"

Mae shot her a look. "You? Starvin'? That'll be the day!" But then she said, "Comin' right up." Mae turned to David. "Want somethin'?"

He shook his head.

"You look like you ain't had nothin' in your stomach for a month. How 'bout a burger?"

"No. Thank you."

"Coffee?"

"All right," he said.

"The two of youse could be bookends. Skeletons!" Mae grumbled as she headed for the kitchen.

When she was gone, Zero noticed David staring at her. "Lying comes naturally to you," he said.

Suddenly she resented him. He's had all the breaks, that's for sure, she thought. "You think you're hot shit, doncha? You got money, education, no real troubles. You look like you never done a day's work in your whole life, all one hundred years of it."

"One hundred and thirty-two. And I'm not insulting you, Kathleen. It's merely an observation."

"Right! You're a liar but don't take it personally." She stared out the window. It was drizzling, and people from the market were hurrying, some with newspapers or plastic bags over their heads. One old guy dozed on a crate in a doorway across the street, oblivious to the boarded-up buildings and garbage surrounding him, a beat-up ukulele on his lap. It's always the same here, she thought. All my life. That guy'll die in that doorway and nobody'll give a shit.

David slipped his hand over hers. She had forgotten for a moment that he was there. His eyes were bright. Too bright. He still looked scary, thin and hungry. She shivered and was relieved when Mae plunked the food down in front of her, although Zero didn't want it. But she ate some, just to keep both of them happy.

As soon as they left Mae's, she took David to The Crack, the bar where Dennis had found her and got her into this mess. From Delancey they walked north, across East Houston. The drizzle had stopped temporarily but the streets were wet.

"Is he here?" David wanted to know as soon as they walked in the door.

There were only a dozen customers, mainly Puerto Rican. Zero recognized a few faces, waved at one, but didn't see Dennis.

"Nope. It's early. He might show later."

They sat at the bar for an hour. Zero drank a Coke, and David let a Budweiser sit untouched before him, as he had the coffee earlier. She chatted with the bartender, a slender guy with a black moustache and a Spanish accent. David said nothing. But she noticed him watching, aware the way a cat is of everything that goes on. Around midnight a lemon blonde with red glitter in her hair and wearing a red leopardskin minidress off one shoulder came up to them.

"Hey, girlfriend! How ya been? Who's your friend?"

"Hiya, Laser. This's David."

"Nice t' meet ya." Laser smiled seductively at David. Then she turned to Zero and winked. "Real nice."

"Listen. I'm looking for a guy," Zero said.

"What's wrong with this one?"

"Nothing. But I need to find this other guy. Name's Dennis. Black dude, Rasta plaits to here, a buncha earrings, wears this jacket with fringe and nipple rings. Know him?"

"Yeah. Middleman, mostly crack. Some H too. Does the baby trade."

"You don't mean children?" David asked, shock registering on his face.

"That's just what I mean. Owns P.S. 91. Says he likes to get 'em when they're teeny so's they'll be customers for life. Twisted, huh? So why ya lookin' for 'im? Wanna score?"

"Have you seen him tonight?" David asked.

Laser snapped her gum and gave him a toothy grin. Zero noticed her rub a knee against his thigh. "Maybe. What's it worth?"

"Who owes who?" Zero reminded her. " 'Member that bust? Last Christmas? Who warned you?"

Laser sighed. "Yeah. I guess I owe you one. Dennis was here. Heard him say he hadda go ta Jersey—big girls flyin' in and he's gotta take 'em to the hospital. He'll be back tomorrow 'cause he's always in before twelve. That's when the ice brains know to find him."

David looked confused, and Zero explained, "Girls are coke, boys junk. He's moving it to a safe place." She took his arm and they stood. "Thanks, Laser. And keep your mouth shut I was asking, okay?"

"No prob. Hey! This a private gig or you wanna triangle?"

"Duo," Zero said, pulling David out the door.

As they walked back to the hotel, she wondered if he was attracted to Laser. "She's pretty, huh?"

"The girl you called Laser?"

"Yeah."

"Yes. Very pretty."

Zero chewed her lower lip. Even though she knew it shouldn't matter, she felt hurt. "Nice too."

"She seemed so."

"Want her to come? We can go back and get her."

David looked down at her and smiled. He let go of her hand to put an arm around her shoulder. The chill from his arm penetrated the leather of her jacket. "I think not."

For some inexplicable reason, she felt relieved. She slid her arm around his waist, walking in step with him back to the Alexander.

When they arrived, some of the kids were out front, but not Frankie. "Lie down," he said the minute they were in the room.

Zero began to get nervous again, and she couldn't figure out why. Sex pretty much bored her, even though she'd certainly done it plenty, mainly for money. Some tricks had been medium to rough trade too, so why David, one of the marshmallows, scared her she didn't know. Maybe because the heroin had nearly worked its way out of her system, reality had started to creep in. Her realization that something was way off with him was becoming impossible to ignore. He didn't look normal and he didn't look like the vampires in the movies. She didn't know what to believe. And she didn't want to think too much about it either, because it just scared her and she had too much to do. She had to think about Bobby.

She lay back on the bed, but before she could say or do anything, he bound her wrists together and tied them to the headboard.

"Why you tying me up now? You into bondage?"

"I must go out for a while," he said, knotting the clothesline so that she would never get it untied. "I'll return in an hour or so."

"Have a hell of a time!" she said bitterly just before he gagged her. Run into any scag, shoot some my way, she thought.

David hurried west along Delancey which turned into Kenmare, then south, through Chinatown, Chatham Square, past the Bowery Savings Bank, until he came to City Hall. Then he took Broadway past the Trinity Church cemetery, where the empty streets narrowed into canyons, buildings scratching the sky, snagging the wind to create a vortex. Along the way he passed only a few people, odd types, the three A.M.'ers in various stages of intoxication, depression, and somnambulance. He avoided looking too closely because he found it painful to stare into the face of humanity's walking wounded and wounding. Eventually he came to Battery Park.

The park was like a cemetery, but he was fine-tuned to every sound and smell. Putrid air stabbed him. A blend of many scents, but one iron-rich odor reached out of the night to strangle his senses. Heart slamming, he sharp-focused. The donor lay on a bench beneath green garbage bags. Filthy, beaten-down, in many respects dead to the world.

David knelt. His throat was parched, his limbs frozen. Beneath the dirty flesh of the man's neck a vein pulsed weakly. Pulse. Pulse. The sound hammered at David's brain. A magnet sucked him down until his teeth fixed to flesh. He cracked dirty, stinking skin. Hot fire bubbled. His tongue lapped at crimson. Salty. A memory. Red meat. He swallowed greedily. He moaned his ecstasy and the man moaned with him as they rocked together. David was lost to the world.

When he finished with this source, he stared at the pathetic waste before him. The man was not dead but he was not clearly alive. The vein, like others in the body, collapsed. David had taken no more than he needed, but he sensed the decrepit form could not withstand the onslaught. He vowed next time to hunt for a healthy body that could afford the loss.

But the blood worked wonders, as always, and he could not help but feel energized. The night crackled. The Atlantic breeze rustled leaves, creating a natural wind chime. A cat yawned, a puppy yapped sharply. Metal pieces of a sculpture beat a syncopated melody. The buzz of ever-present traffic vibrated through new grass beneath his feet and joined the hum in his body. A faint fishy aroma, appealing because of its intensity, swirled up from the river to combine with the powerful sweet-doughy scent of freshly baked bread. I stand on the seam of life, he thought, where everything connects— Heaven, Hell, and all else I can imagine. Where anything is possible.

On the walk back he noticed a man and woman in a car kissing and he thought of Kathleen. Flash-fire eyes. Animated lips, a stage on which every emotion must be played out. He was captivated by the girlish way she tilted her head, sunbeam hair caressing one shoulder, an invitation. But more than her physical beauty appealed to him. Her direct comments and naive questions had caught him off kilter more than once. We're entirely different, he thought; culture, class, even species. Yet those differences seemed insignificant. And most amazing, knowing what he was, she did not seem to find him repellent. She radiated life and all the determination that went with it, and David felt his own will to survive rekindled. He was fascinated; he had never met anyone even remotely like her, at least no one mortal.

When he reached the Alexander, Frankie, the black girl, and another youth huddled together. They stared at him but said nothing, which he found odd. They just laughed and whispered together in a coded language that sounded like a verbal stew composed of Spanish and English slang that David felt no interest in deciphering. As he reached the second floor he stopped, listening. Kathleen was talking to someone.

"Come *on,* Red. He'll be back any minute."

"I'm comin'. Or I will be."

"Fix me first. I'm dyin'."

"I screw you then I shoot you."

"Well, hurry up. Get it over with."

The door had been jimmied, and David easily shoved it inward, splintering the frame.

Red, the fat boy, was positioning himself between Kathleen's legs. His head jerked up. The erection sticking out of his pants shrank like a pricked balloon. A look of surprise and embarrassment filled his face. On the table next to the bed lay a spoon, a glass of water, matches, and a syringe with a needle already fitted into it.

David grabbed the boy and threw him into the dresser.

Red yelled, followed by, "Hey, man, you broke my fuckin' wrist!" He held the injured joint out in front of him like a boy asking his mother for a Band-Aid. The only difference was the depth of horror embedded in his face.

"Send Frankie up here now or I shall break more than that," David threatened.

Red jerked his zipper up awkwardly with his good hand

as he scurried out the door, eyeing David as if expecting to be swatted.

"It ain't what you think," Kathleen said hurriedly.

She was still tied to the bed, but now almost naked, pants off, T-shirt pushed up above her head and bunched around her elbows. She looked frightened.

Frankie must have been on his way because within seconds he was in the room. He glanced at the splintered door frame and then at the bed and laughed. "Kinky!" The boy turned to David with a look of disdain. "I hear you wanna see me?"

"No, I do not want to see you. Nor any of your friends. If I catch any of you in this room again or trying to give Kathleen drugs, you personally will repent the error of your ways. Have I made myself clear?"

"Un-huh, Homes. You gonna break my bones?" Frankie laughed.

He pulled something from his pocket. There was a sharp click and a silvery blade flicked into the air.

David grabbed Frankie's forearm and snatched the switchblade away before the boy could react. Frankie raised his palms and stepped back. "Hey, man, chill!"

David shoved him back even farther. He bent the knife case until the two ends touched, snapping the spring mechanism.

Frankie stared at his weapon. "How'd you do that?"

"Never mind the technique. Just know that you're hardly a match for me, neither you nor your entire gang. As leader, the others will do as you say. If you wish to continue your reign, intact, you'll keep them in line. Now get out!"

Frankie left the room, looking shocked. David was right behind him, calmly, methodically, straightening the switchblade. He bolted the door against the fractured frame, aware of his heart hammering crazily, until he felt it shift in his chest like an engine forced out of low gear and into high. And during that shift something ugly and dangerous uncoiled and wiggled out into the open. He knew he was helpless to stop what was to occur.

He was on her, knife poised above her chest. "What will

it be, Kathleen? What's going to fill this vast existential emptiness you suffer from? You want the needle, but I refuse to give you that. And you won't eat food. So what else will do it? The knife? I can penetrate you with this, right to the heart, just what you had in mind for me. Or do you want my teeth at your throat? That might feel a bit like a needle, don't you agree? A withdrawal rather than a deposit. Or is it my prick you crave badly? Name your poison! How can we fill this huge void inside you?"

"Please! It ain't like you think."

"Do you want the knife? Simply say so."

"No! Please."

He jammed the blade into the side of the night table.

"Teeth, then. Shall I tear into your flesh? Many mortals enjoy that. Are you one of those?"

"David, I'm sorry."

"Then it's my prick. You've been so desperate for me to fill you that way."

"No. Yes. If that's what you want."

"No, this is what *you* want, Kathleen. You're the one with the vacancy."

"Yes. Yes. Stick it in me."

"But which orifice? Your mouth?"

"No. Not there. I mean okay."

"Anus?"

"Yeah, sure."

"And what about your cunt?"

She was silent.

"Which will it be, Kathleen? Hurry. I don't have the night. The sun rises soon, and then you'll go empty another day."

"Anything. Whatever you want."

"No! What do *you* want?"

She looked frightened but said, "Ordinary. But from behind."

Roughly he flipped her over onto her stomach. He made himself hard enough and then, without making an effort to stimulate her, forced himself in.

"Oh God!" she wailed.

He saw himself from a distance and was incapable of intervening. Removed, he felt devoid of any emotion that would put an end to this madness. I'm completely deranged, he thought.

He wanted to hurt her, to tear her apart, to hear her screams. Her fists clutched the rope. Sweat sprouted from the pores in her back. He grabbed her hair, yanking her head back as if she were a horse and not a human being. "This is what you wanted all along, is it not?" he whispered bitterly.

"Harder!" she groaned.

The violence overwhelmed him. It was only when he tasted her blood that he realized what he was doing.

Afterward he sat beside her on the bed, elbow propped against one knee, hand holding up his head. She cried without uttering a sound.

He despised himself. He could barely look at her. It took a long time before he could bring himself to touch her, running a shaking hand down her head and back, stroking her, trying to soothe a wound that he had inflicted.

"I'm sorry," she said, which only made him feel more wretched. She's so accustomed to brutality that she can't even recognize it as such, he thought, which touched a despair so deep in him that he could hardly breathe.

"I always cry after sex. I feel kinda guilty and dirty. I know that's stupid, but I do." She looked at him and he could not meet her eye. I'm the one who's guilty, he thought, not even knowing how to explain this to her. Instead he stroked her hair, his hand trembling uncontrollably.

"My old man started fucking me when I was eleven," she said out of the blue, turning her head away from him, her voice even, emotionless. "I guess I shouldn't've let him do it, but I was so young. And I wasn't really sure what was going on, know what I mean?

"My mom died the year before. He always drank. And he always hit me. Her too. But it got worse. He'd come home in the middle of the night and wake me up, ranting and raving about how bad I was and how he hadda punish me for my own good or I'd turn out real rotten, like her. It coulda been something I did, like breaking a glass, or something I didn't do. Anyways, he'd take off this wide leather belt he always wore and make me lie on my stomach so he could strap my ass, sometimes till there was big welts. If I cried, I got it worse, so I learned how to take it without making any noise. And boy, could he give it. Lotsa times I was raw for days and couldn't even sit at school. After he beat me, he'd get into bed with me and sorta be nice to me, and ... and ... you know."

David felt sick. The idea that he had done what her father had, punished her and then soothed her, revolted him. He had never gone over the edge before. He'd always seen himself as a victim, occasionally as a savior. *And now I've become an oppressor,* he thought grimly.

"He fucked me till I was fourteen, and then I made him stop. A social worker told me I musta shut down. She said I do something called 'displace,' that's why I can't feel nothing inside. And I always cry after. I can't come."

He wanted to cradle her in his arms. But he felt base and brutish, a cowardly predator taking advantage of the weak and defenseless. *And I'm weak too,* he thought. *I let her drag me down into the gutter she's so familiar with.*

Since she had come to Manchester to kill him, David felt more and more out of control, spiraling fast, lower and lower, and this seemed like only the tip of a dark and dangerous iceberg, the depths of which he was terrified to fathom.

"He left when I was fifteen. Bobby was just born, and I raised him alone; it was pretty hard. That's why I dropped outta school. The city sent me to all kinds of counselors and social workers, and I had a buncha shrinks asking me questions and writing down everything I said, but none of it really helped. I guess I'm a hopeless case or something. Anyways, a couple years ago I started doing smack and I got hooked, and now ... I just wish Bobby was here."

"How's Bobby your brother, then?"

"Huh?"

"If your father left and your mother died, how is Bobby your brother?"

Kathleen shifted. She turned her head again to face him.

Her eyes were filled with tears. "My old man knocked up some whore. She didn't want the kid, so I took him. He's all I got." She looked in his eyes. "Can I sleep with you?"

He pulled his hand away; he couldn't bear the idea of having her near. "Not tonight. I need to be alone."

He flushed the heroin and the needle down the toilet, covered her with the blanket, and turned out the light.

"Kathleen," he said in the darkness. "I'm truly sorry I hurt you. I was very wrong to do what I did. You have every right to never forgive me."

"Hey, don't feel bad. That's nothing. I been hurt lots worse. I'll survive," she said, but her voice sounded so small to him.

He lay on the carpet of the closet and pulled the door closed, shutting out the world. His heart pounded painfully, accusingly, in his chest as hot tears burned their way from his eyes. Byron haunted him. ". . . And make thee in thy leprosy of mind/As loathsome to thyself as to mankind!"

It was only in complete isolation and darkness that the full horror of what he was hit him, the knowledge that he was no better than Ariel.

Chapter 7

"Hi!" Zero said. David had slept late, and she thought he looked bad. Strung out.

He went straight to the bathroom without even a glance in her direction. She heard the pipes rattle as the water ran. When he came back into the room, he was naked except for a white towel wrapped togalike around his waist. He walked to the bed and untied her.

"Get ready." His voice was flat. "We're going back to that pub to find Dennis."

She ran to the bathroom and used the toilet right away. Afterward she turned on the shower and wandered back into the room. From the dresser she selected a few things to take with her, then went over to the chair facing the window where David sat. He had untacked the curtains; the glow of flickering red neon reflected on his pale flesh. That skin was a constant reminder that he was unlike her, but Zero could not find him frightening. Even after last night. He'd been a real asshole. Still, most of the time he was nicer than any guy she knew. She knelt by his side and touched his arm. It was cool. He didn't look at her.

"Listen. I been thinking. I'm real glad we're together, know what I mean? I like you." She stopped. "You're ...

you're not like other guys. You're mostly gentle. I ain't saying you're weak or nothing, just, you know, kind. I was thinking that when we get Bobby and you find out who's after you that maybe we could, like, be together and—"

"The only reasons we're together are to find your brother and track down who sent you to murder me. When I've accomplished those two tasks, I'll return to England—alone."

She snatched her hand away as if she had touched a hot stove and stood up. "Yeah. Sure. Don't pay any attention to me. I got a bad habit of running off at the mouth. Mae's always telling me that."

She moved toward the bathroom slowly, feeling like an accident victim, stunned, a little shocked. She dumped what she was holding onto the top of the toilet tank, pulled the shower curtain aside without really being aware of what she was doing, and stepped under the hard spray, mechanically closing the curtain. The water was hot but Zero didn't notice. She picked up the little bar of Ivory and began lathering it in her hands. She felt stoned, not pleasantly so, but the same mental blankness, the same lack of pain. Steam welled around her, swelling over the top of the curtain, filling the room. She listened to the sound of the water on the enamel. The soap slipped through her fingers but she did not bother picking it up.

Whatever sensation she felt on her back from the water had dimmed; her body was as numb as her soul. At some point Zero noticed she felt exhausted. She rested her arms against the cool tiles and her head on her arms. Then she was crying the way she had as a girl when her father beat her, soundless tears, moanless sobs, her body buckling.

Suddenly the curtain was shoved aside and he grabbed her, lifting her out of the tub, pulling her close against him, covering her wet face with kisses. A long cry like the sound of a desolate animal caught in a death trap pierced the air, and she was astonished to realize that it had come from her.

He carried her to the bed, whispering, "Oh, Kathleen. My Kathy. I do care for you."

She felt a violent pain that broke through to the surface as loud racking sobs, a pain worse than the withdrawal she had suffered, any beating that she had endured. The more she cried, the more he kissed her, and the more kisses, the more tears.

"Love me! Please, love me!"

He caressed her hair, her face, her breasts, giving her more than she knew it was possible to get. Soon she began to feel warm and needy, wanting him nearer, pulling him closer. And when he penetrated her, she opened to him as naturally as any flower opens to the sun. "Yes, yes," she cried, unable to comprehend how anything could be so good.

He loved her slowly and passionately. She couldn't get enough of him, laughing and crying at the same time, trapped in a chasm between pleasure and pain. "Stay inside me. Always," she whispered.

As David moved faster and deeper, for Zero the moment was bittersweet. Her limbs clamped around his body as if to ensure that at the last second he would not retreat.

And finally they lay together breathless. He continued holding her tightly, their bodies intertwined. "I could feel you," she said. "Inside." She heard her voice, full of wonder and awe, and felt on the verge of disbelieving her experience. "I never knew. I just never knew."

As they stepped through the door at The Crack, loud rock music grated through an enormous speaker above the door. David hated these jarring modern sounds. They were abrasive to his soul and painful to his overly sensitive eardrums.

Kathleen began to make her way into the room, but he held her back so they were both hidden from view. He turned her head, and she lifted her face for a kiss. "Be very careful. The slightest problem, give me a signal, and I'll be right there." He took a stool at the shadowy end of the bar where he could see the entire place, and Kathleen moved across the room.

While she had eaten at Mae's, they formed a plan. She would approach Dennis alone, get Bobby back, and then David would take over.

He watched her walking in her snug leather pants, hips

swaying naturally, her body drawing eyes like the Sirens' songs had lured enchanted mariners.

She stopped to speak with Laser, who must have asked about David. Zero nodded toward the bar. Then she moved on, circling the room, focusing in on a table in one corner where a brown-skinned young man with bench-press muscles sat surrounded by other youths. His hair was long and tightly braided, Rastafarian style, and hung straight down to his shoulders. He wore a blue unbuttoned work shirt with the sleeves torn out, similar to the ones that had been fashionable in the sixties, designer jeans, tan construction boots, and a dark brown leather vest with eighteen-inch fringe. He talked and gestured in an extremely animated way, constantly tugging on the half-dozen rings and ear clips adorning the outer edges of both ears. From this side view, David could see a large gold hoop hanging from his nipple.

David watched him wet his fingertips, take a pinch of something from his vest pocket, and rub whatever it was onto his gums.

"Want company?" Laser was already seated on the stool next to David. She was attractive, but not like Kathleen. Hers was a rougher beauty, like Athena's. Whereas Kathleen believed she had the upper hand in this jungle, he knew that Laser really did.

"Buy a girl a drink?"

"What would you like?"

"Rye. A double."

After the shot had been placed in front of her, Laser said, "Zero's lookin' pretty good. Clean. And I ain't seen her so happy in . . . jeez, I don't know. You must be some kinda dynamite lay."

David shifted uneasily. "Have you and Kathleen known one another long?"

She had the glass at her lips, about to take a swallow of the rye. "Kathleen? You and Mae are the only ones ever call her that. Yeah, we go back a couple years." Laser took a long drink and set the glass on a paper coaster.

"Has she had many boyfriends?"

"Who, Zero? You kiddin'? You're the first guy I ever

seen her with two nights in a row, even a trick. Never had a pimp. Didn't think she liked guys."

He glanced across the room. Kathy stood at the table and Dennis was on his feet, a startled look on his face.

"Hey, you Crazy-Glued to her or somethin'?"

"Or something," David said.

"My luck."

Kathleen was doing most of the talking. Dennis took her arm and they turned toward the door. They bypassed the bar; she did not look at David as they went out.

He stood immediately and plunked some bills down for the drinks.

"Hey, where ya goin'?" Laser asked.

"I've got to leave now. Sorry."

"Just when we was gettin' acquainted." She caught his arm, pulling him close so that it looked like she was licking his ear, but actually she whispered, "He's filth. Son of a serious bitch. Cut more than one guy. Stashes a blade in his boot. The left."

"Thank you, Laser. I appreciate this."

She lifted the glass. "You and Zero divorce, you know where ta find me." She turned away.

Outside, David picked up Kathleen's scent. Now that he had drunk from her, the blood would always be a lingering memory, a magnetic pull that he could tap into at will. He could separate that scent and follow it like a dog finding a buried bone. Within a reasonable distance.

He turned into an alley that led behind the bar. His steps became stealthy, stalking. At the end of the alley a dim bulb illuminated another turn and he paused. He sensed two warm-blooded beings.

He edged around the corner, blending with the shadows.

The alley was a dead end. Kathy sat on top of a lidded trash can beneath the light over the back door of the bar. She leaned against the brick wall, a strip of ragged fabric tied tightly around her upper arm. Her attention was focused on Dennis, whose back was to David.

From his angle of vision, David saw that Dennis held a

spoon. He watched him spit into it, flick on a plastic lighter, then run the flame under the bowl.

"David!" Kathy yelled when she saw him.

Dennis turned. His face creased; a surprised but nasty look. "Who the fuck be he?"

"My friend."

"Yeah?" Dennis said, as though he didn't believe her, but he went back to cooking the drug. "You wanna hit, man? Green for brown. Clean as you can get. Lemme fix this bitch then I be doin' you."

David stepped into the light. He knocked Dennis's arm. The spoon flew across the yard and clattered onto concrete. Both anger and fear flashed in Dennis's eyes. He tugged on his left earlobe and said, "You be the fuckin' man? Lookit, I pay fuckin' Furguson. Don't be squeezin' me, or I break your head."

David moved in, invading Dennis's space. "Why did you send Kathleen to England to kill me?"

"You the fuckin' dude? Told me she aced you." He turned to Kathleen. "Lyin' bitch!"

"Why are you trying to kill me?" David demanded.

"Hey, bro, not me." Dennis held up his hands in protest. He looked off balance, as though unsure of just who he was dealing with. "I owed a man. He say get Zero. Give me a passport, cash, a plane ticket. Don't know nothin' more, my man."

"You know who you did the favor for."

Dennis didn't answer.

David looked in his eyes. He preferred to use hypnotism, but drugs eradicated consciousness. There wasn't enough to work with. But Dennis saw something. Like a threatened animal, he became cautious.

He tried to put his arm around David's shoulder. "My man, you and me, we sit and discuss the situation. Come on inside. We get a couple beers and—"

"Don't jerk him around," Kathleen warned Dennis. "He don't look bad, but I seen him take six guys out at once."

Dennis considered this. David did not get the idea that the dealer took her seriously, and was surprised to hear him say, "Shit, man, you wasting my time. The Snake Priest, he be the dude you lookin' to speak with. Runs a fuckin' stable on the forty-second parallel."

"Where on the forty-second parallel?"

"He means midtown, Forty-second Street," Kathleen said. She hopped down from the trash can and untied her arm. "Everybody knows the Snake Priest. We can find him. But what about Bobby?"

"Crazy cunt." Dennis shook his head. "Don't know nothin' 'bout no fuckin' Bobby, just what I say. Only passin' this fuckin' shit on, and it sure ain't worth the trouble. The Snake Priest, he tell me not to be expectin' you back."

"Why did he say that?" David asked.

"Man, how the hell I know. The Snake Priest, he sure don't tell me his fuckin' business any more than I tell him mine. I was just, like, doin' the man a favor to even it, you understand?"

"He don't know nothing else," Kathy said. "Let's go."

David let go of Dennis and took her arm. They turned. He sensed movement and spun around in time to see Dennis withdraw a butterfly knife from his left boot.

Automatically David assumed a fisticuffs stance he had learned at Cambridge over a century ago. Dennis threw back his head and laughed. He opened the knife, looking relaxed. "You be cat food, white prick." The blade glinted.

Before Dennis got out another smart comment, David slammed his fist into the dealer's temple, sending him crashing into the metal bins. Dennis got to his feet. He looked deadly. The knife slashed air about stomach height. David rammed his boot into Dennis's left knee and heard the joint snap. Dennis sprawled backward and screamed. The knife clattered to the ground and Zero kicked it away.

David yanked him up by the long braids. He punched Dennis in the face again and again, unable to stop himself, caught up in the motion: arms swinging, fists connecting, popping sound of flesh being mangled. The blood scent flooded his nostrils. Power built throughout his body. A haze, a red filter; only Dennis's blood existed. Long after resistance ceased, David punched. Metallic gore splattered his face, his hands. His tongue lapped at it. He wanted to wallow in liquid crimson.

Kathleen grabbed his arm; her voice penetrating his reality stopped him. "David! You'll kill him."

His fist halted in midair. The young man before him no longer had a recognizable face. David's grip loosened and the wet body slumped to the pavement. He turned to Kathleen. Her eyes filled with horror at the sight of him and she screamed.

"Let it go," Zero said. They were back at the Alexander.

She held his head in her lap. "You had to do it." She picked up his right hand. It had been badly damaged in the fight, and she was startled to see it healing already. He was almost back to himself, but she'd never forget his face. Starved. His eyes furious red demonic lights. Teeth like ice picks. Zero shivered and forced those thoughts aside for a bit. "Look, the guy's a leech. He lives by feeding that crap to kids—kids Bobby's age."

"But Kathy, he's only a human being. I'm not God, although my kind have been known to act as if they were." He sounded bitter. "It was not a fair fight. I very nearly killed him."

David rolled onto his side. A tortured look distorted his features.

"Jeez, what's the matter with you? He was gonna take both of us out, you with a knife and me an OD. I mean, come on! You ain't Mother Teresa! You're a killer, remember?"

"But that's the point, Kathy. I've never killed. I take only what I need to sustain myself. It's enough that mortals kill one another; I refuse to contribute to that madness. I've prided myself on refraining from unnecessary violence. And now I almost murdered a man with not even the excuse of taking his blood. There's no excuse. I'm degenerating here and I can't halt the process."

"Listen, if you'd killed that sleaze, they woulda given you the good citizenship award. How many kids you think'll be dead because of him?" She stroked his hair. "David, you were just defending yourself. And me. Dennis's brain's boiled from years on coke. He woulda killed you without thinking about it. You did him and the world a favor by taking him outta action for a while."

She couldn't tell if what she was saying had any effect, but she knew she was getting mad. "You know, you really piss me off."

He looked at her, startled.

"Yeah, I mean, lookit you. You act like some Holy Roller or something. Life's not like that, take it from me. Some people ain't nice. Sometimes you gotta be mean. You think the rotten stuff's got nothing to do with you, like you're from some lily-white planet or something. Well, it ain't true. I don't know about you being what you say you are, but whatever you are, you're not so different than me. You do what you gotta to survive. Everybody does. And sometimes it comes down to you or the other guy. And if you're a chickenshit, you lie there and he walks."

"But Kathy, I didn't want to hurt him the way I did."

"David, I was there, remember? I watched you punch Dennis out. You didn't wanna hurt him, you wanted to kill him. You just don't wanna know about it."

Chapter 8

"HEY, BRO, WORD'S OUT *YOU* PUT DENNIS IN PLASTER. THEY got a name for him, and it's a human disaster. The homeys north of Houston figure you're one of us. They say heads'll roll and the rest they're gonna bust."

David looked at Frankie. Kathleen had said that Frankie's mother was Puerto Rican and his father, who flew up from Miami once a year around the High Holidays, was Jewish. It explained the unusual features. The tall youth assumed a cocky pose and chewed gum in a careless way. But he was on guard, as if expecting the worst.

"Word travels rapidly in your circles," David said.

"Yeah, hot off the press. Ain't no need to guess. *Newsweek,* newspeak, we got the best."

"And? What are you saying to me?"

Frankie tilted his head. He spit his gum into the gutter.

"I'm sayin' Dennis's a fuckin' son of a bitch. He hooked my kid sister on crack. I'da had 'im myself, but you, like, got to 'im first."

David smiled. "You're welcome." He slid an arm around Kathleen's shoulders. "What about the other gang?"

"They're dust. Fast rust. Put your dollars on Frankie, man. I'll send 'em to la-la land." Frankie snapped his fingers and a cute black girl with her hair pulled up on top of her head through a silver cone came to his side. He draped an arm around her shoulders, a direct imitation. David tried to keep from laughing.

"You want a fav, Frankie's your man." The boy popped a fresh stick of Juicy Fruit into his mouth, holding the pack out.

David shook his head in astonishment. "Actually, I am in need of a favor. I'm searching for a man, they call him the Snake Priest. He's a midtown pimp, so I can't ask the police."

Kathleen looked up at him as if he were exhibiting signs of insanity.

Frankie's mouth dropped open and a big grin spread across his face. "All right! Where'd you learn to rhyme?"

"It's an art form. Older than you might imagine."

"No way!"

"It's true. I'll tell you about it sometime. So, have you heard of the Snake Priest?"

"Who ain't?"

"Do you know where he can be located?"

"His ponies work Forty-second. I can put out the word, see where he feeds, where he beds his herd."

"Thanks. I'd appreciate that," David said.

"No need to mention my good intention." Frankie slapped David's palm several times with his in a complicated series of movements as though they were blood brothers. "Be cool, fool."

As David led her away, Kathy stared at him in amazement. "You're a real charmer. I ain't never seen Frankie so civilized."

David laughed. *"Mano a mano."*

"What's that mean?"

"Hand to hand. Man to man. He already speaks in rhyming couplets. Soon I'll have him studying the bards. Poets."

Now Kathleen laughed. "That'll be the day. You better teach him to read first."

They went to Mae's, and David left her sitting alone at a booth. On his way out he motioned Mae aside.

"I shall return shortly. As soon as I'm able. Will you take care of her until then?"

Mae eyed him as if he had just escaped from Bellevue. "She ain't underage. Howdaya want me to take care of her?"

"Just keep her here. Can you do that?"

Mae scratched her mostly white hair. "Yeah, I guess. Hurry up, though. I can't chain her to the booth, ya know."

While David was gone, Zero sat with Mae, who watched her put away a toasted club. "Honey, I ain't ever seen you eat so much. That guy must be good for you."

Zero looked up and grinned. "He is, Mae. He's real different from the guys around here. He likes me. He's nice."

Mae smiled back and patted Zero's hand. "I'm glad for ya, honey. You deserve somethin' good in life. God knows you ain't had much."

While Zero ate, she thought about last night. David *was* different, but he no longer scared her. If he needed blood to live, well, that's just the way he was; she could accept that. *Vampire* was maybe the closest word she had to understanding him, and it wasn't a perfect fit, but none of that mattered now.

She put down the last triangle of the three-decker sandwich and looked seriously across the table. "Mae, he reads me poems and his voice's so smooth it's like I died and went to Heaven and the angels were playing harps just for me. He talks smart and knows all about stuff I never even heard of. And he thinks I'm smart. He says I got natural knowledge, the kind you can't learn from books. He says I just never had much of a chance." She was thoughtful for a minute. "Howdaya know when you're in love?"

"What am I, Dear Abby?" But Mae's voice held no real sarcasm. Her face softened. "I remember when Willie and me was goin' together. He was the handsomest boy. Used to bring me flowers every Sunday after church, regular like clockwork. You could set your watch by him. 'Course, this was back in the forties, when people still went to church. The war was on and Willie was about to be shipped over.

I'd sit in my window waitin'. My mother'd yell at me that I was the worst trollop in New York, lettin' a boy know I liked him and all. You didn't do that back then. But I never listened."

"Did you feel like you wanted to be with him all the time?"

"That's how I felt. Willie'd come across the river from Fort Dix, where he was stationed. Pretty near every weekend he got passes to see me. He looked real smart in his dress uniform. I tell you, more than one girl had her eye on him."

"When you were near him, did you feel all out of sync, like when you've got a Popsicle and it's melting faster than you can eat it?"

Mae laughed. "Somethin' like that."

Suddenly the older woman's face wrinkled into sadness, and Zero realized what all these years without Willie meant. "Oh, Mae! I'm sorry. I shouldn'ta said all this."

Mae's eyes glistened but she patted Zero's hand again. "Forget it. We didn't have much time together before they shot him up, but what we had was the best times of my life. I've grieved. These is just memories. It's all I got, and they're dear to me." She pulled a napkin out of the holder and wiped her eyes.

"Hey, Mae. Gimme a toasted western and a coffee," a customer who just walked through the door called.

"Be right with ya. You ain't starvin'."

She looked at Zero again. "Everybody says it 'cause it's true. Love's the most precious thing in this life, Kathy. If you found somebody to love and who loves ya back, there ain't nothin' else matters."

Mae got to her feet. Zero looked at her for a split second and then jumped up. The tiny blonde and the old, bulky, mostly white-haired woman clung to each other in a space of time that seemed eternal.

"Mae! How's about some service? Ya want me ta start goin' down the block?"

"Jeez, Al, you're worse'n a baby." Mae turned toward

her demanding customer. Then she looked at Zero and shook her head.

"Men. Can't live with 'em and who the hell wants to live without 'em."

When David returned to Mae's, he found Kathleen sitting behind an empty plate sipping a cup of coffee. She didn't see him come in, so he got a chance to watch her for a few seconds unobserved. Her head was tilted, pretty yellow hair curled across one exposed shoulder. Her skin was as smooth and rich as good ivory, cheeks a little flushed, blue eyes wide and thoughtful, her lips full and ripe. "A living cameo," he whispered.

She seemed absorbed in thought. But when she noticed him, she lowered the cup and her eyes, like a doe's, turned soft and liquid. Her lips parted and curved into a smile he knew was meant for him alone. Byron's most lovely words came to him.

> She walks in Beauty, like the night
> Of cloudless climes and starry skies;
> And all that's best of dark and bright
> Meet in her aspect and her eyes. . . .

"Hi," she said, her eyes glued to his. Despite over a century of British reserve, David could not restrain himself from bending down to kiss her in public. She wrapped her arms around his neck and he inhaled her scent, sweet, almost virginal in a way. And then she was in his arms. He ran his fingers through her hair and kissed her lips passionately.

"You runnin' a hotel now?" the man at the end of the counter grumbled.

"You're dryin' out, Al, if you can't remember love," Mae said.

As they left Mae's, David thought back to the events of the previous night. He felt amazingly good. Without Kathy he knew he would have sunk into depression because of what he had done to Dennis. But she seemed able to contain his darkness. His somber nature did not frighten her as it had so many women. The fact that they were different species held less and less weight.

"You were gone a long time," she said, interrupting his thoughts. "Trouble finding blood? I told you you can take mine. I got lots."

His fingers brushed her throat where traces of the punctures remained. "No trouble. And I will not take yours again. I was gone so long because I met Frankie. He found out that the Snake Priest frequents an S-and-M club in Chelsea."

He laughed. "I had to ask Frankie to explain the letters. He couldn't believe I didn't know. Anyway, he said by tomorrow he'd learn which one. I rented an auto and then drove over there to get a sense of the area."

"Without me?" She looked shocked. "I thought we're in this together."

"We are. But after last night I'm not certain I want you involved to the extent you have been. You could be injured."

"So could you."

"Mortals don't know how to harm me. In any event, I asked a few questions and confirmed that Forty-second Street *is* his territory. I also discovered that he's as protected as a Swiss bank account. It may be impossible to find him alone."

Kathleen stopped. Her eyes flashed. "David, I don't want you doing this without me. First of all, it's stupid. I know my way around lots better than you. Second, even if I don't go, the Snake Priest already knows about me and can find me easy, so I'm safer with you. And I wanna get Bobby back, and I'm going. Besides, I got an idea how we can get to him."

"Well, we can't do much this evening. I don't believe it wise to go from club to club hoping to run into him. I'd rather wait until Frankie comes up with a definite place where he'll likely be." He paused. "Is that all right with you?"

It took a few seconds for the blue fire in her eyes to dim, but eventually she smiled. "Okay. We'll wait. You're right about the Snake Priest. I heard stuff. We should find out as much as we can. What're we gonna do tonight?"

They were near the Alexander. David let go of her waist and took her arm. He stopped in front of a tan Chevrolet and opened the passenger door. "First we'll take a ride. When was the last time you drove along the river at night?"

She shrugged her shoulders.

"What about a moonlight cruise of the Hudson?"

"Never did that."

"Or a carriage ride through Central Park?"

Her blue-crystal eyes sparkled. "I never done none of those things, and I lived here all my life."

"Dearest, permit me to introduce you to New York's lovelier face."

David drove along the East River on the FDR Drive. It was a pleasant evening and they rode with the windows open, Kathy curled up next to him.

It had been decades since he'd driven in New York; one of the last times had been when André had decided to return to France in 1960 and David had taken him to the airport.

When they reached the mid-Nineties, David turned back and drove down to Battery Park. There they boarded the yacht that cruised around Manhattan. Kathleen leaned into the rail. The night breeze blew her long hair so that she resembled Botticelli's Venus to him. He held her from behind; his arms seemed to fit perfectly around her. He would not have been able to identify the point where he gave himself over to long dormant romantic feelings that had somehow been reignited.

"Gee, it's beautiful," she sighed.

"You are far more beautiful," he whispered in her ear.

About one A.M. they snuggled together in the backseat of an imitation Victorian carriage, arms and legs intertwined, a blanket across them. The pungent smell of the horses, the clopping of iron shoes on cement, the ever-present hum of traffic out of sight but always near, the dim arc of illumination from the old street lamps in Central Park, all worked together to weave a spell. She ran her hands up under his

T-shirt along his bare back. His skin was sensitive enough to distinguish the oval ridges on each of her fingertips. He felt his own body respond like dry earth sucking up nourishing moisture.

"Tell me a poem," she said.

> "My blood is all meridian; were it not,
> I had not left my clime, nor should I be,
> In spite of tortures, ne'er to be forgot,
> A slave again of love—at least of thee."

She seemed enchanted by Byron's words, her large eyes inviting David closer.

And David knew beyond any doubt that those words were true; despite his fears and misgivings, he was falling in love with her.

They returned to the Alexander about four A.M. On the way in David tossed the car keys to Frankie. "The tank's full up with petrol and the registration is in the glove compartment. Make certain you have it back here by six tomorrow evening."

The boy looked stunned for a second but recovered quickly. He grabbed his girl, and another couple got in the back, and the four squealed off into the night.

Inside Kathleen asked, "You wanna be alone again?"

He answered by leading her to where he slept. The closet was old-fashioned and large enough to hold them both on the floor comfortably plus block out daylight. He spread a blanket over the carpet.

In the darkness he explored her body. Hot and moist in spots, cool in others, and soft. But it also had a goosefleshy feel. "Are you frightened?" he asked.

"A little."

"What of? Not me, I hope."

"I'm just scared of sex. I want it but I'm scared too."

He kissed her lips then moved to her nipples. Her body quivered. "We've lots of time."

Zero didn't know if she would be able to enjoy this again. The last encounter seemed like a fluke. She wanted so much to give herself, and the more she tried, the less she felt able to.

"Relax," he said again, his lips pulling on hers, sensitive fingers fine-tuning to her flesh.

Years of servicing men had left her with the idea that unless she was running the show, she wasn't doing her job. But she liked his kisses and his touch, which let her know he was aware of more than her skin. And finally she just lay back and let him do things to her. And then something strange happened. She could see him in the dark.

Beyond the lightless closet and the added darkness of closed eyes, she watched him, a shadow, black outlined against black.

She knew when he lifted his arm or turned his head or if he moved up away from her or down onto her. He became like an entity in infinite space that had latched on to her, targeting in, coming ever closer. She felt his energy, a sense of him homing in until she heard herself gasp as his darkness penetrated the light inside her, filling her for the first time.

Chapter 9

THE FOLLOWING NIGHT FRANKIE HAD THE NAME OF THE club—Cutting Edge. David dropped Kathleen off at Mae's. She asked for money to shop with, which he provided. Then he went in search of his kind of food.

The streets were alive with a kinetic energy, the feeling that something was about to happen. It affected him, and he felt a certain expectation. But he wasn't prepared for the shock he got when he returned to their room at the Alexander.

"Well?" Kathy asked.

He looked her over. Orange and purple hair stood straight out from her head, green eyes, four-inch-high heels, a very short white leather skirt, low-cut bustier that her breasts nearly swelled over, and layers of jewelry fashioned into chains and padlocks hanging from her wrists, waist, and neck.

"How did you change the color of your eyes?"

She laughed. "Easy. They got these contacts now that're real soft—they even fold in half—they come in colors. I dyed my hair. It'll wash out."

"What's all this about, then?"

"Well, I figure the Snake Priest knows what I look like,

78

so if he said I wasn't supposed to come back, then he'd be suspicious if I walked into the club. And you ain't gonna get within a mile of him. He's got these bodyguards, big guys; they look like boxers. I know you're strong and everything, but I don't think you can take so many all at once."

David sat down. He didn't like where this was leading. "What are you thinking, Kathleen? That you'll go in there and draw him out?"

"Yeah. I'll get him to take me to his place. You can follow us. Then we got him alone and can ask anything we want."

"And just how are you going to persuade him to take you home?"

"The guy's into S and M. Everybody knows he's the S. I'll be the M. That's what this outfit's about. His bodyguards'll be outside or at least not with me and the Snake Priest. And I figure you can take them out one at a time easy. I'll leave the door unlocked."

"And what exactly do you know about the Snake Priest's sadistic practices?"

She shifted, looked down at the floor and then at David. "He's a lightweight, mostly verbal humiliation. Nothing too physical."

He started to speak but she cut him off. "Anyway, all that stuff's like acting. Nobody ever gets hurt. You tell them how far you'll go and they respect your limits. I've done it with lots of guys. It's the only way, if I can get inside."

"Absolutely not! Do you really think I'd let you near someone like that?"

She took her hand away from him. "David, there's no other way."

"There will have to be because you're not going to do this."

She looked a little dejected. She got up and paced the room. "I'll be okay. You'll be right behind me. Nothing's gonna happen." She sat next to him again. "I know this'll work 'cause I had a girlfriend, Kelly, that went with him. She told me all about it. She said it's the only time she saw him without his protection. Come on, David. Let's just go and get it over with." She kissed him on the lips, and the kiss was familiar, even if the face was not. "Please? It's the fastest way to find Bobby and who's after you."

She kept at him, wearing away his resistance. Despite serious doubts, David allowed himself to be talked into her scheme. But on the drive across town he felt uneasy and could not shake a sense of impending disaster.

The entrance to Cutting Edge was an unpretentious unmarked door on West Twenty-first, factories on either side. While David waited in a car up the street, Zero knocked on the basement door. Someone must have peered through the peephole, because the door opened.

The doorman gave her the once-over as she eased by him.

Inside, the room was poorly lit and dense with smoke, and she had trouble at first even finding the bar. But eventually her eyes adjusted and she sidled up to a structure resembling a prison cell, drinks passed through the bars. An exotic-looking brown-skinned woman dressed in skin-tight silver leather pants with a short riding crop sticking out of the back pocket was on Zero's left. The woman looked her up and down, but Zero turned away, not wanting to encourage anything. On her right stood another woman in a black leather skirt and stilettos. This one had very pale skin, almost as pale as David's when he was hungry. On his knees in front of her a balding man knelt on the tiled floor. He wore a studded dog collar around his neck, and the woman held him in close by a short fluorescent leash. While he licked her calves below the hem of her skirt, she ignored him.

It occurred to Zero that this might not be the right place. She also wondered if the clubs had gotten so specialized that this was a women's S and men's M place. But then she spotted a number of other scenes, like a man leading a young woman with her hands cuffed behind her back, confirming that it went either way.

The bartender handed her a rye and ginger that she paid five dollars for. She took a sip, even though ordinarily she didn't drink liquor. But she was nervous. There were things she knew about the Snake Priest that she hadn't told David because she was sure he wouldn't let her do this if he knew. Like the fact that the Snake Priest was a big dealer of both cocaine and heroin. And that "Priest" was short for "Priest of Pain," while the "Snake" part had to do with his collection. It was rumored he'd beaten a couple of girls to death, one of them Kelly, Zero suspected, when she'd tried to leave his stable. And Zero was worried. But she couldn't think of another way to get at him. She was desperate to find Bobby.

Suddenly she spotted him, and she knew it was him. He was a large man, but large in a different way than Dennis; not so much muscle as height and sheer bulk. He did not resemble a priest at all. Like most of the customers, he was dressed in animal hide, but in his case it was black snake-skin, both pants, and a shirt slit open to the waist. His jaw was very square, his eyes small and piercing, and his face, even across the room, a color that implied he was either stoned or had high blood pressure. Zero thought he looked slick—in a suit he could have passed for the head of a corporation. Certain women might find him attractive in a hard way. His rodent eyes darted around the room as if searching for food. Maybe this isn't such a good idea, she thought, feeling her heart pound in fear. But David's just outside, she reminded herself.

The Snake Priest was surrounded by tough-looking men Zero figured were his guards. He *was* well-protected. He also had a woman with him.

This won't be easy, she thought, but decided to go for it. Maybe she'd just have to set it up for another night.

She took a big gulp of her drink and strolled easily across the room, not in a direct line, collecting glances along the way.

The Snake Priest's table was by a fifties jukebox. As she neared, she walked straight toward him. He looked up. At the last possible second she veered right and stopped in front of the music. She turned her head slightly. He was watching. She shifted her weight onto her left leg, jutting her hip in his direction, and glanced down at the list of song titles.

"Hey, pretty vanilla," came a smooth voice from behind,

the tone the kind Zero had heard in confessionals. She turned her head just a little. The Snake Priest was breathing down her neck. She gave him a qualified smile.

"Like blow?"

"Sure," she said.

He pulled two tiny brown bottles from his pocket and pressed one into her palm. On the fingers of both hands he wore chunky rings, all bearing religious symbols or snakes. "One for later, sugar, one for now," he said, his voice as comforting as his face was not.

In grand gestures he dumped out the contents of the second bottle onto the flat glass surface of the jukebox, used a platinum American Express card to scrape it into neat lines, and then produced a one-thousand-dollar bill which, after he had rolled it tightly into a tube, he offered to Zero. She tried to take it, but he held tight. His eyes roved over her body in a way that made her feel a little sick.

"Lookin' for some tough love?"

"Maybe," she said coyly. She dropped her purse and bent to pick it up, making sure that her rear end faced him.

He ran the back of his hand up the inside of her thigh; the rings were cool against her skin. As she stood, he handed her the rolled bill and grinned. A snake-like white scar running from the middle of his upper lip to his right ear undulated grotesquely when he smiled. His teeth were so smooth she got the impression they were false—the front left had a ruby embedded in it. Against an almost hairless white chest rested a gold disk on a chain, a hologram inside. It depicted a crucifixion, the writhing body hanging from the cross a woman's.

After they did the lines, the Snake Priest led her to his table. The bodyguards made room, but the woman sent daggers of hate in her direction. The woman was a brunette whom Zero imagined had done a lot of pouting as a child. Now, crowding thirty, her protruding lower lip teetered, ready for the disastrous slide from cute petulance to bitter disappointment.

The Snake Priest bought Zero a drink and they snorted more coke. He sat with an arm locked around her neck, his hand down inside her bustier, squeezing her nipple hard, whispering things in her ear that frightened her, promises of pain that would produce a lot of pleasure. She had been with many men, but none as soulless as this one.

At one point he noticed the tracks on her arm. "You go hot or cold?"

"Smack," she said. The coke had raced through her system like a tornado ravaging a sleepy town, freezing her nose and most of her face. Her brain felt on fire, and at the same time, blank. She had a hard time thinking about, even remembering, why she was there, and that David was waiting.

"Got some at my place. And other things bad girls like."

He pulled her to her feet. Immediately the six men stood. So did the other woman, but the Snake Priest shoved her toward one of his guards, a large black man with bleached hair, as if she was a sandwich he had finished with.

Outside, they waited while one of the men got the car, a cranberry stretch limo, and everyone piled in. Zero looked up the street briefly but couldn't see David. That didn't worry her; the coke made her fearless.

They drove north to the west side of Central Park, stopping in front of a glass and steel high-rise apartment complex. The Snake Priest got out, pulled Zero after him, and the rest followed in what seemed to be a prearranged pattern: the driver parked up the block and remained inside the limo; one man stayed in the lobby with the security guard; one took the stairwell; the last two men accompanied the group of four up the elevator to the penthouse. One went to the stairwell there and the other checked the apartment, and, once that was done, waited out in the hallway.

The Snake Priest led Zero and the other two through a door that he bolted securely with a series of chains and dead bolts. There was no way she could unlock it. Maybe if I can distract him, she thought. The black man took the other woman to the left, and the Snake Priest moved Zero in the opposite direction.

He switched on a light, and the room they entered was washed in crimson. The walls and door were padded, except for a glass balcony door that had been blacked out. She had the feeling that whatever went on in here would not be heard by the outside world.

All kinds of torture equipment vied for space—dozens of whips, straps, bamboo canes, and wooden paddles, all sizes and shapes, had been affixed to the walls in neat, orderly rows. The leather looked well-oiled, the wood fine-grained and meticulously varnished. Silver and black bars and chains hung from the ceiling, and a long table with leather restraints and handcuffs took up a corner of the room, but a large, altarlike bed was the focus. Next to it sat a giant snake tank above which hung a silver crucifix.

Zero had a bad feeling about this. She decided she better get out while she still could. "Listen, I forgot something at the bar. I gotta go back for it."

"Get naked, cunt!"

She turned around, about to tell him that she had changed her mind, but before she was even facing him, he punched her in the face. She fell backward against the serpent tank, stunned, tasting blood on her lips. Loud hissing made her crawl away immediately, back toward the Snake Priest.

"Looks to me like you're in need of serious penance, girl. When I'm through, you'll be beggin' the Snake Priest for absolution. I said get those clothes off. Now! Do it!"

Her body began trembling, but she tried to reassure herself—he can't be worse than my old man. When she was naked, he attached her wrists together with leather bands that had metal hooks locking onto each other. "Can I have some smack?" she asked, startled by how frightened her voice sounded.

A mean look crossed the Snake Priest's face, twisting the scar so that it seemed to writhe. But his voice was smooth, silky, almost reassuring. "You'll get all the smack you need. After I draw blood." He hooked her restraints to a chain hanging from the ceiling, then hoisted her off the floor. As her body twisted from side to side, she watched him pick out a whip from his collection, a long cinnamon strip of rawhide connected to a ringed snakeskin handle. He flipped on a CD player; church music screamed from the speakers.

When he approached her, his eyes were on fire, and to Zero he looked possessed.

He rubbed her nipples with the knobby snakehide handle. "You be a real good girl, now, and let me hear some sincere beggin' for forgiveness. You won't disturb a soul, so you'd best try to please me. Make it good and loud, and the Snake Priest give you a hit to take the edge off." He grabbed a fistful of her hair, pulling her head back until she was staring at the mirrored ceiling. He looked up. " 'Cause if I ain't satisfied, you ain't gonna leave here with no skin. Understand me, cunt?"

"Yes," she whispered.

The whip cracked against her flesh and Zero had to unlearn everything she had ever taught herself about repressing sounds. But David was right, she was street-smart. Soon her throat was raw.

David watched the bodyguard in the lobby come back outside. The man walked up the street and stopped at the limousine to lean in the window and talk with the driver. David made his move.

An elderly security guard opened the locked door but did not invite him in.

"Good evening," David said pleasantly.

"Evening, sir," the man in the security uniform said, nodding. "What can I do for you?"

"I'm here on business."

The older man looked him over with the distrust that such a profession breeds. "Apartment number?" he asked.

When David hesitated, the guard began to close the door. The old man had cataracts. He could barely see, and not well enough to meet David's eyes.

"I'm with the party that just arrived. A bit late. I'm expected, of course."

"I'll have to phone upstairs."

"I don't have time for this. Tell them they'll have to rearrange the meeting, and I shall not be back in the States in the near future. I'm sure they'll be mad as hell, given the size of the contract they're losing, but I'm too busy to wait."

David turned away.

The idea of incurring the Snake Priest's displeasure affected the guard, who became obsequious. "Maybe you oughta go right up. Save time."

"Excellent idea."

Two elevators faced each other. The light panels showed that one was waiting to open on the ground floor, while the other had stopped at Penthouse North, obviously where the Snake Priest had taken Kathy. David pushed the button for that elevator. When it arrived, he took it to the thirty-ninth floor, one below the penthouse. He walked to the door marked "Stairs" and opened it cautiously. A large Asian man he recognized as one of the Snake Priest's men immediately started down from the floor above. David started up. They met at the landing.

"Pardon me," David said politely, smiling, adding a condescending tone to his upper-class accent, trying to catch the man's eye. "I find myself a bit confused. I'm searching for Penthouse South."

"Wrong elevator, buddy. Go to the lobby and take the other one."

"So sorry," David said. People like this, so shifty-eyed, rarely met his gaze. But he stood his ground, forcing the large man to challenge him. The weight lifter reacted like any animal obliged to defend its territory. He tried to stare David down.

"I said it's downstairs!" The man's tone was threatening, but by now David had locked on to the mud-colored orbs, focusing on the black dot in the center of each. They dilated and contracted as a battle of wills ensued. David concentrated his will on penetrating the other; he felt the depravity inside this mortal dedicated to destruction. The essence was so sick, so putrid, it almost reeked. David identified it immediately—*killer*.

The light within me, he thought. Focus it. He sensed the beam of brilliance that was the essence of every living thing vibrate inside him and channel its way through his eyes. The light formed an energy that darted out of him and staked the core of this mortal's being.

The guard looked stunned. His pupils had dilated and stayed large, as if he had fallen under a spell. His lids fluttered and he fell back against the wall. David caught him, easing him down to a seated position. He sensed another guard below, probably closer to ground level. He'd only deal with him if it came to that. Concentrating his energy in this way was depleting and he needed time to recharge.

He went up the stairwell to the penthouse floor and surreptitiously peered out into the hallway. Another guard sat beside a door, across from the elevator, reading a racing form.

David moved quietly, and it was not until he neared that the man came to life. "Who the fu—" A sharp blow to the back of the neck and the man was unconscious. David dragged his body into the stairwell and dumped him next to the other bodyguard.

He went back and tried the door. Even with all his strength, nothing happened. Quickly he assessed that it must be a special fire door, metal extra thick, heavily barred from within.

He spotted a window at the end of the corridor. It was double-plated, hermetically sealed, the type almost impossible to shatter. Bracing himself, David flattened his palms against the glass in strategic spots and shoved. The entire sheet popped out of the frame and tumbled down the side of the building, landing in the middle of the side street below.

He peered along the outside wall. A two-foot ledge ran around both corners of the building. Dotting the outside wall were low wrought-iron balconies, designed to imitate garden fences. Each balcony surrounded glass patio doors.

The balcony to the left was about eight feet away. He looked down at the ground, forty stories below. The front of the building overlooked Central Park. From here it was an aerial photo, a mass of green with wavy lines streaking through it and pinpoints of light. Traffic noise was dim. Up this high the wind was strong. He had heard stories, gruesome tales of injuries to others like himself, which had not killed them but altered them severely. What would happen if he fell such a distance? At the least, every bone in his body would shatter. His heart or brain might be pierced, or his spinal cord severed, in which case he would probably die quickly. Otherwise, if he were taken to a hospital ... For once I wish I could turn into a bat, he thought.

He knew he had to work quickly. Kathy was in danger; he sensed it.

He returned to the stairwell and removed the belts from the two guards. As silently as he could, he hurried down the steps.

The guard at the third floor was a bit faster than the other two. He managed to get to his weapon. David knocked him out before he could use it.

He raced back up the steps three at a time, hooking the three belts together so that they would not separate. Then he attached his own, making it into a loop. Back at the window of the fortieth floor he stepped out onto the narrow ledge and looked down. A feeling of vertigo struck. He pressed himself against the building, but there was nothing but the window frame to hold on to. Finally his head cleared and his pulse slowed to a reasonable rate.

He tossed the chain of belts, lariat-style, trying to hook the loop over one of the balcony's spears. After a dozen tries he succeeded. He wrapped the other end of the leather chain tightly around his fist. Gradually he slid his right then his left foot tentatively along the ledge. Sounds of traffic drifted up and he was keenly aware of the scuffing sound his soles made.

The ledge was slippery and his foot nearly slid off once. He clutched, but the steel face offered no support, and secretly he did not trust the leather chain to hold him if he fell.

His movements became agonizingly cautious. Eventually he reached the first balcony and, with clammy hands, climbed over. When he peered through the glass doors he was disappointed. Inside, the black guard and the girl were both lounging back against a couch. Their bodies were limp and they stared at nothing. Between them lay a needle and what looked like enough heroin to keep them occupied for a while.

As he rounded the corner he saw five more balconies, about eight feet apart from one another. He sensed there were only two other people in the apartment; one of them was Kathy, and the vibrations he was picking up did not feel good.

He went to the second balcony in the same painfully slow way as he'd gotten to the first, annoyed with the delay, apprehensive about the danger that Kathy was facing. Inside the second set of doors he saw a kitchen, inside the third a living room. The next was a bedroom—empty. By the time he reached the fifth, cold sweat clung to his body. He gulped air, his muscles quivering, nerves frayed. The last doors were blacked out. He sensed Kathleen within and that something was very wrong. Instinctively he kicked at the glass, sending shards flying inward.

She lay on the bed spread-eagled. Her back was a sea of red and she was moaning. The Snake Priest knelt behind her, about to insert a writhing snake into her vagina.

The pimp turned at the sound of breaking glass, but before he had time to react, David crossed the room with inhuman speed. He backhanded the Snake Priest across the mouth, sending him sprawling across the room.

David's acute hearing could pick up the slightest sounds, even through the soundproofing. The others in the apartment either had not heard, were incapable of reacting, or, as he feared, these sounds were little different from what they had been hearing all along.

The room reeked of blood and sweat. He gathered Kathy in his arms and turned her head. Her face had been beaten so badly that her eyes were already puffy and discolored. "Oh, Kathy, no!"

His voice filled with the pain and guilt he felt. If he had arrived sooner ... No, he should not have permitted her to come here at all. He pulled her close and she moaned.

Beside the bed he noticed the white powder, the needle. He checked the inside of her arm and saw a trickle of blood, grateful, this once, that she was numbed.

He could hardly understand her as she mumbled through swollen lips, "David, I'm a real fuck-up."

"Shhh. Don't talk. You'll be all right. I'm going to take

care of you. I'm a fool, Kathy. I should never have let you come here."

"You're more than a fuckin' fool," came a smooth voice from behind. In his preoccupation, David had not sensed the Snake Priest struggle to his feet. The pimp moved across the room and stood in front of the balcony, a safe distance away. He held what looked to be a short machine gun. "So, fool, you can start by tellin' me who sent you, then I'm gonna blow your fuckin' brains out. And after you that cunt's brains, if she got any."

David stood so that he shielded Kathy. Behind him she mumbled, trying to sit.

Unlike his guards, the Snake Priest seemed to have no trouble looking David in the eye. The dark evil emanating from this man filled the room like poison gas, destroying everything in its wake.

"No one sent me," David said. "I'm here to find out why you tried to have me killed. And where you're keeping her brother."

"What the fuck bullshit . . ." The Snake Priest looked perplexed until it dawned on him and he nodded. "Oh, yeah. The whore. And the English son of a bitch thinks he's a fuckin' vampire." He grinned and a new line of blood trickled from his split lip down his chin.

The blood attracted David. He needed it. His entire body cried out to be replenished. He struggled to bring his obsession under control. Kathy was depending on him. "Why did you send her to kill me?"

"I'm asking the questions, motherfucker. Send the bitch over here. Now!"

Kathleen had managed to stand, and although wobbly, held onto David for support. She started to move toward the Snake Priest, mumbling, "Please, don't hurt him," but David shoved her to the floor behind him.

Rapid-fire shots blasted. One lodged in his right shoulder, another ripped into his stomach.

David doubled over and at the same time forced himself forward. The Snake Priest fired again. More bullets tore into his thigh. And when David still didn't go down, astonishment creased the pimp's face just before he was tackled.

Anger boiled to the surface. David smashed the Snake Priest's head onto the floor. Again. And again. The bullet wounds weakened him, and at the same time sent him nearly out of control. His teeth slashed an artery. Before he knew what he was doing, blood gushed up then down David's throat—a crimson geyser. The quantity of his violence nearly replaced quality, and he checked himself by plugging the leak. He needed this man alive.

"Why did you send her? And where's her brother? None of your guards can help you. Tell me or you're dead."

The Snake Priest spit blood into David's face but his eyes showed shock. "What the fuck are you?" He grinned like a madman. Two of his teeth had been knocked out. "You want her fuckin' brother? Go to the fuckin' bank." He tried to laugh but the effect was a soundless, corpselike grimace spread across his damaged features.

"What's that supposed to mean?"

He pointed toward the serpentarium. "Keys," he said, as his eyes rolled back into his head.

David went to the snake tank and looked in. At least two dozen vipers crowded inside the twenty feet of glass. His stomach lurched and the hairs on the back of his neck stood on end. He heard his breath come in pants. Control yourself! he ordered.

He wasn't an expert, but he could identify the rattlers by their tails, and he would never forget the red, yellow, and black bands of the ringed coral snake. He grabbed a bamboo cane from the wall and nudged the serpents around.

Finally he saw the keys; they were on a key ring attached to the bottom of the tank. A quick glance around the room told him there were no special gloves or other equipment handy. If he reached in to get them, he would be bitten. And poisoned. He had been bitten once as a child in the woods on the estate. And again, this time in Texas, by a deadly coral. It was only his immortal state that had kept him alive that last time. The terror of both memories invaded him now. His body remembered uncontrollable death spasms and mind-chilling hallucinations.

No bloody way! he thought.

He grabbed the sides of the tank and yanked it off the floor. When he got it to the middle of the room, he turned it over and dumped the snakes out. Some slithered quickly, others barely moved, but when the serpentarium emptied, David got the keys.

The Snake Priest sprawled near the balcony doors, crucifixion style. One of the corals headed his way.

David wrapped Kathleen in the satin bedsheet. As he picked her up, she moaned.

Suddenly he heard a low gurgling sound, an unearthly laugh.

When he turned, he was flabbergasted to see the Snake Priest stagger to his feet like a corpse that refused to stay dead. His battered face had twisted into a macabre mask. He had the gun in his hands again, lifting it, and this time David knew he wouldn't hesitate.

"Bitch gets it first." He aimed at Kathy.

David had no time to think, no time to figure out how to protect either of them, only a fraction of a second to react. He leaped, ramming the Snake Priest with the power of his preternatural strength.

The man flew backward through the balcony doors and flipped over the low railing.

Oomph! The impact as David hit him. The deafening gun blasts.

Silence but for the faint din of traffic below filling the room and the incessant rattle of the snakes.

David was unable to move, unable to breathe. The dreadful quiet unnerved him. His acute hearing had picked up the thud of the Snake Priest slamming against the sidewalk. He had died without uttering a sound. That, David knew, would haunt him forever.

He moved through the apartment and into the elevator, Kathy in his arms. When they arrived on the main floor, the security guard was still alone. The old man turned, surprised, suspicious, but David pulled his face close, catching his dimmed eyes, forcing the man back into his chair, erasing his memory.

Out on the noisy street the limo driver and the last body-guard were still talking. David got Kathleen into the car and away without being seen.

At the Alexander, David tossed Frankie the keys. He had lost a lot of blood and his strength was ebbing. He felt off balance physically and mentally. "Can you make this car vanish?"

"You mean for good? Sell the motor, junk the hood?"

"Yes."

"Easy."

"Do it, please. Keep the money." David picked Kathy up in his arms.

"She okay?" Frankie asked, then must have noticed the bullet holes riddling David's body. "Man, are *you* okay?"

"Negative to both inquiries."

Chapter 10

DAVID SENT FRANKIE TO THE DRUGSTORE TO GET MEDICINE and bandages for Kathy's wounds. Relying on a mortal in his condition was risky, but he did not have much choice. His body was already in the process of getting rid of the bullets, and that process caused him tremendous pain.

He washed Kathy, dressed her wounds, and plied her with aspirin. Later, as the heroin seemed to be wearing off, he gave her sleeping pills. He spoke as many soothing words as he could muster, unsure if she heard any of them.

She lay in a stupor, partly from the drugs, partly from shock. Toward morning she started to come around, but his strength gave out and it was all he could do to hide from the sun.

He tied her to the bed to ensure that the desire for drugs didn't overwhelm the instinct to recuperate.

David needed to rest. Like any wounded creature, his body begged for quiet and darkness and time to heal. But he was uncertain whether or not his soul would ever mend. Morally he had sunk into the land of Ulru, as William Blake had termed it, wallowing with the unconscious masses in blame and retaliation, unable to lift himself above it. He felt any control he had ever had, or imagined he'd had, being chipped away nightly at a terrifying speed, leaving him victim of the dark passions that he'd spent his immortal existence struggling to keep locked away. He had to face the fact that he'd killed without giving the act any thought. Even though the Snake Priest deserved to die several times over, that was hardly the issue. He could only wonder what he was becoming.

While he lay in the blackness trying to breathe evenly, he felt the wounds closing from within, pushing the metal out through the muscles, past the connective tissue and up toward his skin. The keys he had retrieved at such a cost were marked "Citibank." They were probably for a safety deposit box at the closest branch. David drifted off wondering what he would find in that box. And whether it would be worth it.

By sunset the next day the bullets had been expelled and David found them lying on the floor beside him. He was sore but nearly healed. As soon as he could obtain nourishment, his physical pain would disappear, but Kathleen was moaning and crying, and he knew his mental anguish had only just begun.

"David, it's all my fault. I screw everything up," she said as he emerged from the closet.

"For God's sake, Kath, stop. This is my fault. I should never have let you go with him. I don't know what's the matter with me."

"No, it's me. There's stuff about the Snake Priest I never told you. I knew he was rough. I thought I could handle him. But we gotta get outta here before he comes after us. He'll find us for sure."

"He can't come after us."

She looked at him.

"He went over the balcony. I pushed him."

"Good." She stopped crying briefly but then began again. "Everything hurts so much. And I'm goin' cold turkey again. It already started."

He stroked her hair and kissed her forehead, the only place that was not black and blue. She looked like she'd been hit by a subway train. "I'll be with you. You're going to recover. And when you're well, I'll get you away from this rubbish heap."

"But what about Bobby? And whoever's after you?"

"There's information in a safety deposit box. I'll see that Frankie gathers it soon. Perhaps we'll learn something." At least I hope so, he thought.

She sobbed. "I'm gonna be sick."

He untied her and helped her to the bathroom. All night long she experienced bouts of vomiting and diarrhea, similar to what he had witnessed in Manchester. But this time she was real to him, someone he cared about, perhaps even loved, and emotionally he empathized, suffering as she suffered.

He went out briefly to get her food and a cassette recorder.

She would not eat the soup, but did manage to drink a little fruit juice. David stayed with her, caressing her, talking about their future. He recorded the love poem Elizabeth Barrett Browning had written for her husband so that Kathy could listen to it during the day. And when morning came and she was sweating and cramping, he had no choice but to tie her to the bed again; he placed the recorder where she could press the buttons.

"You haven't asked for heroin," he said.

"I knew you wouldn't give me any."

A week later David had her up, washed, and then out the door to Mae's. They sat side by side in a booth, with Mae across from them demanding to know, "What happened to you, Kathy?"

"Mae, please," Zero said. She had on large dark glasses that hid most of the destruction around her eyes. But her cheeks were bruised and her lower lip had a nasty cut in it that bled when she tried to eat. David spoon-fed her soup. She sipped a little but was too down to eat. She was stuffed with painkillers and felt drowsy and dull.

Mae was furious. "You do this?" She looked at David.

"Not directly."

"What the hell's that mean?"

"He didn't do it, Mae," Zero said. "It's my fault. I was

in the wrong place at the wrong time. Don't ask, okay?"
She sighed and let her head fall back against David's arm.
She felt utterly and completely exhausted. David had been
so kind to her, kinder than anyone had ever been, even
Mae. And she knew she would heal. She was past the worst
part of the withdrawal too. But despite these thoughts, Zero
felt more frightened than she had ever felt before. Added
to that, the thought that she might never see Bobby again
terrified her. Each morning when David left her alone, she
didn't believe she would get through the day. Only his voice
kept her sane. It stopped her from tearing into the arms of
the madness that beckoned. She sensed that those arms
would lock around her permanently and drag her to her
death. "Hold me," she said.

He cradled her, pressing her against his chest, kissing the
top of her head. Fear quivered through her. When she shut
her eyes, she could still see the room, the red, whips staring
her in the face as one of them shredded her flesh. When
she was alone during the day, she vividly remembered the
cracking sound and the sharp slicing pain, the sight of the
Snake Priest's fist coming at her. And mixed in with all these
images was her father's face.

Her body shook uncontrollably. "I want to go back to
the room."

David told her, "It's all right. I'm here with you. You're
safe. Mae's here too. Don't be afraid, Kath. We'll leave
right now."

When they returned to the Alexander, Frankie was outside. "Hey, lookin' good, Zero."

She nuzzled closer to David and he pulled her in.

"Did you manage the bank today?" David asked the
youth.

"Location's right but they wouldn't let me in to the box.
Ain't rented to Mr. Priest, and that was a shock. But I saw
this girl works at the bank, she got me the records for a
kiss and a thanks. It's rented to somebody named Audrey
Hariman." He handed the keys over to David. "Sometimes
these dudes do that, put it in a girl's name, so's stuff can't
be traced, know what I mean?"

"Thanks, Frankie. You've been a big help." David started to reach into his pocket for a bill, but the boy waved a hand and walked away.

"No, man. That's what bros are for. It's an even score. I acquired some fine currency on that Chevy."

When they were inside the room, Zero said, "I'll go tomorrow."

He shook his head. "I'll find someone else. One of the girls. Or Mae. You're not going."

"Mae ain't part of this. And those girls won't get in. They're too young and dumb. The manager'll call the cops. I can't believe he didn't have Frankie busted."

He sat down on the bed. "No, Kathy. You're still weak. And besides, I think you're too frightened to be out in the world alone right now."

"You think I'll score some junk, doncha?"

"That's a possibility."

"I wish I could tell you for sure I won't, but I know I don't want to. If I go through this withdrawal stuff again, my heart's gonna go ballistic."

She sat next to him. He put an arm around her, and she felt grateful for the constant comfort. "I love you," she said suddenly. "I never said that to nobody except Bobby. But I do, David."

He kissed her lips gently. "When this is over, you'll be with me forever, if that's what you want."

"I never wanted nothing more."

"Kathleen, you must know the truth about my existence. Take some time to decide. There are drawbacks and they're not insignificant. I can't give you children. And although the human imagination seems to demand it, my kind, we are not immortal in the strict sense of the word. Fire, decapitation, a serious wound to the heart or a severed spinal cord, exposure to the sun, these things will destroy you. During the hours of daylight you will be immobile and vulnerable. You'll often feel alone."

"Hell, I'm at my best at night anyway." She laughed, although she was beginning to feel uncomfortable and didn't know why.

"There's more. Our habits are peculiar to mortals, and in the end, they are our prey. For that reason and others we must move frequently. You'll see people around you, people you care about, growing old, suffering, dying, while you yourself remain the same. It's very painful. You'll feel apart from humanity and come to see them as alien, just as they will call you monstrous, should they discover what you are. Their games will be so obvious to you, their pain too real."

"Ain't there other vampires?"

"Yes. But our relationships are unlike human relationships. We threaten one another in ways that keep us apart. I can't explain it, but if you undergo the change you'll understand right away what I'm getting at."

Maybe it was his serious tone that was making Zero nervous. She didn't want to know these things, but he seemed determined to tell her.

"And most important, you'll have to take blood from living creatures, human beings, to survive. Can you face that?"

She knew David drank blood. He'd taken hers. But somehow that didn't have the impact of hearing it stated so directly. The thought of drinking blood made her stomach lurch. She couldn't answer him.

"If you go without blood for very long, it will be far worse than withdrawing from narcotics. You'll feel as though you're starving to death, that each cell in your body is shrinking, dying, and that's what's happening. You'll be driven beyond anything you can imagine. Many of us are driven to murder."

"But you said you never killed anybody for blood. It can't be that bad."

"I am the only one of my kind that I know of who has not been driven to kill by the blood lust."

Feeling his unnaturally cool skin next to hers, the fact that he had no body odor she could detect, that the dark centers of his eyes sometimes narrowed to the point where he looked like something not of this earth . . .

Zero's body began to tremble. She was afraid to look at him, afraid she would see something she didn't want to see, terrified he would know what she was feeling: He could kill her. In a second. Crush her with his supernatural strength. Suck the lifeblood from her body until she was drained dry. What land had she been living in lately? She'd been so high or low she couldn't put it all together until now.

Her heart crashed against her chest in warning and she couldn't breathe normally.

She was about to bolt when, as if reading her mind, he said, "Kathy, I would never take you against your will. You mean more to me than even the blood. And if you reject my offer, I will not leave you, but I will not force you to submit to my will."

The demon she had moments before wanted to flee from evaporated before her eyes into the man who loved her more than any other had, or probably would. Her doubts and fears fled in the wake of the need for him she felt wash over her.

"I wanna be with you, David. And with Bobby. And I want to be like you too. I want to be able to protect myself when people try to hurt me. All my life people've hurt me. I want that to stop."

They talked more about what she would have to give up and how it would be. They also discussed the safety deposit box again. Finally she convinced him that there was nobody else to go, although she knew he didn't like the idea. She wasn't crazy about it herself, but she wanted all this to end so the three of them could be together.

He made her promise to do it as late in the afternoon as possible, to go and return by taxi, and if she felt frightened, to phone Mae.

The next night when David woke, the room was empty. He rushed outside and asked the kids if they'd seen Kathy.

"Not since she went out," Frankie's girl told him.

He headed to the bank immediately, but of course it was closed and she was gone, but recently enough that he hoped to track her. David retreated to an alley where he could be alone.

He concentrated, delved within himself to find that cellular part of him that had been affected by her blood, the part affected by every person whose life source he had consumed during his existence. He focused on the scent of her blood, her essence. And when he had fine-tuned to her source, he was able to follow the trail of the scent.

He found her out on a half-rotted pier, sitting on a stump of wood, a paper shopping bag by her side. Shoulders hunched, head bowed. Tears blackened by mascara streaked bruised cheeks. In her fist she clutched a crumpled sheet of paper.

Chapter 11

"I USED TO BRING BOBBY HERE IN THE SUMMERS. HE REALLY loved watching the big boats come and go. He wanted to sail on one. I told him I'd take him someday." Kathleen's voice was flat.

Tears, like a relentless rain washing down a windshield, poured from her eyes.

David took the crumpled piece of paper from her hand and smoothed it out. It was a photocopy of a grainy photograph, not a very clear one, a picture of a child lying in a shallow, dark pool.

A large shopping bag sat next to Kathleen on the dock. Inside he found a white letter-sized envelope stuffed with money. Scrawled across the front was one name, with another in the upper left-hand corner.

"Kathy, you don't know that this is Bobby."

"It's him." She stared vacantly across the polluted waters. A gull landed on the edge of the pier, squawked pathetically, then took off quickly, as if anxious to get away. "That's what he was wearing last time I seen him."

David looked at the picture again. He could not clearly make out the face of the child or the clothing, and wondered if she could be sure. The background was dark; all that the picture showed was a body. And the dark patch in which its torso lay.

He hooked his hand under her arm. "Let's go back."

He led her to the hotel and put her to bed. She lay staring up at the ceiling. Every once in a while quiet tears filled her eyes and rolled down her face. He sat with her, holding her hand, smoothing her hair back, drying her eyes. But he had few words of comfort. David had witnessed the demise of many mortals. Death was inevitable for them, a reality he had learned to tolerate but to which he could never reconcile himself.

The idealistic part of him thought: If only I could aid all mortals in a transformation process . . . He longed to free these doomed souls as he had been freed from the terror of one's own end and the pain of lost loved ones. He knew those feelings intimately, although as it turned out, death for him had been but a portal to an undreamed-of existence. Perhaps, he had often pondered, death is similar for all creatures, although the gateway normally leads to a different plane. And yet even he was not so lost in the fanciful that he couldn't clearly see the flaw in this scheme. If there were no more humans, there would be no human blood, and his kind could not easily survive. The blood of animals sustained him but was never satisfying. And beyond that lay a starker reality. As much as he empathized and sympathized with these frail temporal humans—and he had been one himself recently enough that he still felt their distress—he also realized that by nature many were vile. Would he enjoy walking the earth as equals with the likes of Dennis, or the Snake Priest? In their mortal state they destroyed one another; what would they do with the powers his kind enjoyed? Even many of *us* cannot handle such powers, he thought grimly.

All he could offer her were hollow-sounding platitudes— the pain will pass, time heals all wounds.

When she drifted into a semisleep, he took the shopping bag to the chair by the window and sat down. The money, all twenties, totaled four thousand dollars. The Snake Priest's name had been written across the front of the envelope. In the upper left-hand corner was the name Donald Reesone.

"Frankie, I need someone to sit with Kathleen. Can one of these girls do it?"

"No prob. Linette!" His girlfriend, a pretty teenager with smooth chestnut skin and sensuous features, came over. "My man Dave needs somebody to baby-sit Zero. Go on up."

"Ain't you heard? The slaves are free!" Her tone was sulky but she turned toward the door. David got the idea that secretly she felt flattered to have been selected.

"Do not let her leave, and under no conditions are you to give her any drugs," David cautioned, handing the girl the room key. "Do you understand that?"

The girl took the key and nodded.

"I'll return as soon as I can. Frankie, I can't tell you how much I appreciate all the help you've given me," David said. "I don't know what I would have done without you."

"Shit, man, it's nothin'. It's def havin' ya on the block. Since you been 'round it's been a real shock. Nothin' much goes down here but a buncha jive. Been lots of action since you arrived."

"You know, Frankie, you're clever with words. You might be wasting yourself here."

"Hey, Homes, you ain't gonna gimme the old 'go back ta school and get a degree, fool,' are ya?"

"Certainly not. I suspect the schools tolerate you no better than you can cope with them. I'm just wondering if there's anything you like doing besides loitering outside the Alexander."

"Homes, I'm your basic well-rounded man. I like gettin' high, listenin' to my music, fuckin' my woman."

"A Renaissance man." David laughed. "Anything else?"

Frankie thought for a second. "Yeah. I liked workin' on my car, before somebody raped and pillaged it." He grinned. " 'Course, that happens all the time in New York, right, bro?"

"Have you ever thought of becoming a mechanic? I understand such positions pay well."

"It's crossed the old mind, but I'm a bit behind. I'd hafta get a Class A."

"That's something to consider."

Frankie shuffled his feet, looking uncomfortable.

"By the way," David said, seeing the need for a change of topic, "have you heard of a Donald Reesone?"

"Negative. But I'll fax it around town."

David headed west and north for food. His injuries had depleted him, and for the last week he'd been feeding three times a night. Once he had found sustenance, he stopped in a Greenwich Village shop with a display of stuffed animals in the window. A small white teddy bear with the name Kathy printed across a heart on its chest caught his eye. Next he went to Mae's to buy Kathy something to eat.

"She still feelin' bad?" Mae asked.

David looked around. The diner was almost empty. "She's had a shock. About her brother."

"Bobby?"

"Yes, I'm afraid I've some tragic news—he's dead."

Mae gave him a strange look but then said, "Yeah, I know."

"How did you find out about it?"

"How?" Mae crinkled her eyebrows in confusion. "Everybody knows. He died right outside my window. It was in all the papers. Hold on! I think I still got it." Mae pulled a metal box from behind the counter and sorted through the contents.

Now it was David's turn to wear a startled expression. "Mae, I'm not clear on what you're saying. When did this happen?"

"Two years ago. Almost to the day." Mae handed him a newspaper clipping that looked exactly like the photocopy minus the caption.

"Bobby died two years ago," David said.

Mae must have realized just how stunned he was, because she took his arm and led him to a back booth. "Come on. Sit. We got some talkin' to do. Wanna coffee?"

David shook his head. "Mae, does Kathy have more than one brother?"

"Not that I know of. Bobby was it. Nice kid, always happy. Got hit by a car one night. The only good part is he died right away, didn't suffer."

"How old was he?"

"Eight. Born the same week they tore down the movie house."

David suddenly had a flash of the date on the back of one of the snapshots Kathy had shown him at Manchester Airport. And now that he thought about it, that date was ten years ago; eight years living and two dead.

Mae interrupted his thoughts. "Lemme ask ya somethin'. Has Kathy been talkin' about him like he's still alive?"

"Yes. But now she thinks that he's dead—murdered—recently."

Mae compressed her lips and shook her head sadly. "She never accepted it. She's been talkin' about him for the last couple years like he was still around. 'Gotta go home now and get dinner for Bobby,' she says. Or, 'Mae, seen my brother?' Most people just look at her like she's crazy or somethin'. Anyway, at first I tried to get her to face it, but she just wouldn't. After a while I'd ignore her or answer her like Bobby was still around. I think the drugs mixed her up."

David was stunned. Poor Kathleen, he thought. Bobby was all she had. That's probably why she started using heroin. The whole thing was getting stranger by the minute. Someone had not only known that her brother was dead, but that she couldn't face it. They'd used the knowledge to get her to go to England. Unless she was in on this plan from the beginning. On the one hand, he couldn't believe that, and yet the thought had occurred to him, and he couldn't deny the possibility.

"There's somethin' else you oughta know," Mae said. "I'm only tellin' you this 'cause I love that girl and I think you love her too. She's been comin' here almost since she could walk. I always felt like she was my daughter. I never had no kids and she never had a real mother; hers died, and she wasn't no good anyways. Her old man was a real bastard too. She told you about them?"

"Not very much."

"Well, what I'm gonna say is only for your ears." She looked at him solemnly. "And I don't want you usin' this against her."

"I wouldn't do that, Mae."

"If I thought you would, I wouldn't tell ya."

Mae stared out the window, her face creased, older, and David sensed the amount of care and love she had put into Kathleen over the years. "I care for her too," he said. "I doubt anything you can tell me will alter that."

She looked back at David. "Bobby ain't her brother."

David waited. The words did not sink in at first.

Finally Mae let out a large breath of air, as though she'd been holding it in a lifetime. "Her father raped her."

When the information finally registered, David blurted out, "Bobby was her son!"

"Her old man had her from the time she was little. It wasn't like it is now, with all the talk about incest. Then nobody knew or wanted to. I suspected. You get a feelin' for somethin' like that. Anyways, when she was thirteen or fourteen, she got real fat. Everybody was teasin' her all the time about it 'cause she's such a little thing. Then she left for a couple months, and when she came back she had Bobby with her."

"But didn't you know?"

"Sure. Most of the neighbors knew. But she said he was her brother, her old man had some girlfriend in Brooklyn that didn't want the kid so she took him. The next year her father left. I think havin' Bobby made her realize just how rotten the old bugger was. She was only fourteen but real feisty. She kicked him out—told him if he came back, she'd kill him, and I think she would have. He must have believed her 'cause he ain't been back since. Anyway, she raised Bobby like he was her brother, and we all just went along with it and, well . . ."

She looked upset, and David covered her worn hands with his.

Now that the words were out in the open, he realized he'd suspected something like this all along but didn't want to face it. "It's all right, Mae. I'm glad you told me. She needs help."

"She's had help. On welfare till Bobby was old enough for her to work. They sent her to all kinds of doctors. She ain't nuts, just can't face what's real. Won't let the dead die."

"She may be starting to," David said. "She thinks Bobby's been murdered. At least she now believes he's dead. That's a way of facing it."

Mae looked in his eyes and hers flickered, as if intuitively she had deduced some truth regarding him that was outside the bounds of her understanding but about which she decided to forgo judgment. She pulled her hands out from under his. "If I only knew you and not Kathy, I'd tell you to get as far away from her as ya can. But I know her, not you. She needs love. She ain't never had none but from me. And from Bobby. All I'm askin' is for you not to hurt her. She's had more than enough of that."

When David returned to the Alexander, Kathleen was sitting in bed, a blanket pulled up around her neck. Her eyes were wide and frightened. "Hi!" she said. He went to the bed and kissed her.

Linette stood, and as she strolled toward the door, David handed her twenty dollars. The girl looked down at it and up at him, her face stunned. "Gee, thanks." She folded the bill and pocketed it as she left.

Kathy jumped up, threw her arms around him, and cried, loud racking sobs.

"I was scared without you," she wailed. "I'm always scared now when you're gone."

He held her, a little china doll, shattered. He did not have the heart to confront her; the broken pieces of her soul would have to mend in their own way, when it was time.

As he comforted her, he closed his eyes. An image of Ariel flashed to mind. A tantalizing image, laced with searing pain and blind fury. Had he learned nothing? Was he still so naive he would again involve himself with a female capable of betraying him? No, it was impossible. Kathleen was not Ariel. And yet Mae's words haunted him. ". . . get as far away from her as ya can."

The sobbing creature collapsed in his arms resurrected both his most tender feelings and his gravest fears. The tension of conflicting emotions turned his body to stone. He felt like a statue, incapable of either pulling Kathy closer or pushing her away. Silently he prayed that if a crucial moment arrived, he would not make the wrong decision. Again.

Chapter 12

"HEY, MAN, CHECK IT OUT. THE DUDE'S GOT CLOUT."
Frankie shoved page eighteen of the New York *Daily News*
under David's nose.

David gestured, and Frankie took the only chair in the
hotel room.

Zero looked over David's shoulder and slowly read aloud
the caption under the picture of a tall gray-haired man in a
business suit chatting with a younger, shorter man in baggy
pants and a Lacoste polo shirt.

> Italian film director Mario Farmacotti and *Kiss
> of Death* star Donald Reesone, both in town for
> the New York City Film Festival.

The article was a short feature on the director. Included
were a couple of quotes by Reesone. At the bottom Reesone
mentioned that he would be at a party Saturday night at the
Italian consulate to honor Farmacotti and his work.

David asked no one in particular, "How in hell can I get
into the Italian consulate for this party?"

"Easy," Frankie said. "I'll get you an invite. It'll cost,
though. Fifty, maybe seventy-five, and a little for blow."

David handed him a hundred-dollar bill. Zero could tell he felt guilty paying for drugs.

"Homes, you printing money?"

"Make sure it's for both of us," she said.

David turned to her. "You're not going."

"David, it ain't a bar. It's just—"

"No!"

His adamance scared her a little, so she kept quiet.

Frankie stood and stretched. "I see youse got stuff to discuss. I'll get your invite. May be the last minute, but don't worry. Frankie's on the job. I'm your man, Stan." With an exaggerated strut he crossed to the door and left.

"David—"

"You're not going, Kathy. I won't discuss it."

He stood and paced. She knew he was upset and decided to let the matter slide for a while. But she had no intention of letting him go alone, and she didn't want him to be away from her that long either. There was the rest of the night to work on him.

She stretched her legs out in front of her and sighed.

Somehow over the last forty-eight hours she had come to accept Bobby's death. Her whole life seemed clearer. And it made her sad. More than sad, really. But Zero was amazed that she was living with the pain. She had cried a lot but eventually felt wrung out, and the whole thing had begun to seem unreal. It was as though she had already known about Bobby and this just finished it. She wanted to look ahead now, to leave the past behind. She longed for the future to unfold as she hoped it would.

Just after sunset Friday evening Frankie brought the invitation.

David turned the ivory card with gold engraving over in his hands.

"The real thing, a regular diamond ring," Frankie said.

"How'd you get it?" Kathleen asked.

Frankie smirked. "A selection of connections. My sister-in-law works in the kitchen. She borrowed it."

After he left she said, "David, please let me go. I don't

wanna be here by myself. It'll be easier for you too. You'll know where I am, and people'll accept you more if you're with a girl. And nothing's gonna happen at a gig like that. Please? I'm feeling better. Don't leave me here alone."

David thought about it. In fact he'd thought about it since the previous evening. The only reason he even considered the idea was that he did not want to leave her by herself for so many hours, and also he felt that being out of the room would do her good. And this would be a different crowd, a safer situation. And at least if they were together she couldn't get into trouble.

"All right," he said, wondering if he was doing the right thing.

Her eyes opened wide.

"Come along. We need to buy proper clothing and rent a car."

On the way uptown David filled Kathy in on the story he had concocted in his head—he would pose as David Newby, a magazine writer from London; she would be his wife, Beverly. "I've been reading up on magazines, doing film research. I'm in New York to interview Farmacotti, and when I meet Reesone, I'll suggest a story on him as well, so I can get him alone."

Kathleen hugged him. "I like the part about being married."

She's the sweetest woman, he thought. Naive, almost pure, despite experiences that would have jaded most people beyond redemption.

They shopped quickly at Bergdorf-Goodman, open late that night; they needed to buy so many different items. He bought himself an Armani tuxedo and Kathy a long elegant dress in gold lamé with big puffy sleeves and a high neck, to hide her wounds. The gown reminded him of the fashions of his mortal youth. In it she looked as if she'd just stepped out of a film, a period piece. They also bought shoes, a small purse for her, and, on the way out, two gold wedding bands at Van Cleef & Arpels.

Saturday afternoon, Kathy went out alone to get her hair

and face done. After sunset, David picked up the rented Bentley and collected her at Bergdorf's.

She took his breath away. A vision in shades of gold, her ocher hair swirled around her head in curls reminiscent of the classical Greek women depicted on artwork. Her makeup was subdued, perfect, covering the facial discolorations, and she looked radiantly beautiful to him, a princess in a fairy tale, a virgin bride. He felt like a fool quoting poetry on the sidewalk, but Byron's words burst from him.

> "And, oh! the Loveliness at times we see
> In momentary gliding, the soft grace,
> The Youth, the Bloom, the Beauty . . ."

He could not keep his hands to himself, and she laughed her airy laugh, blue eyes twinkling like stars, forgetting for a time the sadness and cruelty of which she had so recently been a victim.

At the fenced-in graystone Italian consulate, David handed the doorman the invitation. The man barely glanced at it before ushering them, with a note of deference, past very ordinary, almost severe, offices, each with its requisite red, white, and green flag. They ascended a highly polished wooden staircase to a room on the second floor. There they entered into an elegant, magical world, the kind from which fairy tales are spun. A short, classical marble pillar with a neo-Italian floral vase full of gladioli greeted them. In fact, the air was thick with the intoxicating scent of hundreds of cut flowers.

David watched Kathy's eyes grow wide and her lips part. First she looked down at the black and white tiles beneath her feet, then at the peach walls with white wainscoting, and finally she was staring up, almost mesmerized by the crystal chandelier glittering above them. She clutched her purse in front of her the way a little girl would. Clearly she'd never seen anything so grand except in films.

He took her arm and led her to the reception line. "David Newby, sir." He extended a hand to the man he knew from his quick research was the consul general of Italy in New

York. "I'm a writer with *Fame and Wealth,* out of London. May I present my wife, Beverly."

"Ah, yes. I read the magazine regularly," the consul general said graciously, shaking first David's hand and then kissing Kathy's. He introduced his wife, who commented that she loved David's articles. He thanked her. Kathy said nothing. She seemed too startled to speak.

The consul general introduced David and Kathleen to Farmacotti, whom David asked to interview. The director, a bone-thin man of at least sixty, first pulled on his nose and then gestured wildly toward the main room, saying, "Speak with my press agent. He's the one with the messy beard, wearing a blue blazer."

After the introductions, David led Kathy into the main area and over to a long table of hors d'oeuvres. "Eat something," he told her.

"I can't," she whispered, her eyes glowing blue coals. "I got butterflies taking off in my tummy." He kissed her instead.

They mingled for about an hour, and then David maneuvered them over to a group including Farmacotti, Reesone, and a woman.

"Ah, the writer," Farmacotti said. "You know Don?"

"We've not met, although I've been a fan for years and eager to interview you. Perhaps we can arrange something while I'm in New York?"

"My wife." Reesone's tone was studied as he presented the painfully thin brunette, chicly dressed in a couture outfit with padded shoulders that could have been worn by a football player. She twisted her mouth into what was obviously intended to be a smile and said, "Call me Ellen." She extended a skeletal hand covered in gold rings embedded with precious stones. "I read you all the time. You're so witty."

"Thank you," David said.

Reesone was muscular, about five-eight, with thick hair the color of roasted coffee beans, and close-set brown eyes that would not meet David's. He was smoking black bitter-smelling cigarettes. Even though he was dressed in a tuxedo, he looked like a mafioso, which, as David had read, was typical of the roles in which he had been cast. And he was smoother than the silk bow tie he wore. "Call my agent. We read you all the time," he said indifferently, then turning to Kathleen, said, "And who's this glamorous creature?"

"My wife, Beverly."

Kathy extended a hand, and Reesone brought it to his lips.

"Hello," she said softly, the first word she had spoken to anyone other than David, all traces of her heavy New York accent gone. David was amazed.

"You're a lucky man." Reesone stared at Kathy, looking in her eyes, which he clearly had no trouble meeting, still holding her hand.

"Yes I am." David took her arm and broke the contact between them.

The small group chatted amiably for ten minutes or so, mainly film gossip, until Farmacotti was dragged away and Ellen excused herself, leaving only Reesone, David, and Kathleen.

"You look familiar, Beverly. Where have I seen you? The newspapers? Television? Have you done some modeling?" Reesone became charming and suave, and David found himself irritated at the transparent veneer. He recognized another predator when he saw one.

Kathy didn't answer instantly. But when she did, it was in the same soft voice devoid of accent. "I study poems."

"I'll bet you're attracted to the Romantics."

David didn't care for Reesone's sharklike smile. He broke in to change the focus. "Bev has a rather literary mind, and I'm encouraging her to write. Perhaps one day she'll publish. I understand *Kiss of Death* is under way."

Reesone's eyes hardened, but still he managed to avoid eye contact with David while maintaining a facade of friendliness. "We fly to Canada tomorrow morning. We're shooting on Vancouver Island and in a little town outside Vancouver called Revelstoke. The town had a rockslide last winter and it looks like the moon. This is an SF thriller, loosely based on a Bradbury story. I play a gangster of the future."

"Interesting," David said, "and convenient. Bev and I will be visiting Vancouver then Victoria, on Vancouver Island. They say there's a large population of former Brits there. We've been married several months but, you see, this is our first chance away together. A bit of a honeymoon."

"Delightful," Ellen said as she rejoined the group. She was a little tipsy and the champagne glass she held tilted too far, spilling bubbly wine onto the tiles. She didn't seem to notice. "Newlyweds. How quaintly romantic."

David smiled. He glanced at Kathy, but her attention was riveted across the room on a small group of people clustered around a coffee table in a corner secluded by potted palms. They were bent over its mirrored top, surreptitiously sniffing a white powder through short gold tubes. Her face paled and her body quivered.

"Are you all right?" Ellen asked.

Kathleen turned back to the group. Her startled eyes reminded David of an animal caught in the glare of headlights. Beads of perspiration pushed their way through the makeup on her forehead.

"If you'll excuse us," David said. "My wife isn't feeling well."

"Nothing serious, I hope," Reesone said smoothly.

"No. She's expecting our first child. She just needs fresh air."

"How marvelous," Ellen exclaimed. "When are you due?"

"Not for a while," David answered for Kathy, turning her toward the door.

"Nice to have met you both," Ellen said.

"Maybe we'll see you up in Canada," Reesone called as David led Kathy away.

Once they were outside she said, "I'm sorry, David. I don't know what happened. Watching those people do that blow, I just wanted some."

When they reached the car, he opened the back door. "Get in."

"Why in the back?"

"Sit on the floor," he said, taking off his bow tie. He bent her knees and put her arms underneath her legs, then crossed them over and bound her wrists together. He used his handkerchief to join her wrists to the metal frame of the front seat.

"Why you doing this?"

"I must get his number in Canada. And also I want to ask a few questions. And watch him. I need to get a feel for him. He's rather too slick. There's something about him."

"But why tie me up?"

David took off his cummerbund and tied it around her mouth.

"I'm sorry, Kathy, but it seems as though you're on the verge of becoming overwhelmed by your craving. I don't want to leave you alone, but you should not be in there. You're about to fall to pieces." He kissed her on the forehead then stood and buttoned his jacket. "I won't be long." Her eyes blazed.

David returned to the party and for the next twenty minutes covertly observed Reesone. The man was sly, his persona slippery as ice. But under that was something dark and dangerous, waiting like a scorpion beneath a rock.

They spoke briefly, the tension between them palpable. David wondered if Reesone knew his identity or was always wary, cautious, hiding behind a mask of pleasantries. At one point David attempted hypnosis, but Reesone would not hold the eye contact.

"Why don't we do the interview in Canada?" the actor suggested, jotting a telephone number on a cocktail napkin. "I'm renting a retreat on the island during filming, mainly for weekends. Call when you're in Vancouver."

"Yes," Ellen said. "Come for dinner. We'll have a marvelous soirée."

"And make sure you bring Beverly," Reesone added.

When David returned to the car, he untied Kathy. She climbed in the front without a word and they drove back to the Alexander in silence.

"Holy shit, man!" Frankie and the others gawked openly when they saw first the car and then the couple.

Kathy brushed past them all and entered the hotel like a queen refusing to acknowledge her subjects.

"Will you return this for me? It needs to be logged in by tomorrow evening at nine," David said, reaching into his pocket. "You'll require petrol."

"Sure thing!" Frankie took the keys and the money, his eyes as glossy as billiard balls.

David caught up with Kathleen outside their door. He grabbed her arm, turning her to face him. "What's wrong?" But the princess had turned into the witch.

"Wrong? Nothing. I'm crazy about being tied up."

"I did it for your own good. You were becoming a victim of your cravings, and I was fearful of leaving you alone. I thought it likely you'd go after the drugs."

"Thanks. All my life men been doing stuff to me for my own good. First my father and lately the Snake Priest and now you."

They were inside the room. David slammed the door. "You're being unfair. The situation is not the same. You were beginning to shake and perspire. Reesone's wife noticed something was amiss."

She slipped out of the gold dress and shoes and left them in a heap on the floor. She dressed in her black miniskirt, boots, and T-shirt. Slipping on her black leather jacket, she said, "It would've passed. You could've just taken me outside for a couple minutes."

"How do you know it would have passed? I don't. I thought it better to make an excuse."

"And tie me up!" Her voice was sharp.

"Look, Kathy, undoubtedly you're still upset over Bobby's death. And all you've been through lately. That's natural and I understand. It takes time to recover from traumatic events."

She glared at him then grabbed a hairbrush and began brushing her hair out with long quick strokes. "Stop tying me up!"

"I'll stop tying you up when I'm certain you can be trusted."

Her eyes were hate-filled, the same look she had given him back in Manchester. It startled David and he found himself feeling defensive.

"Screw off!" she shouted. "Who the fuck're you to decide when I can be trusted? Besides the junk, and that's physical, I've been trustworthy."

"The hell you have!"

"What's that supposed to mean?" She tossed the brush onto the bureau.

"You're about as trustworthy as a coral snake—pretty on the outside and poisonous within." He regretted that immediately. Suddenly everything had gotten out of hand again.

"I'm sorry, Kath. I didn't mean what I said." He reached for her, but she backed away.

"If it wasn't for you, Bobby'd be alive. If you weren't a fucking vampire, if you didn't exist, if somebody didn't hate you enough to try and kill you."

"That's ridiculous—"

"Fuck if it is! You never cared if I found Bobby. You just want whoever's on your ass."

"Bobby died two years ago." It came out before he realized what he had said. And he knew he'd spoken more from anger than caring.

She took another step away from him. "That's a lie." Her voice was very even, controlled.

"No, Kathy, it's the truth." He did not want to sound hard, yet he did. "Bobby died in a car accident outside Mae's restaurant. That photocopy was of a photograph in the newspaper. Whoever is after me used you and your refusal to admit Bobby's death."

Before his eyes her face changed, the features shifting until he began to wonder if he had ever seen this woman before.

"Maybe I was confused, but I ain't no more." Her voice was still too calm, too controlled.

She picked up her purse and walked to the door without looking at him. Her hand was on the knob when he said, "Kathy, don't leave. Please!"

She turned, her blue eyes a frozen ocean, chilling him.

"If you walk away from me, I will not be here when you return. And don't try to find me." The tension was driving him to say things that he didn't want to say.

But before he could even begin reversing gears, she opened the door. "Don't hold your breath. This is the last time you're gonna see the back of me!" She slipped the gold wedding band off her finger and threw it at him, then slammed the door shut behind her and was gone.

David stared at the knob, expecting to see it turn any second, almost unable to believe that she had left him.

"Hey, Zero, what's happenin'?" someone down below asked. There was no reply. He forced himself to walk to the window and look out. She was crossing the street, her boot heels clicking angrily against the hard asphalt.

David sat heavily in the chair, watching her walk away quickly until she disappeared around a corner. The scent of her perfume clung to the air, taunting him throughout the remainder of the night. A pain in his chest, one he had expected never to feel again, intensified as though an old scar was slowly being ripped open. When the ache became unbearable, he cried into the stillness of the night Lord Byron's lament:

> " 'Tis time this heart should be unmoved,
> Since others it hath ceased to move:
> Yet, though I cannot be beloved,
> Still let me love!"

Part 2

Who could save me from plunging
   into a sea of shame
but the love god
who teaches us how to faint?
          —Vallana
           (circa A.D. 900–1100)

Chapter 13

ZERO HURRIED ALONG DELANCEY TO ALLEN STREET, WHERE she caught a cab. "Take me to the East Village—First Avenue."

She counted her cash, $855, the rest of the money she'd been given to go to England. She'd be okay for a little while.

On the ride across town she sat fuming. He's a real prick, she thought. Thinks he can push me around. Well, he can just fuck off, for all I care.

But even as she painted him the darkest shades of black she could envision, another voice inside was shrieking "Danger!" As they neared Eleventh Street she caught a glimpse of a familiar form up the block and yelled, "Stop!"

The driver pulled to the curb and Zero shoved some cash at him, then jumped out shouting, "Hey, Laser!"

"Zero! What you doin' out and about? Heard about the Snake Priest? Shame, huh?" She glanced at her nails.

"Where you headed, Las?"

"Trot around the track. You? Hey, where's your man?"

"Can't I go out by myself no more?" She felt uncomfortable at the mention of David.

"You two split, didya?"

"I needed air, okay?"

123

"Sure. If you say so. Hey, honey, got any cash? I'm seein' my sister. Her new boyfriend runs a crack shack. And she's got some dynamite smack too. Almost pure. You want?"

Zero thought for a minute. "Why not?"

The two headed down First then east into Alphabet City. Zero followed Laser up the half-dozen steps at the front of a neat but nondescript brownstone. A tough-looking security guard with a gun admitted them to the building. The door to a studio apartment on the first floor was opened by a man holding a not-quite-hidden automatic.

The place was a mess, but no worse than others Zero had seen. Fast-food wrappers, cigarette papers and butts, and a general assortment of trash littered every surface, already cluttered with the equipment necessary to transform cocaine into cheap, powerful crack. A metallic smell of ether hung in the air, the aftersmell from freebasing. Laser's sister, Connie, whom Zero had met before, was a mousy-haired woman of barely thirty who looked forty and had very gray teeth. Instead of a greeting, she pulled out a cookie jar shaped like a pink hippopotamus wearing a blue tie and sporting one gleaming white tooth. She shoved aside what was already on the coffee table and plunked it down. Inside were two-inch-by-two-inch zip-top Baggies of white powder.

"How much?" Zero asked.

"Fifty a deck. Three for one-forty. You need works?"

"Naw. Gimme three. How much you wanna borrow, Las?"

"You got fifty?"

Zero handed her two twenties and a ten, then paid Connie for three tiny bags. Connie, taking on the role of hostess, prepared a speedball—a mix of coke and heroin—and injected it into a vein at the back of her sister's knee. Zero watched Laser's face redden, her breathing quicken, and her eyes temporarily roll back into her head. Then a smile spread across her friend's face. "Now, that's healthy shit!"

Connie offered the needle to Zero.

"Uh-uh. I'm late," she said, surprised at herself, since this was the first time she had ever turned down a hit of anything. But she felt agitated, still angry, and needed to get out of there and be alone.

She headed to a bar on the corner, thinking she might pick up a little trade. I don't need this crap, she thought, meaning the heroin. And I don't need David. I had good times before him, and I still can. Besides, he ain't even human. But she was not convinced by these thoughts.

It was a local straight bar, and she took a seat. Within five minutes a skinny man past forty, with a potbelly and boils on his neck, came on to her.

"Here on business." He slurred his words a little.

"I don't do S and M or B and D. Hundred buys you anything from a hand job to a straight fuck, plus forty for the room."

He looked her over. Salesman, she thought. From the Midwest. A real dink. Probably try to bargain me down.

"You're fast," he said. She could tell he was nervous. "A hundred dollars is a lot of money."

"Don't waste my time."

"Okay. Let's go for it."

She took him to a Bowery hotel. Once inside the room, it was Zero's turn to feel nervous. What if this guy's weird? she thought. That's crazy. He's peanut butter and jelly. You've done hundreds like him. You're losing your nerve, girl.

The salesman decided he wanted a blowjob. She collected the money and then sat him on the edge of the bed. Zero got on her knees in front of him. It was all over in half a minute. When she finished, she felt a little sick. What the hell am I doing with this potato? she asked herself. She rushed him out of the room and locked the door. Then she sat on the bed and thought about David and the junk in her purse.

She couldn't remember why she was mad at him. He'd tied her up, but that wasn't really so bad. He only did it because he was concerned about her. She knew that, so why'd she jump all over him? She opened her bag and looked at the white powder.

It's Bobby, she thought. It's what he said about Bobby already being dead. No. She didn't want to think about it.

She opened one of the Baggies and sniffed a little of the powder. A rush was followed by a calm that rolled up from her toes. When it reached her chest, she felt her heart slow and seem to stop. Soon she felt nothing.

Eventually she picked herself up and left the hotel.

"Coke?" somebody whispered as she passed.

She wandered along looking at the crowds. There were a lot of people walking around the Village because the weather was so nice. The happy ones seemed to be with somebody. The sad ones were alone. But she felt estranged from them all, as if she'd just landed on another planet and didn't know what to do with this culture. But hidden beneath that feeling was another—she sensed an all-too-familiar emptiness. A feeling that *she* was the one who was alien and might not even exist. Suddenly she was hit by the need to see David, to talk to him, to touch him and have him touch her. She hailed a cab.

Back at the Alexander, Louie caught her on the stairs. "Hey, Zero, where you goin'?"

"To the room."

"He checked out."

She didn't think she'd heard right, and repeated, "He checked out?"

"Yeah."

"Louie, gimme the key, willya?"

"You want in, you gotta pay."

"Just lemme in for a minute. I forgot something."

"Fifty bucks." He held out his hand.

She reached in her purse and pulled out five tens, too upset to care that she was being robbed. He tossed her the key.

She raced upstairs and opened the door. The room was empty. She checked in the bathroom, the closet, and even under the bed. The night-table drawer and all the drawers of the dresser. It was only because she happened to glance down that she saw the cassette David had made for her lying at the bottom of the wastebasket. She picked it out and sat on the floor, holding it to her heart. And even though the junk kept the sadness at bay, still she felt tears, like drops of chilling rain, wetting her face.

As she left the Alexander, Zero saw Frankie leaning against a street lamp, struggling to read a book. She didn't need to be told that it was the book of poetry.

"Hiya, Mae." Zero sat down heavily on a stool at the far end of the counter.

"Kathy, honey, what happened? David was here. He said ta give ya this."

Mae handed over a large manila envelope. Zero ripped it open and peered inside. There were big wads of bills and nothing else. It looked like the money from the safety deposit box. She glanced up. "Did he say anything?"

"Just that you left him. Why, Kathy?"

Zero stretched her arms over the counter and lay her cheek against the cool Formica. "We had a fight. He said stuff about Bobby, that he died two years ago, and I got mad and ... I don't know what happened, Mae."

"But honey, you remember the accident. You know Bobby's been dead for two years."

Even though she felt angry at hearing it from Mae, Zero knew it was true. She realized now she'd already known. Why couldn't she have accepted it when David told her?

"Oh, Mae, I really screwed up this time."

"Honey, if you love him, don't let your pride stand in the way."

"He told me not to look for him."

"That's just *his* pride talkin'." She took Zero's hands in hers. "Know where he went?"

"I think he left the States."

"Back to England?"

"Uh-uh. Someplace in Canada. *Van* something. I can't remember."

"Vancouver," came a voice from the other end of the counter.

Zero looked over. "Yeah. I think that's it."

"Where's that, Al?" Mae asked.

"Up in Canada out west. It's their California." Al turned back to his coffee.

"There ya go, Kathy. I'll give you the money. You get yourself a plane ticket and find David."

"I got money."

"Here." Mae reached over, pulled the black phone out from under the counter and set it in front of Zero. But Zero just stared at it. "Well, go on! Get yourself a ticket."

"I don't know how."

"Jeez, you're like a kid," Mae said as she leaned over and pulled the Manhattan yellow pages up too, but there was little irritation in her voice. "Look up travel agents and call one."

She found the right page for Zero and propped the book in front of her.

Still Zero hesitated. Finally she said, "I don't think he'll take me back."

Mae shot her a dangerous look. "Kathleen, stop feelin' sorry for yourself and stop playin' games. There ain't many like David, and it'll be the biggest mistake you ever made if you let him get away."

"He's not what you think, Mae. I mean, yeah, he's special. But there's things about him you don't know. He ain't like regular guys."

"You sayin' he hurts you?"

"No, nothing like that. He's good to me."

"He ain't *funny,* is he? You know, in bed?"

Zero laughed a little and shook her head.

Mae put a hand on her hip and was silent for several seconds. Finally, like a mother laying down the law, she said, "Kathy, if he's Lucifer himself, it don't matter. What matters is he loves you and you love him, and you ain't gonna find that every other Monday. Believe me, I know. Now get on that damn phone before it's too late!"

Chapter 14

ZERO CAUGHT A FLIGHT THE NEXT MORNING TO VANCOUVER. Because of the time zones, she arrived at eight A.M. Pacific Time. She wasn't comfortable with traveling, and felt entirely out of her element. How'd I ever go to England alone? she wondered, then realized it had been the heroin that had gotten her through that and so many other terrors. But now she was laying off, although she still had it with her, buried in the crotch of her underpants, just in case.

She took a taxi to the city and was surprised to find a civilized metropolis. For some reason she'd had visions of Canada as being snowbound, even in summer. There were no Mounties on the streets either. Instead she found a modern, fast-paced city of high- and low-rises in pastel colors accentuated by the brilliant sun, bordered on one side by a bay and on the other by snowcapped mountains.

"Hey, I gotta make a bunch of phone calls. There a place I can do that?" she asked the cabbie, a young guy with spiked hair, tattoos on his biceps, and pale, watery eyes.

"How 'bout B.C. Tele, main office?" he suggested.

"Sure. Let's go."

The driver was happy to exchange ten U.S. dollars for twelve-fifty in Canadian money, giving her two handfuls of coins. At the phone company she stopped at the first booth, but the yellow pages had been stolen so she tried the next one. Finally she settled in with a directory and opened to "Hotels," starting with the A-Budget Inns. By the *L*'s she got lucky.

"Yes, Mr. David Newby is registered here," the receptionist at the Lloyd Hotel told her.

"Thanks," Zero said, not bothering to have them ring his room.

She caught another cab. It was a short ride to the small hotel situated near English Bay.

"I'm Beverly Newby," she told the preppie desk clerk. "My old man, David, is staying here."

He looked her over as if he didn't quite believe her but was too polite to show it, then checked his registration book.

"Mr. Newby's in Room 402." He turned toward the key slots. "He must still be in his room."

"Thanks," she said, almost skipping to the elevator. But when she reached 402, Zero found the door locked and realized that since it was day, David couldn't answer. She went back downstairs to the lobby, a very British-looking room furnished in stable blues and serious greens with the barest hint of pink. She knew her midnight-black leather outfit must have looked sinister in this staid environment.

"I guess he ain't in," she told the clerk.

"Then I'm afraid he has the key with him," the man said, his tone reserved, his face settling into a look that Zero interpreted as "down his nose."

"Well, I gotta get in. Got a spare?"

"I'm afraid not, Mrs. Newby."

She could tell he didn't believe she was who she said. She felt dejected. It wasn't even ten o'clock in the morning, and she'd have to wait until eight or nine for David to get up. "Got a coffee shop?"

He busied himself with the registration book and absently pointed across the room.

"Thanks. You're a real player." She strolled casually over the conservative carpet between chairs holding an assortment of dried-out severe-looking guests. Zero figured that the movement of her hips was more excitement than this place could handle.

She hadn't eaten on the plane but decided she might as well eat now because she had nothing better to do. She sat over the remains of two eggs sunny-side, three coffees, toast, and Canadian bacon, which she didn't like, until eleven, the waitress passing her dirty looks for taking up a table so long.

For the first time in her life she was worried. Up until yesterday, being on her own hadn't mattered. But now, for some reason, it was hitting her just how alone she really was. She had no family, no real friends. Mae was the only person she could count on to care about her, and *she* wouldn't be around forever.

She saw a woman carrying linen, realized that in a fancy place like this they'd have chambermaids, and was relieved that she could *do* something instead of sitting and worrying about things.

She took the elevator to the fourth floor, but there was no maid there. She then went up a floor, then another, finally finding a girl on the seventh lugging an armload of bedding to a cart in the hallway.

"Hey, listen! My man's out and he's got the key and I gotta go real bad. Can you let me in my room?"

The young girl, who looked like a college student with a summer job, eyed Zero as if someone was playing a joke on her.

"What's your room?"

"Four-oh-two."

The girl looked skeptical but followed to the elevator.

Downstairs she unlocked 402 and Zero handed her three dollars in quarters.

Inside she noticed familiar things on the dresser—the hair dryer, shaving equipment, toothbrush, and David's clothes.

All of it made her happy. She flipped the bathroom light switch. His comb was next to the sink. She picked it up and held it. She felt really excited and wanted to go right to him, curl into a ball against him, but she knew she shouldn't expose the closet to light.

She checked her watch; it was only eleven-fifty. There didn't seem to be anything to do but sleep. And now that she thought about it, she realized she hadn't slept in two days. The floral drapes were already shut. She pulled the matching bedspread and top sheet down, took off her clothes, stashed the heroin in her purse, and then got into bed. The sheets were pleasantly cool and the mattress soft. She thought about David, how handsome he was, and she was dreaming about him even before a church clock finished chiming out noon.

"What are you doing here?"

She was jerked out of bed and to her feet. Only the bathroom light was on, but she did not need to see him to know he was angry. "I came back."

"Yes, I can see. I told you not to follow me. Why are you here?"

She was upset by his anger. Immediately her thoughts turned to the smack in her purse, but she pushed those ideas out of her mind. "I wanna be with you."

"You didn't want that the other night."

She reached for her clothes, feeling awfully naked under his harsh look. "I made a mistake. I thought it over. I wanna be here."

He grabbed her arm and shook her a little. "And what about what I want, Kathy? Did it occur to you that you're no longer welcome?"

She said nothing, feeling hurt by the rejection.

As soon as she finished dressing, he said, "Come along," leading her out the door.

"Where we going?"

Instead of answering, he took her down to the lobby, past the desk, then outside and into a taxi.

"Stanley Park," he instructed the driver. "The Georgia Street entrance, please."

His body was tense, rigid, and she felt a little frightened. He's so mad at me, she thought. Maybe it's too late.

At the park he paid the driver and pulled her along the walkway between the flower gardens and an urban forest of spruce, oak, and cypress trees. This place's gotta be as big as Central Park, she thought. Eventually they came to a zoo.

"Wait here," he said, stopping her in front of a cage. "And don't wander off! Do you understand?"

She nodded and watched him hurry down the path. He was dressed differently, in jeans, a red T-shirt, and a short, unlined, dark brown leather jacket. She liked how he walked, his long strides, the way his hips moved with just the right touch of tension. His shoulders were broad, and that excited her. He turned a corner and was out of sight.

Zero looked through the chain-link fence at what, on first glance, appeared to be two big white dogs snarling at and circling each other. Information posted beside the cage told her they were Arctic wolves. "Jeez," she said out loud, "you guys sound like people. You eat, sleep, mate for life, and sometimes you gotta fight for what you want." She wondered how angry David was, hoping he'd get over it soon. But what if he didn't? What would she do? Instinct told her things had somehow changed, *she* had changed. Whatever happened, their relationship would never be the same again. That scared her, and she thought about doing a little H while he was gone. Just a bit wouldn't hurt, just enough to relax her. But she decided not to. He'd know. Somehow he could tell. And it would just make him madder.

The male wolf suddenly sank his teeth into the female's furry neck and mounted her. Zero watched, mesmerized, as they copulated right before her eyes. The encounter was brief, and when it was over the female eased down on all fours. She fell onto her side and then her back, rolling and stretching luxuriously on the ground as though in ecstasy.

"Let's go." Suddenly David was beside her. He seemed fuller now, his skin had a little color; she figured he'd gone off and found blood.

Maybe it was because her brain was clear for once, but the idea of drinking blood suddenly struck her as really strange. She wondered about his victims, if they recovered or if they became vampires too.

She felt her neck—the bite marks had almost disappeared. It occurred to her that she might have changed because he bit her, and she began to wonder just how much.

At the park's exit she waited on the curb while he looked for a taxi.

"Where we goin' now?"

"You're going to the airport. Back to New York."

She took two steps back. "No! I wanna stay here. With you."

"You're not staying. I don't want you here." He turned away but not fast enough. She caught something other than anger in his eyes.

"I'm hungry," she said.

"Food is normally served on commercial aircraft, is it not?"

"Please. I ain't had nothing in my stomach in a while."

"Eat at the airport."

"David, I feel sick. There's a place across the street. Can't we go there first? Please?"

He hesitated, then said, "Come along, then," guiding her by the arm toward the outdoor café.

They were seated in a corner under a Cinzano umbrella, and Zero ordered a well-done hamburger, fries, and a Coke. When the waitress left, she turned to David. His face was hard, unforgiving.

"It's nice here," she said cheerfully. "There's a beach and everything by the hotel."

"Why did you come back?"

"I told you, I wanna be with you."

"And I told *you* not to look for me. You walked out.

134

That's a game mortals indulge in, and I refuse to play it. Game over, as Frankie would put it."

She sucked in her lower lip and looked down. "I was wrong to do that. I came back later but you already checked out." She wanted to see love, but there was only distrust in his eyes.

"David, please listen to me. I screwed up, I know it. When you told me about Bobby, I don't know, I just went psycho. But it's true what you said. I just couldn't see it then. It's not like I was lying to you, it's like I was lying to myself."

He said nothing, but that didn't discourage her.

"I thought about it after and Mae said it too. Bobby did die in a car accident. I'm sorry I didn't believe you."

She felt something inside her shift, as if the ground beneath her feet had turned into a sinkhole and she were being sucked down. Saying it somehow made it real. She couldn't remember feeling so vulnerable.

David watched her, filled with hesitation, afraid to trust her again, afraid not to.

"I wanna stay. I love you. Please take me back," she said, her eyes round as twin moons, as blue as the Aegean.

"You listen to me, Kathleen, and listen carefully, because I do not intend repeating myself. I've been soft with you, far too soft. You've twisted me 'round your little finger again and again, and I've allowed it to happen."

"David, I didn't, I—"

"Don't talk! Just listen."

She closed her mouth and stared at him, but he wasn't sure if she was taking in what he said. "You've never had a man who loved you," he said. "Your father was a brute, not a real father, so how can you know what to do with love? I understand that. Half the time you're rough as a lorry driver, and the rest you're helpless as a sparrow with a broken wing, wanting me to look after you. And when I do, you resent me for it. I'm not your father and I can't make up for what he did. All I can be is your lover, your friend, but I doubt that's enough. The damage is too great. You're continuously on the verge of self-destruction."

She looked forlorn, frightened. Her lower lip trembled.

"But you need a father figure, there's no way 'round it. I can play that role, but I don't want to do it forever. I'll show you what it means, but I want you to learn and take over and do it for yourself. You don't know how to care for yourself, to set limits with yourself. If you wish to stay with me, there are going to be limits which you will respect and learn from or we shall part ways permanently. Do you understand what I'm saying?"

She nodded, her eyes so large that he expected her to cry.

"You tried to kill me, both body and soul. I have little reason to trust you." He paused to let the words sink in. "All right, this is how it will be. To start, these are the things I want changed. First, stop looking like a tart."

"But David—"

"Be quiet! I want you to dress like an adult, and wear less makeup. Also, no more drugs. Of any kind. If I see you looking at drugs, I walk, to use a colloquialism. You will consume at least two nourishing meals a day and I will not listen to excuses. And lastly I insist on the truth from you. No more lies, no more omissions. If you have any pertinent knowledge, for example, what you knew about the Snake Priest and didn't bother telling me, I want it out in the open. Stop trying to protect me or con me or manipulate me. You're not making unilateral decisions, do I make myself clear?"

She just stared at him, her lips parted a little, a shocked look on her face.

"Well? Do I?"

"Yes," she finally said.

"Good! Now, please go into the ladies' room and wash ninety-nine percent of that makeup off your face."

She didn't move. "David, maybe I don't understand. Sounds like if I wear too much lipstick or a dress you don't like, you'll leave me."

"I'm telling you that by looking the way you do, you draw

a lot of attention to yourself, and, consequently, toward me, all of it unsavory. Just look about. Everyone in this restaurant has been staring at you. You're begging to be rejected, except by pimps, johns, and drug pushers."

She turned slightly. No one met her gaze, but he could see she noticed a few covert glances. When she turned back, she looked embarrassed.

"Okay," she said, standing.

"One moment." He took her purse away and rummaged around inside, finally taking out the two remaining envelopes of heroin. He slipped them into his jacket pocket. "Is there more?"

She shook her head and he handed back the purse.

David watched her walk across the patio and disappear behind the door marked "Femme." While she was gone he canceled her hamburger and ordered baked sole and a salad.

What am I doing? he asked himself. This is madness. She's no more trustworthy than two nights ago. She's an addict, a human wreck who can't face the reality of her life. What would she do with eternity? You know she'll walk out on you again, he warned himself. Why are you setting yourself up to be hurt? Hadn't Ariel been enough?

On her way back to the table he saw her notice people watching her and she looked self-conscious. Her hair had been brushed straight back, her face scrubbed nearly free of the thick makeup she usually wore. The fading bruises were clearly visible. She wore her black leather halter and miniskirt like a second skin, exposing much of the first, and as her body swayed sensuously across the patio, all eyes were drawn to its movements, including David's.

"Hey! What's this stuff?" she asked as she sat down.

"Eat it. It's healthier than the garbage you ordered. From now on I want you selecting better food for yourself."

She picked up the fork and knife and began cutting into the fish. She took a small bite and then ate a forkful of salad, chewing slowly. He watched her silently as she devoured most of it.

When they left, they walked along Denman Street, and David steered Kathy into a shop specializing in Mexican cotton imports. He picked out a long skirt, the color of the inside of a honeydew melon, and an off-white peasant blouse, and also a pair of huaraches. When she stepped out of the dressing room, she was a different person. "What a hippie!" He laughed. And then he almost cried, thinking, Why must she remind me so very much of Ariel?

"How come you're staring at me like that?"

"You resemble someone. Someone I knew long ago."

"A girlfriend?"

"Yes."

"What's her name?"

"Ariel."

"Didya love her?"

"Yes."

Kathleen looked fragile when she asked, "Still?"

"Not love. Not now."

As they were leaving, the salesgirl called, "Hey!" She held up Kathleen's black ankle boots, her miniskirt, halter, and black leather jacket.

"Keep 'em," Kathy said.

They strolled along the beach of English Bay. The tide was out, and at first they walked close to the low waves that rolled in, but then moved back to the dry sand. The moon, fickle mistress of the night, was just a fraction over half full. David felt he had fallen out of favor with this celestial mistress nearly four decades before. Tonight he could just make out her ancient, impassive face. Despite Vancouver's lights, the beach was dark, and there were plenty of stars, like chips of white crystal, sprinkled across the black sky. Few people were out walking, and eventually they found a strip of deserted sand.

"Look!" she cried, scooping up a tiny spiral shell, feeling it because it was too dark for her to see it clearly, then holding it out to him, then to her ear, her face full of wonder and delight. She's like a child, discovering everything for the first time, he thought. Like one of us, changed, seeing the world the way we view it.

He sat on a stump of driftwood and watched her walk to the water's edge, her hips swaying a little. A slight breeze blew both her long skirt and corn-silk hair to the left. She stretched her arms slowly from her sides to above her head, an invocation. Then she turned. Like Aphrodite rising, he thought, and she came to him.

She knelt between his legs and rested her head on his thigh near his right hip, holding him around the waist. He ran his hands through her hair. His sensitive fingers explored the ridges and contours of her face, tracing bones beneath pliable, porous skin. Her scent overwhelmed him. He lifted her to him, sucking her soft lips, embracing her warm flesh, loving her as though they had never parted.

Chapter 15

"YES, DON. GOOD OF YOU TO RETURN MY CALL." DAVID gestured for Zero to keep quiet. "Vancouver Island? Fine."

She watched him write something down on the top piece of notepaper from a pad with the hotel's name printed across the bottom. He tore the sheet off and stuffed it in his shirt pocket.

"Friday evening at ten. No, Beverly won't be able to join us. She's come down with something. I'm afraid not. She's rather ill. On antibiotics." Zero started to protest, but he gave her a severe look that shut her up fast.

"Right. See you then."

The second he put down the phone, she said, "You're going without me?"

His face hardened. "Yes. And this time I mean it. I want you to stay put so I'll know where you are and that you're safe. And I won't discuss it further."

"Okay." She flopped onto the bed. If that's the way he wanted it, she wasn't going to argue. She was just so happy to be back with him that she didn't care about a lot of things they would have argued about before.

He sat down and she wrapped her arms around his neck and pulled him to her. As they kissed she felt him relax. He stroked her hair and his hazel eyes glided over her face lovingly. But then he looked faraway.

"You're looking at me like that again. Like I'm reminding you of your old girlfriend."

"I'm sorry." He cupped her chin. "Perhaps it's how you're dressed. Or your face without makeup. You look a bit like her at times." He brushed hair back from her forehead. "Like now. The way you're smiling, the tilt of your head."

"How'd you meet her? What's she like?"

"She said her name was Ariel. Ariel Moon, although I was unable to discover if that was her true name.

"We first met Ariel when I was living in Manhattan with André and Karl. It was 1955, I believe. Spring, but a cold, damp, drizzling evening—the sky dark. I remember the weather because we went to one of the first games of the baseball season. The Yankees beat the Washington Senators an astonishing nineteen to one, and we were part of the smallest opening-week crowds in the stadium's history. At least that's what André assured us. He's a great sports enthusiast, and that was the first game he took Karl and me to. And the last. We three were close; we spent most of the hours of darkness together.

"When we left Yankee Stadium, we decided to ride the subway back to our apartment. We had barely walked a block, hurrying because of the chill, and were waiting for a light to change, when a black car drove up. It was Karl who noticed her.

"She was glowing, an extremely white glow, on fire with waves of pulsing light."

"Whatdaya mean?" Kathleen asked.

David leaned back against the headboard and slid his arm around her shoulders. "She's one of us. Like me. One of our kind." He paused. "There's a belief that at death the spirit or soul leaves the body. Many cultures think that's accomplished within three or four days. My species, we have a theory of our own. Our spirit bodies begin to depart our physical bodies, but because of the cellular changes, and likely spiritual changes as well, we return to life. It's a bit like people who've been pronounced dead but then revive.

But in our case the soul is partly in, partly out; that's why we see the light. We can see one another's souls. Blood sustains us because it is life reduced to its essence."

Kathleen nodded, but he knew she could not understand exactly what that meant. And how could she? Her concept of his existence was based on something she had seen in a movie. And there were enough similarities to overshadow the differences.

"Ariel looked at us and we at her. Without a word she opened the passenger door and we got in, André and I in the back, Karl in the front. This was very unusual. Our kind, we generally avoid one another."

"How come?"

"It's complicated, Kathy. Let me put it this way. There's almost an innate distrust. You see it with some animals. A male and female will come together occasionally to copulate, but that's about all."

"But you had friends. Those two guys."

"Yes. Karl, André, and I were exceptional. We always wondered why we three were able to be together. It might have had something to do with the one who created Karl and me. We believe he was the same predator. For both of us the attack was shockingly quick, like a hit-and-run, and we never saw him again. We also think he transformed André's aunt. It's the connection, you see."

Kathleen nodded but she looked confused.

"As we drove, the four of us were silent. I sat behind Karl and could observe Ariel's profile. She was the most exquisite creature I'd ever seen, and I could not take my eyes from her. None of us could. Fine-boned, like you, her hair was blond but an unusual shade, the color of saffron, and her eyes ... I don't know how to describe them. They were such a pale shade of blue that at times they appeared completely white. The effect was similar to the eyes of a blue-eyed husky—startling, unearthly.

"She looked to be twenty, but Ariel wore a perpetual smile on her full lips and had an aura of confidence about her that was centuries old. And there was something mischievous too, or so I thought at first. Later I came to know that it was cruelty. But even when she was being cruel, that beatific smile never deserted her, and because everything about her was so mesmerizing, it was difficult to react to her in a negative way.

"She took us by her small cabin cruiser to Fire Island, where she had a house. She was a bohemian, dressed in sandals, a long skirt that the Atlantic breezes blew about, and a Gypsy shawl caressing her shoulders. That was an unusual costume then. But she was the most beautiful being I'd ever seen. In fact, other than Ariel and André's aunt, I have not met a female of our kind. Neither had Karl nor André. There's something about one of our own that we find impossibly appealing, despite the distrust. Mortals do not hold the same attraction for us. With a mortal, the blood is all, and unless the mortal changes, any relationship is doomed."

"Is that how you feel about me?"

"Unless you change you will die. My two lifetimes have been as brief as a year seems to you."

She looked like she didn't want to think about that now. "What happened next?"

"When we entered the house, the first thing I noticed was her sculptures. The place was cluttered with her work, large plaster forms, all nude, all male, resting on pedestals standing amid a hodgepodge of furniture. Most of the house was a studio, including the bedroom.

"She built a fire and we sat and watched her. None of us dared turn our eyes away. She was breathtaking and each of her movements so fine, so delicate, even magical, that the thought of looking away was painful. When she finished, she stood and glanced from one to the next. 'I'm Ariel,' she said with an accent I came to believe was Irish, but she never verified that or anything else. 'I want you,' she said.

"This jolted the three of us. We stared at one another like schoolboys. Finally André ventured the question we all were thinking: 'Which?'

"Ariel laughed, and the sound was like slivers of cut crystal joined by the caress of a breeze. 'All of you,' she said. 'At once.'

"She was more liberated than the three of us together. She must have realized that quickly because she laughed again and nodded. 'All right. You first,' she said to André, and took his hand, leading him to the bedroom.

"Karl and I sat together by the fire unable to speak. The two of them were in there for what seemed like hours. We heard laughter. Moans. Her cries. When they returned, André sat down and she took Karl's hand. Her light was brighter, her skin richer with texture. And her eyes! She was even more alluring than before.

"When André and I were alone, I studied him. He was pale. I wanted to ask him if he'd given her blood but couldn't bring myself to do it then. Later he assured me he hadn't. But it wasn't just the absence of color that I noticed about him. He seemed angry. But André was often angry, particularly at mortal women.

"Eventually Ariel and Karl returned. Karl too was pale, but I sensed he was more stunned than anything else. And then I looked from him to Ariel. She was watching me, amused, her lovely lips curled into a smile, I suppose, although later I would remember that look and call it mocking. But that night I was enraptured.

"She held out her hands and I placed mine in them. And then she led me to her bed. The room was warm and the air humid with the scent of bodies.

" 'You're the poet.' She seemed to know about me from the others. She untied the belt of the coral dressing gown she wore and let the silk fabric slide down her body. Her skin was the color of alabaster and her shape so perfect that I found myself unable to breathe. I was totally paralyzed by her classical beauty. If you could see the way we do, Kathy, you'd understand. Mortals find us attractive, there's no question about that. But it's a surface perception. We see beyond the surface, the subtle shades of color, the fine movement of curves, the pulsing of the light that emanates from our bodies. Ariel was like a statue of an ancient goddess come to life.

"She opened her arms to me and said, 'You're the one who will love me most.' I found myself embracing her and being embraced by her, lost in an ecstasy that afterward I could hardly recall. In dreams I've caught snatches of it. Her body so yielding. And at the same time the intensity of her muscles clamping around me, pulling me in, leaving me without air. I only know that the feeling was a fine line between pleasure and torture. With Ariel I came as close to bliss as I ever expect to experience. And other than the change itself, what I felt with her has been my most intense experience."

Kathleen took his hand. "Don't you feel that with me?" She looked hurt, as if she couldn't compete with such a divine fantasy.

"It's different with you, Kath. And it will be different again once you've changed. I know I've made Ariel sound like a dream. And in many ways she was. But she was a dream that turned into a nightmare.

"That was a strange evening. As soon as we returned to the others, she led us all without a word back to her boat. Once we'd crossed the water, we got into her car and she drove us into the city. And then she disappeared, and we three stood in the rain outside our apartment building looking to one another for confirmation that what had happened had really occurred.

"Oddly enough, we did not discuss it at that time. It was as though each wanted to cherish the memory of Ariel and by sharing with the others, the experience would somehow have been diluted.

"It was two months before we saw her again.

"One night Karl brought her home. She was dressed as before, flowing skirt, off-the-shoulder blouse, long saffron hair streaming behind, thin gold hoops dangling from her ears, looking just like a Gypsy. And, as with the first time, she slept with each of us, or tried. André refused. 'You two divide the spoils,' he said to Karl and me, and Ariel laughed at him as he stormed out.

"And like the first time, it was so wonderful an experience that I couldn't remember much afterward. I just know that for me it felt like returning to the womb, like dying, or joining with the stars in the sky. For those brief moments I lost myself, and the pain I carry with me each night, the ache that has always plagued me and kept me apart from mortals and immortals alike, disappeared.

"We saw Ariel often after that. She would come to our apartment or Karl and I would go to her house. André refused to join us. He told us that he not only disliked Ariel but didn't trust her. 'Don't be surprised if she plays you against each other, *mes amies,*' he warned. Of course, the idea had occurred to both Karl and me. And Ariel may have tried to do just that. Yet we did not feel competitive. It was a peculiar arrangement.

"But the situation changed. Ariel became disenchanted with Karl. Months later he confided that initially he had felt they had little in common but something had 'caught him.' I remember he described it as feeling 'like a fish that's been hooked, but the hook is embedded so deeply it's almost impossible to get free. I felt that if I struggled, I would only tear myself apart.' And when he said that, a chill ran through me because I then realized I had felt the same way.

"But it was Ariel who released him. She seemed to just grow tired of Karl. She told me that both he and André bored her. I remember her laughing, 'I can have them easily, they're so transparent. Their suffering does not run as deep as yours, dear David.' As with much of what she said, I only understood in time.

"I talked with Karl once, thinking that he was upset. 'On the contrary, I'm relieved,' he assured me, although I didn't believe him and certainly didn't comprehend until much later what he meant.

"Now Ariel turned her full attention on me. I've never been able to understand why she preferred me over the others. But even then I recall feeling a little frightened. There was something about her, like looking directly into the eyes of the Medusa. I spent every evening with her and soon moved into her house on the island. I couldn't resist her. It would have been impossible for me to have done otherwise.

"For me our life together alternated between Heaven and Hell. Hunting was always a painful affair with Ariel. She had a way of enticing mortals that grated on my nerves. It seemed the more she could convince them to trust her, the greater her pleasure in the kill. And she did kill—always—in hideous ways. I never saw her spare one, and it disturbed me. But she couldn't persuade me to kill, and believe me, she tried. Her obvious disappointment caused me a great deal of agony. It was not our only difference, but probably the most obvious. Because of it, I was thrown into a constant state of turmoil and insecurity.

"Other than looking for food, we spent much of our time in bed. Even today the memory of the sex is vague, hazy, the way I imagine a patient etherized must remember an operation. During our lovemaking she often insisted on drinking from me, and I permitted it. But she never allowed me to drink from her.

"How can I tell you what she was like? She was so restless. Her work never satisfied her. I couldn't satisfy her either: She seemed to want something from me, but I didn't know what. I think she found immortality painful but could not admit that because she thought it a weakness. Consequently she was attracted to and repelled by me, for the same reasons. Once I recall her standing by the window just before daybreak. Unlike André, Karl, and me, she seemed more tolerant of dawn, but not, as far as I know, in a way that permits movement outdoors. I was across the room, sluggish, lying in darkness, waiting for her to secure the shutters and join me. As she stood in the shadows, peering through the filtered window at the predawn light lifting itself above the horizon, I heard her say very softly, 'I think I would give anything to be free.' That was as near regret as I'd heard her come.

"When we weren't in bed, I watched her sculpt. Each time we made love, she jumped up immediately afterward to begin work on a life-size model of me. She must have begun hundreds, but would abandon them partway through, smashing them in a fury that burst from her like a sudden volcanic eruption. I asked her why this obsession to reproduce me when she had me in the flesh. 'Because, my love, I must capture you exactly as you are now, at your most vulnerable, at your weakest, when I possess you so completely.' Rather than enraging or frightening me, I was so under her spell that these words sent a shiver of urgency through me and I had to make love to her again. I was a prisoner with not even the desire to escape.

"Without being aware of it, my energy was draining from me night by night. Karl and André tried to talk to me, but I thought they were jealous and not only did not listen, but began to avoid them. I stopped writing poetry, stopped reading, no longer attended the theater. Pleasing Ariel became my sole *raison d'être*. If she bestowed one of her enigmatic smiles, I felt existence worthwhile. But she often became upset with me, and the hint of a frown on her enchanting face left me feeling that extinction was my only alternative. Now I'm amazed at how much energy I expended trying to please her. And the more I tried, the less I seemed to succeed. But that only made me try the harder. Frequently she tormented me with stories of former lovers, even André and Karl. But there was one in particular, the one who had changed her. She compared me and invariably I fell short.

"Not only was Anthony a superior lover, but he was fearless, brilliant, ruthless, not plagued as I am by a sensitive nature. As her mentor, he taught her everything, including, I imagine, her callousness, although perhaps even now I'm making excuses for her. When I asked why they parted, Ariel never answered, just gave her cryptic smile. Why did I put up with all this? I don't know. What I do know is that she had only to wish for something and, with the exception of killing, I would do it. Had she asked me to lie in the sun, I'm certain I would have, without question. The power she held over me was so complete that I still can't make sense of it.

"We had been together six months. It was fall then; Fire Island was deserted because the weather had turned cold. One night, just after we had made love, as I watched her shaping the torso of yet another effigy of me, I remember feeling utterly exhausted. Almost near death. Suddenly the image of the succubus flashed to mind, the creature of mythology that drains a man's energy through sex. My thoughts must have been clear to her because she turned and gazed at me with her mysterious otherworldly eyes and said, 'This is my last model of you, David. Our males are so much more difficult than mortals. Even you, my pet, weak though you are.'

"I had no idea what she meant. Later she drove into the city with that statue.

"By sunrise I was frantic but immobile for the day and could do nothing, although I got no rest. The following night I went to Karl and André. I hadn't seen them for a fortnight. I knew from the way they stared, their faces shocked, that I looked peculiar, acted strangely. But I was so desperate that I ignored those looks. When they said they hadn't seen Ariel, I accused them of lying, of hiding her, of being jealous, trying to keep us apart. I think that during those first weeks without her, I was insane. If it hadn't been for my friends, I doubt I would have survived. Initially they tried to reason with me, but I wouldn't listen. They helped me look for Ariel. And we looked everywhere. It took a year for me to understand that she was gone forever.

" 'It's her game,' André told me. 'She does it with mortals, bewitching them, draining life away slowly, keeping them helpless until they're dead. And they don't have a hope in hell. We're too strong for her to deplete so completely.' Of course, I was furious with him. I wouldn't believe it for a long time. Karl wasn't as adamant but he did agree.

"Eventually I realized just how much I'd been under her spell. I also realized that it was the blood. Of the three of us, I was the only one who had given it to her; I hadn't been strong enough to resist. But by the time I understood all this, things had changed again.

"Karl was desperately lonely. He decided to return to his native Germany. André, who had always been bitter when it came to women, became even more so. I found it difficult being with him. He liked to play with mortals, especially the females. He'd get them to fall in love with him and then abandon or kill them. I think he saw Ariel so clearly because they were alike in that regard."

Kathleen shuddered. "You ain't gonna do that to me, are ya?"

David realized that he'd been so lost in memory he'd forgotten she was in the room. He pulled her close. "I'm telling you about André. I don't feel that way."

"But this girl, Ariel, she left you. Maybe you're gonna do that to me. To get back at her."

"I'm not going to leave you, Kathy. Unless you drive me away. And I'll only change you if you agree to every step of the process." He kissed the tip of her nose.

"After Karl left for Germany, André and I stayed together a short while, then he returned to France. I remained in the United States for another five years before going home to England and the house I had always kept there. But it was as though I'd become someone else. I'd always been unhappy, but now I was inconsolable. Ariel had taken more than the time we spent together. She also took my will. Existence has always been painful to me. But after Ariel, I felt an emptiness, a flatness that I couldn't shake. Eventually I just didn't care anymore about anything, even the blood. I stopped leaving my house, except when I became absolutely desperate to feed. If you hadn't come to me, I'd still be there, lying in that coffin, passively trying to die, I suppose."

Kathleen stared at him, her eyes clear and honest. "David, I wanna be like you. Make me like you so we can be together always. Please. Do it now."

He sighed.

"Don't you want to?" she asked, her voice hesitant, afraid of rejection.

"Yes, I want that. But I'm not sure it's the right thing. I've never changed anyone, but I know the process. Often it's done in one violent encounter, yet there is another way, more difficult and painful, at least for me, but I'm told it works, and I will not do the other. The change can be brought about over several nights. You drink from me and then I take your blood. But sometimes it doesn't work out."

"It'll work!" she cried, grabbing his hands. "Please do it.

We can start tonight. I'm tired of being alone. And you're alone. I want us to be together forever."

"There's something we need to discuss first. Something about you."

"What?" Her eyes were fearful. He felt disconcerted.

"It's important that you enter this life clear. Do you understand me?"

"Uh-uh."

He hesitated. It wasn't altruism but fear. Once she faces her demons, she may no longer love me, he thought. "Clear in the sense of not carrying any unnecessary burdens along. This life is difficult enough. It's best to resolve your mortal problems and leave them behind."

She looked terribly frightened, and he sighed.

"What I'm saying, Kathy, is that if there's anything painful you need to face, anything you should rethink, any emotions unresolved . . ." But he couldn't go on. She looked too vulnerable. He decided to wait until Saturday night to make her confront the truth, even though he well knew that if he let her drink now, it would probably be too late for her to go back.

Immediately he rationalized: He'd have seen Reesone, who, David was convinced, knew what this was all about. Once that was out of the way, he would talk with her about her father. And her son. He wanted her free of pain. He wanted to give her the chance he had not been given to unload the concerns of mortality and to enter this existence free and clear. But more than anything, he wanted her with him. He wanted her as much as he was capable of wanting a mortal for more than the blood.

And why not? he thought bitterly. If she ceases to love me, I can always go back to playing out the role of the living dead. It's a role I've perfected.

He bit into his wrist. Blood trickled down his forearm, two crimson streams. I'm a coward, he thought. Afraid to wait, afraid of losing her. But all he said was, "Are you afraid?"

She looked shocked but shook her head.

He offered the burning wounds, and she took his arm in

her hands and immediately pressed her lips to them. While she sucked the blood from his veins, he thought about Byron's bittersweet words.

> Yet did I love thee to the last
> As fervently as thou,
> Who didst not change through all the past,
> And canst not alter now.
> The love where Death has set his seal,
> Nor age can chill, nor rival steal,
> Nor falsehood disavow:
> And, what were worse, thou canst not see
> Or wrong, or change, or fault in me.

Chapter 16

THE FOLLOWING EVENING, DAVID TURNED OFF THE NARROW two-lane blacktop just twenty kilometers north of Tofino, a fishing town on the Pacific coast of Vancouver Island. Within minutes he was heading toward a large two-story red cedar house surrounded by a dense wood of wide hemlock and three-hundred-foot Douglas firs. A black Lincoln was parked out in front.

He did not have a plan. But the fact that the house was isolated helped. He didn't want to spend much time here, just enough to find out what this strange plot was about and then get back to Kathy. She had been doing all right, fearlessly drinking his blood for the last two nights, but he knew she was beginning to feel changes, minor though they were at this point. He planned to get her away from the city, somewhere in the country, or maybe by the ocean, so that he could wake her in peaceful surroundings. He wanted her transformation to be as pleasant as his own had been shockingly violent.

Before he reached the door it opened. "David. Welcome!" Reesone said in his smoothest voice. "Here, give me your jacket."

Behind Reesone stood two large men who looked like

bodybuilders. David heard a warning bell go off somewhere in his brain. But he stepped through the door into the main room.

"Harry. Bill." Reesone's tone was bored. He hung the jacket on a peg. "David Newby, a writer from *Fame and Wealth*, isn't it?"

To David's relief, the two men nodded and then headed up the stairs. It wasn't that he thought they posed a threat—they were only mortal, after all, and he knew he could take both of them and Reesone, even if the three came at him together—but there was something building here and he wanted to get a handle on it.

The place was a hunting lodge. There was a fair-sized fireplace with an antlered moose head towering above it. A varnished walnut and glass case stocked with rifles took up most of one wall. The building stank of decay and rancid blood, at least to David's sensitive nose.

"Interesting, isn't it?" Reesone said, lighting a black cigarette, avoiding looking directly at David. "They hunt game here, large game. Impossible game. Ever hunted, David?"

The man's eyes seen in profile almost glowed, and David wondered if he was on drugs, although he could not smell anything but after-shave, and blood.

But before he could wonder further, Reesone said, "Let me show you around before we get started. Maybe you can work some of the ambience into your piece. There's one room in particular I think you'll find interesting." David decided to play along. There were only the three of them, he could sense that. And he still had a hunch, but couldn't get an edge on it. He needed time to feel things out.

They began in the basement, a musty-smelling root and wine cellar, moved to the enormous kitchen cluttered with copper pots and three oversized ovens, and then on to the library, crowded with unread books, forest-green leather chairs, trophies, and more stuffed animal heads. There were also three bedrooms, and another five on the second floor, where Harry and Bill joined them. As they approached the last room, Reesone motioned and David stepped inside. The polished hardwood floor was bare, as were the exceptionally high white walls. Overhead, the ceiling was a domed sky-light. This room seemed to be a greenhouse, but something did not feel right. The walls were too high, the floor too polished.

As David turned to get an explanation, the door slammed closed. He rushed to it but there was no knob on the inside. He heard it being bolted from the other side with what sounded like iron bars sliding into place. He shoved, but the door itself must have been a foot thick, like the door of a bank vault. No matter how much he pushed, nothing happened. Yet even through the thickness he heard Reesone laughing.

"David Newby. Really! I knew right away who you were, you and your hot little whore. The Snake Priest's death didn't make the papers, but word gets around. Incidentally, you didn't have to kill him. He was supposed to lead you to me."

David pounded his fist against the door. "Why are you after me?"

"Oh, it's not personal," Reesone said smoothly. "I don't even know you, although I'm sure you must be fascinating. A man who thinks he's a vampire. Who falls for a psychotic slut. How could you be anything but interesting? Tell me, is she as good a piece of ass as she looks? Never mind. I'll find out for myself."

"If it's not you, then why are you doing this?" David tried to wedge his fingertips between the door and the frame, hoping for enough leverage to pull it inward. But the gap was too narrow.

"Let's just say I'm doing a favor, and you're it. Nothing personal, as I say. It's been favors all along the way, but you can see that, can't you?"

"Who?"

"Sorry. No can tell."

David backed up and rammed the door with his shoulder.

"It's twelve-inch leaded steel," Reesone said. "The walls are reinforced with steel. They tell me you're very strong, although from your size that's hard to believe. But it was guaranteed you wouldn't get through."

"Who's behind this? And why?"
But there were no more answers.

David spent hours trying to break through the door, then the walls. But even with all his preternatural strength, he couldn't make a dent beyond the plasterboard. The ceiling was thirty feet high, the floorboards were thick, and when he got through them, he discovered even thicker sheets of steel underneath. It was almost as if this room had been designed to kill his kind.

When he wasn't trying to force his way out, he was castigating himself for being so naive. Of course Reesone would have known about the Snake Priest. And Dennis. He wouldn't make eye contact; that should have told me something, David thought. He just wasn't tough enough mentally for this kind of deception, but then, he never had been. That's why Ariel had gotten to him. And the one who changed him. That was the reason both his mortal and immortal lives had been so dismal. I'm emotionally weak, he berated himself. Always have been. And now I've brought about my own death, in one of the most painful ways possible. The sun would kill him, but slowly. He'd heard stories from André, who knew. It would fry him during the day. And at night, without blood, he would not be able to recover, only to suffer. If he was lucky, it wouldn't take long. And if he was unlucky . . .

The worst thing was not understanding who or what was behind this torment. This made no sense. As inept as the initial attempts using Kathy to destroy him had been, this last bit had been well-planned. And executed. He couldn't think of who hated him this much.

At least he had insisted Kathy stay behind. When he thought of her, of never seeing her again, her blue eyes, her silky hair, never holding her, hearing her speak, making love to her, feeling her laugh swirl through his soul . . . whatever control he possessed crumbled. Reesone could find her, and David knew he would. He'd have to kill her. David just prayed that it would be quick and permanent and that she would not suffer.

As the sky lightened and his limbs grew heavy, he huddled in the corner farthest from where the morning sun would shine when it rose. He took off his shirt and covered his head and as much of his upper body as he could. But it didn't matter. The power of the sun would penetrate the fabric's weave and burn him anyway. By the time the sun set, he would be on fire.

Zero paced the floor. She checked her watch again. It was eleven A.M., four hours after sunrise. David should have been back long ago. I shoulda gone with him, she thought.

She was stressed out with worry and indecision. Hours earlier, with the first wave of panic, she had used a pencil to trace over the sheet underneath the one on which Reesone's address and the directions to it had been written. Now she had that information in her pocket. Four or five times she had almost rented a car and gone there, but the thing that stopped her was knowing how furious it would make David. He told her to stay here, and that's what she would do. She stepped out onto the balcony. The rain had turned into drizzle, but the sun peeked out now and then. For some reason the brightness annoyed her and she went back inside. Maybe he's on his way home, she thought. But as the hours had come and gone and the sun rose, Zero had a bad feeling in her gut.

She slipped her bag over her shoulder. I'll just go down and make sure he hasn't called, she thought. Maybe it didn't get through. At least in the lobby she could see the front door. It was better than sitting here alone, worrying herself to death.

Suddenly she heard a key in the lock. Her heart immediately went from heavy to light. She was about to run to him when she heard two voices, both male. Neither one sounded like David.

A cold chill shot up her spine. Instinctively she darted onto the balcony, despite the rain, and quickly pulled the glass doors almost shut. She put her hand over her mouth out of nervousness, but within seconds locked her hand over her mouth for another reason. Two men were talking.

"She ain't here."

"Gotta be. Reesone said she'd be here."

"Check the closet."

She heard the closet door slide open.

"Now what?"

"I'll stay, you go tell him."

"*You* go tell him! He ain't gonna like it. He wants her back at the house by sunset."

"Fuck him. Since when's he paying enough for two contracts?"

Zero's heart pounded wildly. It seemed so loud that she wasn't sure if she heard the door close or not. She tried to breathe softly. Already she was drenched and the light made her nauseous. The balcony was not very large, but she edged farther to one side so that if the man in the room did open the glass doors, he might not see her unless he stepped out. She heard him rechecking the bathroom, sliding the shower curtain along the pole, the closet being checked again, and it sounded as if he was even looking under the bed. And then he pushed the drapes aside. She held her breath. He slid the glass doors apart. If he took a step out, he would see her right away.

Suddenly she heard the room door open and the other one say, "Come on. He wants us in the limo. Says we'll get her outside."

Zero heard the room door close again, but she waited for several minutes until she was certain they were gone. Quickly she made her way to the door and eased out into the hallway. She took the five flights of stairs to the basement, one floor below the lobby. There was one door there, locked, but she pounded on it until it was opened by a frail-looking East Indian man. Her wet hair and damp clothing clung to her, and he looked at her strangely. He might not have been able to speak English, because he pointed up. Zero shoved a ten-dollar bill into his hand and gasped, "Outside? How can I get outside?"

He pointed up again, but she shook her head. "From here. I wanna go from here." She nodded into the room behind him. When the man still pointed up, she brushed past him. Inside, a whirl of industrial washers and dryers filled the space with noise and intense heat. She edged by the machines and the immigrant women loading and unloading the hotel's linen, finally finding a door with a press bar that read, EMERGENCY EXIT—ALARM WILL SOUND.

She pressed the bar and peered out. Instantly a high-pitched alarm blared. She hurried up the four steps to street level, then along the sidewalk to the corner. A shiny black Lincoln sat parked at the hotel's entrance. She had no idea if it was Reesone's, but ran around the building the other way to avoid it.

Within thirty minutes Zero had rented a car and gotten directions to Tofino. An hour-and-a-half ferry ride across the Strait of Georgia and three hours of tense driving in the downpour on a desolate blacktop, her nerves on edge, wilderness pressing in on both sides, finally brought her to the fishing village. She turned north toward Clayoquot Sound and the lodge.

Zero had no idea what she would find, but something told her it was not going to be good.

Chapter 17

"DAVID?" SHE CALLED SOFTLY. ZERO HAD FOUND THE FRONT door unlocked. Hanging on a hook just inside was David's jacket. Convinced he was there, she made a thorough search of the place, first the main floor, including calling down a trapdoor to a basement that was nothing but a hole in the ground the size of a walk-in freezer. On the second floor she checked out all the bedrooms, even the closets and bathtubs, calling his name. This house was so quiet it was eerie. She half expected the animal heads to come to life.

The last door on the second floor was heavily barred by six metal beams. She pushed but was not strong enough to budge even one of them. She put her ear to the crack and listened. Nothing.

He probably ain't in there anyway, she thought. But just as she was turning to leave she noticed a butt on the floor, the remains of a black-papered cigarette. Reesone had been here.

She struggled with the bars again but they were beyond her abilities. Maybe there's a fire escape, she thought, and went outside to look. She didn't find one, but where that locked room was located she saw bricked-in windows, reinforced with prisonlike bars. That struck her as pretty weird. The roof above the room was a bubble of glass. For some reason that worried her.

If I go up on the roof, maybe I can see what's inside, she thought. She returned to the second floor and found a movable panel in one of the bedroom ceilings. But she had to search for a ladder, finally finding one in the toolshed behind the house.

The rain that she had driven through had barely wet the ground here, and the early afternoon sun was just beginning to sink behind the trees. The heat prickled her skin slightly, and the glare hurt her eyes. Zero had a sense that she should hurry, although she didn't know why she felt this way.

With the ladder she was able to get through to the attic, not much more than a crawl space. She found another door that led up, and finally was walking across the tarred roof to the dome.

At first she almost missed him. But when something caught her eye, she pressed her hands onto the glass and leaned against it, partly to get a better look and partly to steady herself because she suddenly felt light-headed. There, down in one corner of the room, lay what looked at first glance to be a heap of old clothes. But then she recognized them.

Even as she began to shake she was bringing herself under control. Cut it out, she told herself sternly. You gotta get in there. He's covered. Maybe he's okay.

Quickly she made her way back down through the crawl space and to the toolshed again. There she collected a crowbar, a glass cutter, and rope, and as she went through the bedroom, grabbed two blankets.

It took a while to score and shatter the thick double glass then tie the rope to a chimney. By the time she lowered herself down into the room, the sun was behind a cloud and it was drizzling.

She approached him cautiously, afraid of what she would find. There was a peculiar smell in the room.

"David?" He didn't move. Carefully she lifted the shirt

protecting his head and peered under. The harsh odor of burnt meat nearly knocked her over. She gasped at the singed scalp and charred skin. Instinctively she dropped the shirt and spread the blankets over him. And then she cradled David in her arms, using her body to shield him from the remaining light. "Oh, David! Please don't be dead. I love you so much."

She sat that way for what felt like hours while the room darkened, but there were no signs of life. She felt no heartbeat, heard no breath, saw no movement. Yet she refused to leave him. She couldn't.

Eventually a plan formed and she climbed back up the rope to the rooftop. She would use the car to bring him to the roof and then lower him to the ground.

It was a long process. She had to find more rope, tie it to the rope she already had, tie it to the car, slide back down into the room and tie it to David, climb back out again.

More hours dragged by and she was exhausted. As darkness set in, it began to rain seriously. The lights in the house and the headlights were barely enough. But worse than anything else was the struggle to keep the fear and pain at bay. But she wouldn't give up. She refused to abandon him.

It was nearly midnight when she finally lowered David to the ground in the downpour. She backed the car up slowly, the same system she'd used to haul him to the roof. Soon she was dragging him across the gravel driveway and then lifting him into the trunk. Finally she just sat behind the wheel, depleted, heartbroken.

She stared into the woods; their darkness threatened to engulf her. The rain pounded heavily against the car as if demanding admission.

"God's tears," she said, remembering how Mae had explained it to her as a child. And then, "How come one life's got so much misery?"

She almost broke down.

But again she checked herself, quickly shifted the car into drive, and pulled away. She was three miles from Tofino when another vehicle came into sight. As it passed, she glanced in the rearview mirror. It was a black Lincoln.

"Ohmagod, David! What're we gonna do?" She jammed her foot down on the gas pedal and sped along at 110 mph. Soon she was at the highway heading east, thankful that the slick road to the ferry had relatively few curves, hoping that it was not radared.

She caught the first boat of the morning, and as it neared Vancouver, Zero spotted another black Lincoln parked by the wharf. She tried to tell herself there were plenty of black limousines in the world but she panicked anyway and avoided the city.

Zero found her way onto the Trans-Canada Highway heading east. She didn't know where she was going, but she wanted to put space between herself and Reesone.

Over the next day she wove through the lush Fraser Valley, climbed the Canadian Rockies, and rushed through the chrome-and-glass oil city of Calgary. After that the land flattened considerably.

It was around Medicine Hat, Alberta, about four A.M., when she realized she couldn't go on. A homemade wooden sign read CABINS, and she drove four miles off the highway to the turnoff. At the end of a dusty pitted road, near a small clear lake, she found a smattering of crude stack-wall buildings scattered amid clusters of evergreens. She pulled up to the one marked OFFICE.

"I need one of these cabins."

"By yourself?" asked a slow, reedy man, well past retirement age, with a weather-worn face and kind brown eyes.

She hesitated. "Yeah."

"Stayin' long?"

"The night, I think."

"Just passin' through, eh?"

"Yeah."

He gave her a card to fill out. She used a fake name. When she handed it back with forty dollars in U.S. bills, she said, "I want a place away from the others. I'll pay extra."

"No need. All the same," he told her, handing her a

key on an oversized ring. "Down the road a bit, past the boats a little ways, and there you are. Number's on the door, eh? Checkout's eleven A.M. Got a restaurant opens at six, and there's some in Medicine Hat, oh, five, six miles back."

She thanked him and took off to number 22, relieved to see that there were no other cabins nearby. Inside she found a single musty-smelling room with a nook for cooking and a tiny bathroom. Two old-fashioned La-Z-Boys, the upholstery worn, were accompanied by a scratched veneered coffee table and matching end tables. A small Formica-topped kitchen table and two chairs, the vinyl split and the stuffing seeping out, and a brown tweedy chesterfield that she realized must convert to a bed, completed the furnishings. Four logs were neatly stacked next to a rustic fireplace. She dropped her purse onto the tiny kitchen table and stood for a moment. Her body felt as if it were still in motion. Emotionally she was ravaged.

Zero backed the car up so the trunk faced the door. She looked around. It was quiet.

Very carefully she pulled David's body from the trunk and half lifting, half dragging, managed to get him inside. There was a closet, the door as thin as a cardboard box. It wasn't big enough for him, so she just draped the bedding over the windows and closed the bathroom door. Then she opened the bed and pulled David up onto it.

She was exhausted but not tired, empty but not hungry. Outside she heard the last of the night's crickets and the first morning birds and a single pond frog croaking. All of it made her feel lonely. She left the bathroom light on but turned the rest off, then locked the cabin door.

With great care she pulled the blankets from David's body, then the clothing, bits of which had melded to his charred flesh.

Around his waist was a soft leather money belt containing thousands of dollars, pounds, and his identification. She stuffed it into her purse. Then she just sat and stared at him, or what was left. The shape of the face was his, all right, but the features were unrecognizable. Blackened skin, blistered eyelids, cracked lips, singed hair. His fingers and toes had curled under, his body pulled up into a fetal position, as if at the last moments he remembered the safety of the womb and wanted to return there.

In the dim light, chilled by the cool, quiet prairie air, Zero broke down and wailed like a baby.

Chapter 18

For the next three days Zero stayed in the cabin by David's body. Other than short trips out to pay the rent for another night, buy coffee and sandwiches, and a couple of bottles of rye, she would not leave him. She knew he was dead, and in more lucid moments realized that not burying his body was strange, even gruesome. But she felt unable to abandon him, almost as if a will greater than her own compelled her to stay.

She took it day by day, unable to make any major decisions. Partly she just couldn't think of what to do, and partly she was caught up in grieving. So she kept the room dark and hung on tenaciously, refusing to really come to terms with the situation, in much the same way she had not believed that Bobby was already dead. She talked to David as though he heard, almost expecting him to respond. But as the days and nights merged, hope dimmed.

Even through a liquor-soaked perception, reality was too sharp. On the fourth night at the cabin she sat on the end of the bed, staring at the fire in the fireplace, drinking from a fifth of Canadian Club.

"David? I ever tell you how I got my name?" She took another swig from the bottle, wishing she had some heroin.

But the fiery liquor no longer burned her throat; she didn't feel it at all now.

"When I was just a kid we used to play hopscotch in the schoolyard. You know how the numbers go from one to ten? Well, we just learned adding and it was my turn again and somebody starts adding up my turns. 'You got ten.' 'Cause I got a seven and a three. But I said, 'I got zero,' because I was making a joke, adding the numbers sideways. Well, everybody was arguing with me and then Tony Alvarez says, 'No, she's zero,' because he was in on it. And then after that everybody just starts calling me Zero." She laughed a little and took another swallow, spilling the rye down the front of her shirt. Then she sighed heavily.

" 'Yeah, zero,' they all said. Nothing. They got that right."

Suddenly she felt very sober. "You know, David, I don't think we oughta stay here much longer. This ain't right. I just wish I knew what to do and where to go. I don't wanna go back to New York. I just dunno."

She turned and looked at him. He was still on the bed, where she had placed him that first night. But she had rearranged him so he was propped up against a pillow. He seemed to be looking at her. Suddenly Zero thought she saw movement.

"David, I'm scared! I think I'm really losing it this time. I know you're dead and all, but I just saw you move. I'm scaring myself." But again the first finger on his right hand twitched.

"Oh, God!" she cried, clamping her hands over her mouth. "If you ain't dead, move again so I know I ain't drunk or nuts." The finger moved, slowly, hesitantly, but she realized that this time she was not hallucinating.

She climbed up onto the bed and crawled to him slowly, afraid to have her hopes rekindled. "Do it again!" And when he did, she burst into tears and threw herself onto him sobbing, cradling him in her arms, pressing his singed hand against her cheek, coating it with her tears.

By the time she had regained control over her emotions, she figured out that they needed a way to communicate.

"Listen," she said, her voice trembling, half laughing, half crying. "Move your finger once for yes and twice for no, okay?"

She waited and he moved once. "You ain't dead, are you?" she asked, just to check on his response, and he moved his finger twice. She broke into tears again.

"David, what do you need? What can I do for you? Are you gonna be okay?" Then she realized he couldn't respond to those questions and that she'd have to think carefully, wording everything so that he could answer yes or no.

"Need anything?" He tapped once.

"Does it hurt?" Again one movement.

"Is it too bright?" One movement.

Immediately she doused the fire, switched off the porch light, and closed the bathroom door except for a crack of light so she could see him.

"Better?" He tapped once.

"I don't know what to do!" She looked around helplessly, but immediately said, "I'm such a baby. Mae's right. I gotta grow up." She sighed.

"David, you must need blood, huh?" she finally realized. He indicated that he did.

She jumped up and went to the kitchen area. There was a paring knife on the drainboard and she snatched it up. Already David was furiously tapping his finger twice, pausing, then twice again. She saw it. "I know you don't wanna take mine, but it's an emergency. Just tonight. I'll get you some other blood later. Please, David? I gotta do something for you."

He moved his finger once.

Barely flinching, Zero sliced into her thumb. The severed skin parted and blood welled out. She placed her thumb between his charred lips and tilted his head back. There was no movement, no sucking. She couldn't even detect swallowing. Some of the red gore leaked out of his mouth and dribbled down his chin, but she knew there must still be enough saliva in him to keep the anticoagulant working; she could feel the wound seeping. Most of the blood was sliding down his throat. Throughout the night she gave him more, reopening the cut that was rapidly turning pink and infected.

And Zero did not care. She would have done anything for him, even sliced a vein, giving her life if it would mean his. And she would do it happily.

But the blood did not seem to have any effect. Still he didn't move, except for the finger, nor could he speak. His burnt eyelids would not even flutter, nor his scorched lips so much as part. Yet all night long she talked to him. She told him what had happened, about the men in the room, how she found him and got him out of the lodge, the car she had passed as she was driving away, and her decision to head east to where they were staying. She told him over and over how much she loved him, between bouts of tears. She would have held him but earlier had asked, "Does it hurt when I touch you?" He had tapped yes.

At daybreak she made sure that the windows and doors would not let even a single ray of sunlight in, and then curled next to him on the bed, just letting his finger rest on top of her palm.

"David, I was so scared," she told him in the dark. "I love you more than anything. And you love me, don't you?" His finger tapped weakly onto her skin.

By the following evening she had worked out a system whereby he could communicate with her. It was like the word game Hangman she had played so often with Bobby. First she got the vowels and their places, and then guessed the consonants. David tapped out yes or no. It was a long, tedious process to form even one sentence. She learned right away that he needed a lot of blood and that animals would do. Also, he wanted almost complete darkness, so she bought candles and lit one at a time.

She had no idea how to find animals for him. At first she tried catching the small wild ones behind the cabin, but had no luck at all. That second night she drove into Medicine Hat and found an SPCA. She wanted to get rats or guinea pigs, but all they had were cats and dogs, and she was forced to adopt two cats, old ones. She hated to do it but David's life was more important. He was all that was important to her.

Crying, she slit their throats, getting badly clawed in the process. With the first she was covered with blood. But by the second one she had refined the technique a little and caught almost all of the gooey red liquid in a bowl. She filled and refilled the eyedropper she'd bought and fed him throughout the night. Before morning she asked, "Is it enough?" He tapped twice.

The next night Zero rounded up four stray animals, enticing them into the car with food. The fourth day she found a slaughterhouse and purchased jars of cow blood. "Mom makes lotsa sausages," she told the beefy man in the white coat who gave her a peculiar look but nevertheless seemed delighted to get rid of his excess. She also bought two white rats from a pet store.

Zero could not get used to the killing. But what was equally hard, although not as repulsive, was disposal of the corpses. Some she buried, scooping out shallow graves with a large slotted kitchen spoon. Others she left in the woods in inconspicuous places, next to fallen trees, under piles of leaves, returning the animals to the arms of Mother Nature.

On the eighth night of their stay at the cabin David was able to move most of his fingers and toes, his eyelids and his lips. But he still could not utter a sound. That night she spent the whole evening translating this message: *Drive Montreal. Me well covered. Change car Winnipeg Toronto.*

She had no idea where Montreal and Winnipeg Toronto were. Casually she asked the man at the office.

"Hey, Will! Ever heard of these places?" She handed him a piece of paper onto which she had neatly printed *Montreal* and *Winnipeg Toronto* in block letters.

He took it from her hands, read it and then laughed. "You Yanks are somethin'. If it ain't in the U.S. of A., you ain't heard of it. And us Canucks saved your bacon more'n once in W.W. Two. Well, just take Number One east. That's the Trans-Canada. You'll come to Winnipeg first in, oh, two, three days, less if you drive straight through. Then keep goin' and you'll hit Toronto, though why anybody'd wanna go to a crowded, noisy place like that beats me. Then half a day later you're in French land."

"How many days altogether?"

"Oh, six, seven, 'less you got somebody helpin' with the drivin'."

"No, there's nobody else. Not yet."

Part 3

From the wreck of the past, which hath perished,
   Thus much I at least may recall,
It hath taught me that what I most cherished
   Deserved to be dearest of all . . .
          —George Gordon, Lord Byron
            "Stanzas to Augusta"

Chapter 19

As Kathleen drove through Canada's prairie provinces, past the endless honey-colored grain fields of Saskatchewan and Manitoba, so flat that the sky became a dome, David saw none of it. He lay in agony. She had followed his instructions and rigged up a tent in the backseat before they left Medicine Hat.

On her own initiative, Kathy told him, she had covered it with something called a "space blanket," material designed to block the sun and reflect its heat back out and keep him cool. Her efforts were virtually wasted; he was in torment.

During the day he slept. But even in sleep he was aware of searing pain. It was like living a nightmare. Or being in Hell.

Each night, shortly after David woke to a tentative consciousness, she stopped at a motel. He was constantly ravenous and suspected that if he were not immobile, he would kill for blood. He also realized that she gave him as much as she could find; it was never enough. He needed the blood to heal. And yet it was the blood that triggered the grueling pain. Without it, those first days, he had been in a kind of shocked limbo. But as he began consuming nourishment, he felt more alive, and more tortured.

He could not see. He could barely hear. Her voice came to him in echoes, as if through a long hollow tunnel. The sound kept him sane, and at the same time the vibrations grated on his nerves. All stimuli were painful. Occasionally she forgot and touched him, sending electric shocks charging through his system.

He was barely breathing as it was, but when the pain intensified, he held himself completely still inside. It was odd. He could not make a sound and yet he distinctly heard himself screaming.

In Winnipeg he gave her the message to switch vehicles. She rented a van from Avis, loaded David and the equipment into it, and then returned the car to Hertz. He wanted to make sure that neither Reesone nor anyone else could pick up their trail. He had her cover the windows with the space blanket material because it kept his body cooler. But the constant motion was another torment. Everything was a torment.

"We're nearly in Toronto," she told him one night. He heard her rustling paper, probably a map. "I see big buildings. It looks like we can go right past without going in." Her voice was clearer; she must have turned. "That okay?"

He tapped twice.

"You wanna go into the city?"

He tapped once.

"Oh, yeah. The van. You want me to change it, right? I almost forgot."

He tapped once.

"I'm sorry, David."

He knew this was confusing and stressful for her. And he couldn't explain his plans, because it would have taken too long. But he needed to get to Montreal fast and find André and Karl.

They were there, or at least he hoped they still were. He had received a letter from André just before Kathy arrived in Manchester. André wanted David to come to them. He said things were different for both him and Karl and that David should come right away. David had noted the address, partly because it was in Canada, and partly because, with a photographic memory, he tended to recall everything that he saw written down. It wasn't because of the content of the letter that he needed to find them, it was that they would know what to do. Kathy, for all her care, could only accomplish so much. He required a specific type of help to heal. And input to figure out what this was about; it was beyond him, and he was not ashamed to admit to himself that he felt frightened. Other than when he'd been under Ariel's power, he could not recall being so afraid, especially since he had changed.

"You want me to get another van?" she asked.

He tapped once.

"I guess you're hungry too?"

He indicated that he was.

"Listen, I got an idea. We won't find no places to buy blood here, especially now 'cause it's so late. But in a big city like this they got a blood bank. Why don't I go there and act like I'm giving blood and I can probably steal some while I'm waiting."

He was angry. He tapped no emphatically.

"You think I'll get caught?"

He tapped yes. He couldn't tell her the real danger. If her blood was analyzed, the technician would notice immediately that its molecular structure was strange. She had already begun changing. The cells of his kind, including blood cells, contained human, animal, and plant components as well as other elements that no mortal scientist had seen. Even the most research-oriented minds in his community had yet to establish the whys, but the wherefores were clear: allergy to sunlight, the inability to digest solid food, a distinct preference for mammal blood, and an extended lifetime, like that of whales and elephants. In the old days André, Karl, and he had speculated. They knew of some who had survived five centuries. They had no idea how long they would live, but none of them seemed to age. Damaged tissue regenerated at an astonishing rate. They were strong and quick, aided by an uncanny intuition that enabled them to sense others of their kind and to hypnotize mortals—at least those who were not too guarded. And even though

Kathy's cells had altered only slightly at this point, still, it would be evident immediately to a trained eye that something was amiss.

"Should I go to the SPCA again?" she wanted to know.

David tapped yes.

Within an hour they were in downtown Toronto. The traffic was heavy, and the stopping and starting nearly sent him to the limits of his endurance. Blaring horns, the nauseating odor of gasoline, snatches of loud music, voices, and the density of bodies surrounding him was excruciating. So many stimuli, and the scent of an ocean of fresh, pulsing blood, finally drove him over the edge. He lay wallowing in unrepressed cravings. Only his nearly immobile body kept him from rampaging through the night and tearing open flesh to sate his overwhelming desires.

As before, Kathleen exchanged vehicles, and once that had been accomplished, headed for the animal shelter. There she discovered that she was ineligible to adopt a pet because she was not a resident of the city. She drove around back streets and alleys but the stray animals were more paranoid than the ones in small towns, or sensed her ulterior motive; she could not entice one to come near the food she offered.

When she returned to the vehicle, she said, "I don't know what to do. Why don't you drink mine again? We'll be in this other place—I don't know how to say it—tomorrow night."

He tapped twice. He then tapped three times, their signal that he wanted to give her a message.

She got a paper and pencil. "How many words?"

He moved his finger once.

"Vowels?"

He moved twice.

"A?" He didn't respond. "E ... ? I ... ? O?"

David tapped once.

"First letter?"

Two taps.

"Second?"

One tap.

"Okay. Second vowel? "A ...? E ...? I ...? O?"

David tapped once.

"First place? No? Third, then?"

He tapped once.

"Blank ... O ... O. What kinda word's that?"

If he could have expressed any humor he would have laughed at the irony. He, a Cambridge scholar, a man of letters. Well-read. A lover of words. Encased in a body nearly destroyed. And now at the mercy of a woman whose vocabulary would scarcely fill five pages of the *Oxford Dictionary*. At least she knows what a vowel is, he thought wryly.

She had to go through the entire alphabet. Even when she got to Z she wasn't sure what the word meant. He felt a grim satisfaction knowing that he was forced to remain silent; he couldn't yell. If we get through this, he promised himself, my first project will be to teach this girl English.

Finally, as if a light bulb had gone off in her head, Kathleen yelled out, "Zoo! It spells *zoo*, right?"

Wearily, David tapped yes.

Forty minutes later they were in the suburbs, pulling to a stop on the road leading to the zoo's parking lot.

"They probably got guards. Should I try to sneak in?"

He tapped yes, hoping she'd remember to take the equipment.

Zero drove down the long desolate suburban road with green and white signs pointing the way to the Metro Toronto Zoo. She parked in one of the lots in an unlighted corner and got out of the van quietly. A high chain-link fence with barbed wire at the top kept visitors off the grounds, but she wasn't about to go through the turnstiles at the entrance.

She walked along the unlit fence for what seemed like miles—this zoo was enormous. Eventually she found fencing that had been loosened from the ground, probably by children, and she scuttled under it, knowing she'd been awfully lucky to find this.

Zero stumbled her way through the dark bushes and eventually came to a poorly lit path. She stayed in the woods, though, parallel to the path—she didn't feel safe even under such sparse lighting.

After walking for quite a while and not finding even one animal, she decided to cross the path and the still-green grass beyond, sprinkled with the first multicolored leaves of autumn. This ain't like any zoo I ever seen, she thought. The open concept, the idea of keeping animals in surroundings as similar to their natural environment as possible, specifically regarding space, baffled her, although she liked it. But it meant a lot of walking.

She found a dimly lit paved path and kept to the edge of it. There were woods on both sides that she could dart into quickly, if necessary. To her right she saw cages of tigers, and a little farther on a camel gazing at her curiously, its eyes sparkling eerily red in the artificial light. She crossed the path once to try the door of a pavilion, but it was locked. It was an outdoor animal she'd have to find.

Eventually she came to a sign with a picture marked BISON. In the faint moonlight she couldn't read the information, so she wasn't sure what kind of animal a bison was, but it looked like a furry cow. And big enough so that giving up a little blood wouldn't hurt it. Carefully she climbed over the low barrier and then felt her way down into the ditch that kept the animals from escaping. Away from the path it was dark; she couldn't see a thing.

Once she was on level ground again, Zero wandered over the dirt stripped of grass by constant grazing. She worried that she might not find one of these bisons; maybe they were indoors now.

"God, it stinks!" she said out loud. A response came from her left. A low snort, almost an exhale, and then the clomp of a hoof.

She had with her a pack containing a large needle, a syringe, and several dozen big vials to hold the blood. Somewhere outside Winnipeg she had decided that if she couldn't buy blood, she'd rather take it this way, so the animals would live. One night she stole the necessary equipment from a veterinarian's office, but so far she hadn't been forced to use it. This would be a slow process, but she didn't mind. Besides, she was an expert with a needle and had no trouble finding veins.

"Oops!" she cried, walking into a beefy wall of fur and flesh. "You gotta be a bison," she said, feeling its side with her palms. "You're a big guy." She couldn't reach very far over his humped back, and below, long strings of matted fur hung down nearly to the ground.

The animal snorted again and then relieved itself, splashing her leg. "Hey!" She jumped back. "Jeez, couldn't you've waited?"

With a sigh, she opened her shoulder bag and pulled out the equipment. One container was already fitted into the needle. She felt along the animal again, in the direction she'd heard the snort. Finally she discovered what she figured must be its neck and probed with experienced fingers. Most of the skin was covered with fur, and what wasn't was thick and rough. "Boy, you ain't makin' this easy," she said. Finally she felt a pulsing and quickly pushed the tip of the needle into the hide. The animal moved forward a little. "Whoa!" she said. And then, "Hold still, bison. This ain't gonna take long. And it's for a good cause. I'll pay you back when I'm done, okay?"

Fifteen minutes later she had two liters of bison blood in her bag. "Stay here," she told her donor, who didn't seem greatly affected by his contribution. "Be right back."

She climbed down the hill, into the gully, and then up over the railing. The woods were dense. Many trees still had what felt like softer, still-growing leaves, and she gathered a big armload, then carted them back to the bison.

"Here you go," she told him. But the bison made no effort to taste the leaves.

"Hey, I went to a lotta trouble for these. Don't be like that. Eat some, okay? David says you gotta eat your greens or you get sick." The bison seemed to consider this statement and then apparently made a decision. He nibbled experimentally.

"Is someone there?" a firm but frightened male voice called.

"Holy shit!" Zero whispered in her animal friend's ear, dropping the leaves onto the dirt. "I gotta get outta here."

She moved away but turned back briefly. "Hey! Thanks!"

She was long gone by the time a flashlight beam streaked across the 1,300-pound buffalo munching the mound of juicy leaves. Only the bison heard the security guard wonder, "Now, how the . . . ?"

Chapter 20

JUST AFTER SUNSET ZERO DROVE INTO MONTREAL IN THE pouring rain. The windshield wipers clacked, squeegeeing sheets of water off the front windows rhythmically, but the ride was far from relaxed. Boulevard Décarie, a main road leading downtown, was bumper to bumper with the last remnants of rush-hour traffic.

"These guys don't know how to drive," she called over the backseat to David, then swerved sharply to avoid a Datsun that had skidded in front of her. She had to concentrate very hard because of the bad weather and also because the drivers in this city did not seem to respect lanes. In fact, this road didn't even have white lines on it. And in addition to the normal difficulty of being in a strange place and finding her way around, here all the street signs were in French.

Most of the colorful three-, four-, and five-story brick residences she drove past, when she got a chance to look, were interesting. Long rows of iron steps led to charming iron balconies. Shuttered French windows and sloped chateau-style roofs. And everywhere there were crosses. They even had one stuck into the top of a mountain.

She wondered if David was afraid of crosses, like the vampires in the movies, then she remembered he said he wasn't.

"I'm gonna get some gas." She pulled into a PetroCan service station. "Fill 'er up," she instructed the attendant.

The boy, dressed in a yellow slicker with a hood, asked, *"Plomb ou sans plomb?"*

Zero just stared at him, her mouth hanging open.

Finally he said, "Leaded or unleaded?"

"Unleaded." She shook her head. Then she called out the window, "How come you didn't ask in English the first time?" But there was no reply.

While he filled the tank, Zero talked to David. "I'll find a place to park so's you can tell me where you wanna go, okay?" She figured he must have a plan; after all, he wanted to come here.

She switched on the inside light, lifted the space blanket and then the flap of the tent. His finger tapped yes. He still couldn't speak, but he was now able to move his arms, legs, and head, and even open and close his eyelids and mouth, all of which were encouraging signs for her, although his eyes were kind of flat and zombielike and his skin was still black. He looked horrible, like an animal that had been roasted on a spit.

"Want me to get a map?" she asked. He indicated that she should. "I don't know how I'll read it, though. Everybody here talks a foreign language."

She heard a cough to her left and turned. The gas station attendant stood quietly, rainwater dripping off the tip of his nose. He was looking at her strangely. "I like talking to myself. That way I don't get into fights," she told him, handing over a Canadian twenty.

"You're from the States," he commented, counting out the change in soggy colorful bills.

"Yeah! How'd you know?"

"Lucky guess," the boy said and walked away.

She pulled to the side of the station, used the washroom, bought a map, and then conferred with David.

"So, where to?"

He tapped out one word and she guessed the letters, coming up with *Redpath*. It took her a while to find it, but she finally circled the street in pen on the map.

"The guy inside says we're here." She held up the map, pointing, but then realized he couldn't see it. "It's not far. Should I go right there?"

He tapped yes.

By the time they arrived on Redpath Crescent, a street of large expensive homes built of gray fieldstone and brick and set high up on the west side of Mont Royale, the rain had stopped. "Want me to park?" He indicated that he did. She backed into a space, pulled up the emergency brake, switched off the ignition, and climbed into the back. She turned on the inside light again.

"Now what?"

He tapped four times, their signal that he wanted to write something down. She wedged a pen between his fingers and placed a notebook in front of him on the floor of the van.

Agonizingly slowly, he scrawled out a message.

777. André and Karl. André left NY 1960, Karl 1958.

"I don't know what you mean. You want me to go to 777 on this street?"

He tapped once.

"Then you want me to ask for Karl and this other guy, I don't know how to say his name. And . . . er. Is that right?"

David tapped twice.

"Well, I never saw this name before. How'm I supposed to say it?"

He tapped for the paper again and wrote out the name phonetically.

"Ann dray? Like the wine?" she asked.

And he tapped once.

"And Karl?"

One tap.

"What's this stuff about them leaving New York?"

She noticed his hand twitch and felt even more frustrated. She knew writing was painful for him. It was so hard to understand him. And she couldn't figure out why they were here, although she knew that these two were David's friends. He wrote another note.

Ask André when he left NY. Ask Karl. If answers correct, bring them to me.

She read this note aloud, nodding in understanding. "But what if they gimme the wrong answers?"

He wrote one word—*run*.

As she walked up the steps at the side of the three-story house numbered 777, Zero was memorizing "Ann dray 1960. Karl, 1958," hoping she would remember.

She knocked on the walnut door and waited. Within ten seconds it was opened by an attractive woman in her thirties. Her eyes were the clear color of sapphires, her hair dark and wavy, skin pale. *"Oui?"* she asked.

Behind the woman a man appeared. He was handsome and well-built, like an athlete, with gray eyes and black hair streaked with silver. He took one look at Zero and said, *"Mon Dieu!"*

Both women looked at him.

Zero piped up, "You guys speak English? 'Cause I don't talk French."

The woman turned back to her. "Yes, we speak English."

"Great! I'm lookin' for two guys—one's name's Karl and the other one's ..." Damn! She couldn't remember. She glanced at the piece of paper she was holding. "Ann dray," she pronounced slowly, feeling pleased with herself, and then looked back at them.

"I'm André," the man said. "Who are you?"

"I gotta see you and this guy Karl. He here too?"

"I asked who you are!"

The woman touched his cheek. He slipped an arm around her waist and seemed to relax a little. Then the woman turned to Zero again. "Step inside."

She followed them to the living room. A man about her age with rich brown hair and eyes was seated on one of two couches next to a pert slender girl with mahogany hair. Like the others, these two were dressed casually. The man jumped to his feet immediately, his pale skin turning even paler, his mouth gaping, surprise registering on his face. His reaction caused the redhead to stand too. *"Was ist es?"* she asked.

"Ich sehe ein geist!" He stared at Zero.

"Sit down." The woman who had answered the door gestured toward the same couch.

Zero could tell that the four of them were strange. They had skin like David's, or at least the way it used to be, pale, bright. Their eyes were very intense. They made her uneasy. It was like watching wax figures that had come to life.

She took a chair close to the door, but they remained standing. She felt nervous and struggled to hold her own. David was relying on her. She also thought about the quickest means of escape, just in case. She decided she'd flip the chair behind her to block them as she ran to the door, hoping to make it out before they knew what was happening.

"Look, I gotta ask you guys some questions."

André took a step toward her. "Your name?" he demanded.

"Zero. Please, I just got two questions, then I can tell you everything."

"What do you want to know?" Karl asked.

"You're Karl, right?"

He nodded.

"I gotta know when you left New York."

He looked surprised. "Is that all?"

"Yeah."

"I left in 1958. In the fall."

"Been back since?"

"Well, no ..."

Zero turned to André. She found him intimidating. She got the feeling he was only restraining himself because of the influence of the woman with him. "When did you leave?"

"Why do you want to know?"

"Why don't you tell her," the woman next to him said softly. "She seems harmless enough." André looked at the woman, and Zero watched his boiling anger cool. She's like a safety valve on a pressure cooker, Zero thought. If she wasn't here, this guy'd explode.

Finally he said, "Nineteen sixty."

She exhaled loudly, suddenly feeling exhausted with relief. "Boy, am I glad you guys are who you are."

"I want to know what all this is about. Now!" André said.

"You're David's friends, huh?"

"David? Yes," Karl said. "But who are you?"

"I'm his girl. He needs help. That's why I'm here."

"What kind of help?" Karl asked.

And André wanted to know, "Where is he?"

"Outside. In a van. You gotta help him. He's hurt. Bad."

André and Karl looked at each other, then André said to Zero, "This better not be a trick because I wouldn't want to be you if it is."

"It's no trick." Zero stood, suddenly elated. Things were going to be all right. She wasn't alone with this. "Come on. I'll show you."

The two women waited inside while the men followed her down the street. When they came to the van, she unlocked the back doors. André jumped in and Karl stayed outside, as if on guard.

"Sacrement!" André said softly. Then, "Karl, drive up to the door. And back in."

Zero got in the passenger seat and Karl drove the short block to the house. The two women were waiting just inside.

André said to the one with the blue eyes, his voice urgent, "Carol, use the satin sheets and make up our bed. Quickly."

The redhead laughed. "Desperate for love?"

André turned to her. "No time for humor, Gerlinde. We'll need ice, a lot of it. Buy at least twenty bags."

"Sure thing," she said, grabbing a jacket and heading for the garage.

Zero stood aside while the men lifted David carefully onto the space blanket and carried him inside. They turned right, went through the modern kitchen and then downstairs. She followed, suddenly feeling both ignored and useless. They walked through a clean, finished, empty basement and then through a doorway into a bedroom done in black, silver, and gray. Carol was just smoothing a silver satin sheet over a king-size mattress. "Oh my God!" she said when she saw David.

"Turn off the lights," André instructed, and immediately she switched off the overhead and then the rectangular reading lamp above the bed, leaving them in darkness but for a strip of illumination coming from the main basement.

"What happened to him?" Carol asked softly.

"I'm not sure," André said. "It looks like he's been exposed to a lot of sunlight. He's badly burnt. David, can you speak?"

"He can't talk yet," Zero said.

"When did this happen?" Karl wanted to know.

"About a week ago. Maybe a little more. Out in Vancouver."

"You drove all the way here by yourself?" Carol asked.

"Yeah."

David was shifted to the bed. "We need an IV setup," Karl said. "Gerlinde will help me when she gets back."

"Maybe I should phone Chloe," Carol offered. "She's probably at Jeanette's by now. They'll both have some suggestions. And Julien will know the best way to handle this."

"Good idea," André said. "I'll start defrosting plasma."

Amid the general buzz of activity, Zero didn't know what to do with herself. André left the room, and so did Carol. And then Karl started out the door too, stopping briefly to tell Zero, "Don't touch him. It will be painful."

"I know," she said, feeling resentful. It's because of me David's alive, she thought. And now I'm being shoved outta the way like I don't belong.

When they were alone, she perched on the edge of the big bed and slid her hand under David's. As always, he lay perfectly still.

"Glad to be here?"

He tapped once onto her palm.

"You're gonna be okay, huh? Now that you're with your friends?"

Again he tapped once. Then he drew something with his fingertip onto her skin.

"Is it a heart?"

He tapped yes.

"I love you too," she said. But she felt lonely and wished more than anything that she could crawl into the safety of his arms.

Chapter 21

ZERO SPENT SEVERAL WEEKS LIVING WITH A HOUSE FULL OF vampires—using that word made it easier for her, but the two times she let it slip out, it annoyed the hell out of them.

Besides the four she'd met, there was a child, a boy about ten years old, the age Bobby would be. And although he didn't look anything like Bobby, Zero fell in love with him. The feeling was mutual.

His name was Michel, which she had a hard time believing because she had only heard girls called that. When she discovered it translated to Michael, she just called him Mikey, which he seemed to like. He was a bright, attractive child with black hair and clear blue eyes. Carol was his mother and André his father. She knew from David's stories that André had been a vampire for a long time, so at first she couldn't figure out how he was Mikey's dad. And she hesitated to ask. Eventually she decided that Carol must have had the child before she changed, and André was probably his stepfather. And although Mikey slept in the daytime, just like the rest of them, there was something about him that was thoroughly human. And very special. He was like them but different.

During the night hours, she spent a lot of time with Mikey

while David recovered in solitude in the total darkness below ground level. They kept her from seeing David, saying he needed rest and blood and that the stronger he got, the more blood he needed. She would only hinder the healing process. Zero accepted it, because they gave her no choice, but she didn't like the way they were treating her.

During the day, they locked her in a big room on the third floor that seemed to be a painter's studio. They all slept from sunrise to sunset, and she couldn't sleep that many hours, so the time dragged. But at night, when she was with Mikey, time flew. They played games, sang songs, watched videos together. She felt like a child herself. When she wasn't with Mikey, she was with one of the others; at night they never left her alone, even to go to the bathroom.

The women weren't too bad, and Karl seemed to be losing some of his initial distrust. But André still made her uncomfortable.

He and Karl interrogated her every night about what happened, the same questions over and over. She was intimidated by André's hostility and felt a lot better when Carol was around.

"Tell us again about this man Reesone," Karl asked.

She was on a green two-seater couch. Mikey, at her feet, worked a Sandman puzzle. Karl, Gerlinde, Carol, and André, in that order, sat on a long couch on the other side of the coffee table. Gerlinde sketched her in charcoal while the rest watched her silently with that same glowing immobility.

"He was in the papers, that's how we found out who he was. He's some actor or something. Looks Italian. David did all the talking when we saw him. I wasn't paying much attention."

She felt embarrassed that she didn't have more details to offer. First, she had been so awestruck at the Italian consulate, and second, the longing for drugs had hit, and by then she didn't even know what was going on around her. It made her feel dumb, and she wasn't being much help to David.

"Describe him again," André said.

She looked at André. The way he stared, it was as though he hated her. But that can't be, she thought. He doesn't even know me. She sighed. "He's short. Hair like yours," she said, pointing to Karl. "The color, I mean. And he smokes these black cigarettes. I bet you could get one of his movies at the video store."

"I already have," André said, still watching her.

"So how come you're asking me, if you know what he looks like?"

"Because there are things you're telling us that we don't believe."

Zero shifted. She had told them the truth, except for a couple of things. One was about Bobby already being dead. Another was that it was she who had tried to kill David in Manchester. She just skipped that part, said she met him there, and that somebody else had tried to kill him. They'd gone back to New York together and managed to track down Dennis. She knew she shouldn't have lied but didn't know how to say those things without making herself look stupid. Also, she'd been afraid they wouldn't trust her if they found out that all this started with her. But now it seemed they didn't trust her anyway.

"Look," she said. "David's almost better, right?"

"He's recovering," Karl said.

"Well, why doncha ask him, if you don't believe me."

"I intend to." André looked at her coldly. She glanced down at Mikey. The boy was an angel. She could see how he could come from Carol, but definitely not from this guy, although André was okay with Mikey, and everybody else, for that matter. It was just Zero he seemed to dislike, and she couldn't figure out why.

"Can't I see David tonight? Please?"

No one spoke for a few seconds, but then Karl stood. "I'm going down to change the plasma bag. I'll ask him if he wants to see you. He's in a lot of pain. He doesn't want to see anyone."

As he left the room, Mikey piped up, "Zero, help me."

Immediately she slid to the floor and began trying to fit

the puzzle pieces into the remaining spaces. She was busy with that for several minutes until Carol asked, "What's your relationship to David? Are you lovers?"

She looked up and grinned. "Yeah. We're lovers."

André stood. She couldn't believe how much anger came off him. He walked to the window, shoved the curtain aside and then looked out.

"Are you thinking of becoming like us?" Carol asked.

"Yeah. I already started."

André spun from the window to face her. Zero looked down.

"Open your mouth, kiddo. I gotta check this out," Gerlinde said, flopping onto the floor.

Zero opened her mouth, and the redheaded vampire peered inside, like a veterinarian examining a horse's teeth.

"She's on the verge, all right. I'd know baby fangs anywhere."

André came across the room quickly, shaking his head. "This doesn't make sense. Why would David do this? Has he lost his mind?"

Zero jumped to her feet, hands on hips, a full blast of defensiveness rushing out. "Because he loves me. Is that so hard to figure? And I love him, even if you don't think I'm good enough for him. So he's smart and rich and I'm poor and stupid, right? Well, there's other things between people besides that stuff, so you can go fuck yourself, because I don't give a shit what you think!"

Everyone was still, even Michel, who held a piece of the puzzle, his hand poised in midair.

André folded his arms across his chest. In a voice dangerous with restraint he said, "Whether you're good enough for David is between the two of you. Has David mentioned Ariel?"

"His old girlfriend? Sure."

"Then what I want to know is—"

"David wants to see you," Karl interrupted from the doorway.

Zero ran from the room, raced down the kitchen steps, and flew across the basement.

The bedroom was dark and cold. She shivered; it was like walking into a refrigerator. "David?" she called softly.

A low, raspy voice said, "Over here."

She walked in the direction of the sound, soon banging into the side of the bed. Two hands reached out to steady her.

Instinctively her arms went around him, her heart pounding with excitement. Her fingers brushed his bare back and she felt large patches of dry, crinkled skin peeling away.

"No!" he said, and she jumped at the sound. "Don't touch me. Let me touch you."

She dropped her arms to her sides. His hands moved hesitantly down from her shoulders to her fingertips and then up again. He felt her face, her neck, her breasts, and then he was unbuttoning her blouse. "I need you, Kathy. I really need you."

The words sent a thrilling quiver through her body, and she had to force herself to keep from touching him.

His fingers became urgent as he pushed the skirt and underpants down her hips. Both of them were breathing heavily.

She kicked off her shoes, and then his sensitive hands, which seemed stronger now, pulled her onto the bed. "Lie back," he said, kissing her lips. His were cool, and she shivered from that and the chill in the room.

He hovered above in the darkness, not touching his body to hers, only caressing her with his hands and lips. "It's so hard not holding you," she said.

"I know."

His lips moved down to her right nipple and lingered there.

Then he licked her stomach and thighs. Her body was jolted by the sensations. She did not need to be stimulated for long.

He eased to the end of the bed. She sensed him kneeling. He bent her knees and pushed her legs straight up in the air, holding her calves, pulling her toward him. He lifted the lower half of her body off the sheet a little and eased into her.

She was hit by a spasm of pleasurable pain and cried out; all the agony she had gone through in the last few weeks, and the intensity of desire generated by wanting him so much, crashed together.

"I need you, Kathy," he said again, the desperation in his voice acute.

He held her legs away from him so their skin-to-skin contact was minimal. The sensation for her was strange; she could not see him, she couldn't touch him. But she heard and felt him, and what she felt was a little frightening. There was an aggression coming from him. He moved fast and thrust hard; her thighs were close together and it was a snug fit, the stimulation intense. He must have sensed her fear.

"I'm still me, Kathy. Please! Don't hold back. I need you so much."

And his need touched her, dissipating the fear into a wave of passion. Heat burned up her body. She grabbed on to the headboard to brace herself. He thrust so fast all she could do was fall back and let him take her. Her breathing was quick, little cries pulsing out of her. And then she felt herself slipping down, down, as waves of hot pleasure raged through her body.

Afterward he sat beside her, kissing her, touching her, as she lay quietly. He allowed her to hold his hands, the only area he felt comfortable having her touch.

"I love you," she said softly. "When you gonna make me like you?"

"Soon. When I'm stronger."

In the cool darkness they were silent until suddenly she said, "You're different."

He knew it was true. His appetites were intense. Already he wanted her again. And his desire for the blood verged on depravity. If he had allowed lust to overwhelm him, he would have pierced her artery tonight, ravaging her more violently than he had been victimized when his blood had been stolen.

But David was aware of a new appetite as well, spawned by pain, nurtured on hate. It had grown like a fungus, spreading inside him, obliterating nearly everything else and blossoming into an obsession. For the first time in his existence he hungered for revenge.

Chapter 22

"HEY, ZERO! WANNA PLAY ROCK STAR?" MICHEL CALLED from the doorway of the living room.

David looked across at the boy. "Her name is Kathleen. Kathy."

Michel ran into the room and squeezed between André and Carol, who sat on one couch. Karl was in a high-backed chair nearby. Gerlinde, cross-legged on the floor at his feet, draped one arm over his knee, letting her fingernails dry.

"You said your name's Zero." The boy looked at Kathy accusingly, his face, in David's eyes, a younger version of André's.

David raised his arm, the one with the needle stuck into it.

The tube attached to the needle led to a plastic bag half full of the greenish plasma that dripped steadily into his veins. He took Kathleen's chin in his hand and made her look at him. "Don't ever call yourself Zero again. Do you understand?"

She stared with big round eyes. He could feel blood boiling beneath her hot skin. He wanted to be inside her, in more ways than one.

"You saved me, Kathy. All of you saved me. I'd be truly dead without your help." He looked around the room at his friends, but turned back to Kathy. "But especially without yours. The white walls and the glass caused the sun to be extremely intense. It would have destroyed me sooner than normal exposure to sunlight. If I had been in that room much longer, I would have been unable to recover."

"Kiddo, you shoulda caught yourself when you arrived," Gerlinde said. "I wouldn't have bet two bats' wings you'd be walking around now. Although if I were you, I wouldn't enter any beauty contests for a while."

David had seen himself in a mirror. He looked raw. Most of the crusty blackened skin had been shed, leaving a sensitive new layer, scarred, possibly permanently. Under the lightweight clothing Karl had loaned him, his injured body was cooled and soothed by a blend of healing natural ingredients Chloe suggested over the phone—English marigolds, calendula, and chamomile. The lights had been dimmed, enabling him to come upstairs tonight for the first time.

He watched Gerlinde French-polish the nails on her right hand. She had already applied two coats of clear polish on each nail with meticulous care. Now she was painting white just on the tips with the practiced movements of an artist. She was a perky redhead with twinkling chocolate eyes, not the type he would have selected for Karl. The two were so different. And yet he could see the attraction—Karl's intellect balanced by her humor, his quiet by her light and sound.

Even more astonishing was this woman Carol, and the fact that André had a relationship with her. It seemed a good one. And they said the child was theirs.

"Tell me about Michel," David said.

As André talked, David realized how much his friend had mellowed. His hair, once white only at the temples, was now black shot with silver: maturity. We're all different, he thought, André, Karl, and I. They've softened, I've hardened.

"Ten years ago," André began, "Carol and I met in Bordeaux. We had a . . . relationship. It didn't work out. It was my fault."

Carol touched his cheek. "It was both of us," she said.

Immediately his arm went around her shoulders. "No, it was me." André leaned over Michel to kiss her lips.

"Don't mind them," Gerlinde said. "They're still on their honeymoon."

André focused on David again. "We don't understand why it happened, but I managed to impregnate Carol. The legends say that a child born from such a union can be either mortal or immortal. It's really a choice. Michel's at that age now, the age of decision. But either way, the child is exceptional. A divine child, with unusual powers. We've already seen signs in him."

"You were a vampire and she wasn't?" Kathy interrupted, excited.

"Yes."

She turned to David. "Maybe we can do that."

"It's a rare occurrence, Kathy," David told her.

"Extremely," Karl added. "Before Michel there were only legends of such offspring. None in our community has encountered such a child."

"Carol and I parted," André continued. "Because of me."

Carol took his hand.

"But she was determined. She found us last year when we moved here, God knows how. Miraculously, I was able to change her. I couldn't have done it without help," he said, nodding toward Karl and Gerlinde.

"Chloe was here too, and one you haven't met, Morianna," Karl said. "And Julien. He has a wife now and children. Not by birth."

David was astonished by all the changes in his community. While he had been out of touch, avoiding contact, giving in to despair, much had occurred. His ideas of the world, in retrospect, seemed to be as rigid and distorted a reality as he had so often accused others of possessing. "You're both happy," he said.

"Yes." Karl ran his fingers up the back of Gerlinde's fiery hair.

David looked at André, Carol, and Michel. André nodded.

"And you?" Karl asked.

"With Kathy, yes." And then David felt icy burning hatred eat through him. His tone hardened, and he noticed shocked looks on the faces of his friends when he said, "I want Reesone. And whoever's behind him."

Everyone was silent until suddenly Michel asked, "Dad, how come he looks like that?"

"He was burnt by the sun. You know that, Michel," André said.

"But how come?"

"Someone tried to hurt him."

"Must have been a mortal."

"Yes."

Michel looked frightened, and David attempted to reassure him. "This would never have occurred if I hadn't blinded myself. I walked into a dangerous situation. I knew it was risky but failed to take proper precautions. In a real sense, I've only myself to blame."

But Michel still looked upset.

"Are you worried someone will try to hurt you?" Carol asked.

Michel shrugged and shook his head too quickly.

"We'll never let anyone hurt you," she said.

André added, "All of us will protect you, Michel. I've taught you how to protect yourself. And as you grow up you'll learn more. No mortal's going to harm you. Ever."

Relief flooded the boy's face. He jumped up. "Can we go to the park?"

"Later," André said. "We want to talk with David for a while."

"But they got this band on. Can we go now, please?"

"I'll take him," Kathy offered.

André and Carol looked at each other. Finally Carol said, "All right. Which park is it, Michel?"

"Mont Royale."

"It's not far," she told Kathy. "Michel, don't eat a lot of junk. You know too much solid food makes you sick. One candy bar, one Coke, that's it, okay?" The boy nodded. To Kathy she said, "His system can't handle it."

Michel grabbed Kathy's arm and dragged her to the door.

"I won't let him eat junk," Kathy promised just before the door slammed.

As soon as Carol sat down, Karl said, "I've formed a theory. I think one of our kind is behind this."

"I've thought that too," André said.

"Why?" David asked. "It's been mortals who've tried to kill me all along the way. First Kathy, then Dennis, the Snake Priest, Reesone—"

"What do you mean, first Kathy?" Karl asked.

"I thought she told you the whole story, from when she came to Manchester to kill me."

Everyone shifted uneasily. Finally Karl said, "She told us Dennis tried to kill you in Manchester. She met you there one night and helped you track him down in New York."

David didn't know what to make of this. "I'd best tell you everything," he said, and started at the beginning.

Halfway through his story, Carol stood. "I'm going to walk over to the park."

André caught her hand. "Wait. It's early, just nine-thirty. Give them another half hour." She sat back down.

Thirty minutes later, David's story was complete.

"*Mon ami,* I wish we had heard all this from the beginning," André said.

Carol stood abruptly. She looked nervous. "I want to go over there. Michel's probably got Kathy buying him everything in sight."

André walked her to the door. Meanwhile Gerlinde said to David, "God! You two've been to hell and back."

"Kathy didn't tell us she was addicted to heroin," Karl said. "And she lied about something else too. About her brother dying in a car accident."

David was worried. He thought she'd accepted that, and now she was denying it again. And was she also denying that she'd tried to kill him? She seemed clear. So clear that he had planned on talking to her about Bobby being her son. He thought she was strong enough to face it now. And he wanted her to face it before he changed her.

"Look, the theory still holds," Karl said. "This is too well-planned, even down to a room that seems designed to kill our kind. I think only one of us could arrange all this."

"But then why use mortals?" André asked as he sat down.

"Because it's too difficult for us to kill each other," Karl said.

"Any one of us could've shoved David into that room," Gerlinde said. "I mean, we have the physical strength, not that we'd ever do it."

"Yes, but because we sense our own, David would have been more alert. With mortals you never think they can harm you, so you don't pay close attention."

Gerlinde nodded.

"But it's all so sloppy," David said. "The note to arrive after dark—"

"That's an example," Karl interrupted. "Every mortal's seen *Dracula*. You kill vampires *before* dark. Whoever wrote that knew you'd be awake and able to defend yourself."

"But why would Kathy go, then?" Gerlinde asked.

"Because she was a junkie," Karl said, "so desperate for drugs and confused about her brother that she couldn't think clearly. And they chose her because they knew you'd stop her. And let her live. Whoever's behind this knows you well."

"There's another reason they knew you wouldn't kill her." André paused. "She looks like Ariel."

David felt slapped in the face. "Perhaps a bit. I've noticed similarities, sometimes, occasionally her mannerisms . . ."

"David, they could be twins," André said.

David shook his head.

"It's true," Karl added. "André and I both saw it right away."

"But her hair, her eyes . . ."

"Different coloring, that's all."

He ran a hand over the top of his head. The old hair had been singed, the new only grown about an inch so far. "Perhaps I've forgotten what Ariel looks like." He stared around helplessly.

André came and sat next to him. "Whoever sent her knew about you and Ariel."

"But who else besides you two? And Chloe."

Suddenly the door crashed open and Carol raced into the room. Her face was a mask of terror.

"André! They've taken Michel!"

"What are you talking about?" He grabbed her arms, searching her face.

"Michel's been kidnapped. He and Kathy got into a truck."

"What happened?" Gerlinde was already on her feet; they all were.

Carol's voice quivered and she was out of breath from running. "They were in the park. An old man saw them. He wouldn't come with me, but here's his phone number." Hands shaking, she handed André a piece of paper. "He's French. He didn't speak much English and talked too quickly for me to understand him."

While André made the call, the others surrounded Carol. André talked only a short time. When he returned to the group, he looked frightened. And angry.

"He says a blue van pulled up. A woman got out of the passenger side. She spoke with Kathy and then the three of them got in. Michel and Kathy went willingly. The van was driven by a male. The old man couldn't see him, but the driver tossed a black cigarette butt out the window. The woman . . ." He turned to David. "It's Ariel."

Chapter 23

"I HAD A FEELING," CAROL CRIED. "IF I HADN'T LET HIM GO with Kathy, this wouldn't have happened."

André held her. "No. You wanted to walk to the park earlier. I stopped you."

"It's neither of you. I should have realized they'd follow us." David sat down grimly. He felt more than guilty. Horrible thoughts nagged at him. Kathy had gone willingly. She had lied when she told André, Karl, and the others about what had happened.

And something else occurred to him too. When she'd first confessed in Manchester that his own kind were behind this, he'd dismissed it as a story concocted to get the drug. And now he wasn't so sure that she hadn't known the truth all along.

"Look, all of you, stop blaming yourselves," Karl said impatiently, running a hand through his hair in exasperation. "We've got to get out there and search."

"Of course you're right," André agreed. He still held Carol but turned to face the others. "We'll return to the park and find out if anyone else noticed anything. The van is dark blue. The old man said it was large, so it's probably an American make. With dark circular windows on the sides.

Will you two drive around the mountain? You know who to look for."

"Sure thing," Gerlinde said. "Karl, you take the Volvo, I'll drive the Fiat."

André turned, and David could hardly stand the look of pain and accusation in his friend's eyes. "Will you wait here? You're not in any condition to run around. And we need someone so we can call in."

David nodded. He took a step toward his friend. "André, I don't know what to say."

"I don't blame you. It's Ariel. And Kathy."

"Not Kathy. I'm sure they were taken against their will."

"She's just like Ariel."

"No. There's got to be an explanation."

"The lies," Karl said. "She went willingly. And they look so much alike."

"She's not part of this. I'm certain of it."

"You were fooled before, *mon ami*," André said. And before David could respond, he added, "We'd better go."

The four left David by the phone. Karl had suggested he call Austria, tell Chloe and Julien what happened. While David waited for the connection, he sat back thinking.

This was too peculiar. It must have been set up so that an exchange could be made—Kathy and Michel for him. But why? They could have kidnapped Kathy before now. And Michel. Also, they could have made certain he died in Vancouver by stopping Kathy. It was obvious they didn't want Kathy. Or did they? But the lies she's told, David thought. And, as both Karl and André kept pointing out, she looks so much like Ariel. With Ariel involved, the motives would be very twisted. His head hurt trying to sort it all through.

Julien—one of his kind whom David had met in New York, just after World War Two—came on the line. David sketched out what had happened to him and then told Julien about the abduction.

"Yes, it is very strange," Julien agreed, traces of a classical French accent in his English.

"Maybe you should come here?"

"Perhaps. Chloe will certainly want to return to Montreal, although I think it best that the rest of us remain, until we learn more. Ariel could be anywhere. Tell me about her, David. Ariel and I have met, but our contact was brief. And it was many many years ago. She soon discovered she could not gain power over me, and I tired of her efforts to reverse that situation."

David winced. "Yes, she prefers males she can control. She's secretive. To me she appears Irish. I'm certain she's from Europe, and several hundred years old."

"Our encounter was at the end of the eighteenth century. In Venice. She had an old aura about her then," Julien remembered, then chuckled. "Although not *ancien régime,* as I am."

"She told me once she prefers Europe to North America," David said, "and that if she didn't dislike flying she would be back and forth more. She also mentioned someone she'd been with before me." David was surprised by a stab of pain and anger that hit at the memory of how Ariel had brought up her former lover only to torment him. "He's one of us. She called him Anthony."

"Anthony? Italian?"

"I'm not certain."

"I do not know the name, but of course with us names convey little. Tell me, David, in your relationship, did you take from her? Can you track her through the blood?"

He felt ashamed. "No. She took mine, though. She can track me."

"Then she knew where you were all along, which is something to consider. You may not have yet discovered this, but taking the blood from one of our own is entirely different than drinking from a mortal, where the connection is direct. Between us the blood must always be secondary. She can track you, but not as quickly nor reliably as you can track Kathy."

"Are you saying I can find where Kathy is now, even if she's taken against her will? How can that be? The range I have when I sense mortals is based on their thoughts, feelings, and memories, extracted from the blood I've ingested."

"The process is identical. When you capture her essence within, focus on the future rather than the present and the past. The blood will guide you."

When David got off the phone, he delved within himself, meditating on Kathy, the core of her being. The taste and scent of her blood became a sensory hologram. The room still held vestiges of her, and he allowed the oral and olfactory images to move forward in time, like a three-dimensional movie, and he moved with them, as though he lived inside her skin and had become a part of her. She was with Michel, at the park, getting in the van, driving, stopping, walking. Looking around. Waiting.

He unhooked the plasma, defrosted two pints of whole blood in the microwave and drank it, and buckled on his money belt, which also contained his own and Kathy's passports. Then he left a note for the others.

David hurried down from the mountain to a main street as fast as his wounded muscles could move him. He caught a taxi to the train station.

He raced through Gare Centrale, hurrying up Track 2, where the train would come in from the west, heading east to Halifax. As he ran he scanned his platform and the passengers on the opposite platform, waiting for the train going in the other direction. He glanced quickly up and down but could see none of his kind. But the feeling of them, and of Kathy being near, was intense; the air crackled.

Suddenly, at the end of the opposite platform, he caught a beam of light darting into an enclosed waiting room. As he reached the end of his platform, Ariel emerged from behind the waiting-room door. She gripped Michel tightly by his upper arm. The boy looked frightened.

Seeing her again, after so long, threw David off balance.

She smiled across the expanse, speaking seductively and so softly that no mortal could hear. "I knew you'd come. I felt it. You're incredible. So very reliable."

Behind Ariel stood Reesone, now a form of light himself—she'd changed him. Reesone had come out dragging Kathy behind him.

"David!" she cried.

Seeing both Kathy and Ariel side by side shocked him. He had thought about the similarities before, but the realization had not clicked until this moment, and he wondered how he could have avoided making a connection that had been so blatantly evident to both André and Karl. It's almost as if I've been hypnotized myself, he thought.

Reesone locked an arm around Kathy's throat. "Make another sound and I'll snap your pretty little neck."

Behind them were six more of his kind, none that he had seen before, which made eight, far too many to attack even had he been at his peak.

Ariel seemed aware of his frustration and laughed. "There are many more of us, David. A veritable army."

"Why?" His voice rang with impotence, and Reesone grinned.

Ariel smiled cryptically at the actor. To David she said, "Why what, my love? You who were always so curious."

"Why did you take Kathy? And Michel?"

"Long ago your little mistress and I tasted one another. It's so much easier tracking a mortal. You've always been under my spell, haven't you, my pet?"

She stroked Kathy's hair, and Kathy pulled back, crying, "David, don't listen to her. I really love you!"

"Charming!" Ariel laughed. "A romantic. She thinks of you as her Romeo and herself as Juliet. Tragic yet beautiful."

"I don't understand this." He stalled, trying to figure out what to do. Down the track he heard a whistle. As if calling to its mate, another blasted from the opposite direction. Soon there would be two trains between them.

"I sent this charming girl to charm you, dear boy. And look at her. How could she fail? When we heard of the child," she stroked Michel's head, and he too pulled away, "we knew we must have him. He's unique. Their house in Bordeaux was empty. No trace of André. You know how thorough we can be. The only way to find the child was through André, and the only way to locate André through you. I couldn't very well ask for the address. You would have alerted him, and he's naturally suspicious. I considered force, but in many ways you're incredibly stubborn, an appealing but infuriating trait. And David, you know how the role of martyr suits you! Would you have left your comfortable crypt without a good reason? Well, she proved an excellent catalyst for change, did she not? We're distant relatives, separated by centuries. And blood is thicker. They say she looks like me. Do you think so?" Ariel laughed.

The trains neared and David screamed in his head, Think! How can I get them? He had an urge to just throw himself across the track, but even if he avoided being crushed by a powerful engine, he would be instantly torn apart by Ariel's seven guards, and then Kathy and Michel would be lost.

"You did all this to get Michel?" he asked, incredulous.

"Of course. I had no intention of destroying you. What a waste that would be. You're too attractive, or at least were."

Her smile became coquettish. "I would have sent her to the lodge by sunset, but she took the initiative. Unfortunately the atrium was necessary. One of Donald's ideas." She turned a little, and Reesone looked pleased with himself. "One that worked," she added, and Reesone's face dropped.

"You're such a loner, David," Ariel continued. "We had to force you to lead us to your friends. You have no idea how special the boy is. A hybrid that will alter the future of our race. I intend to breed him and begin the development of a new life-form, an exquisite blend of mortal and immortal. Think of the possibilities—a submissive race that walks in sunlight, easily. They'll be able to thrive on more than the blood and yet live forever. The ultimate in genetic engineering."

"But this makes no sense."

The roar of the engines nearly obliterated Ariel's voice.

"It's so simple. But David, you've never been able to see the obvious. This new race, they'll be so fragile. Vulnerable. They'll need guidance. And who better to aid them? I'll feed off him, and eventually his blood will change me."

He couldn't think clearly—the noise, the confusion, it was all becoming overwhelming—but he knew he had to hold on. "You're insane!" he shouted.

She laughed. "Not insane, a genius. Once I've changed, I'll enjoy daylight, like even the lowest life-form, and yet still be immortal. The worlds of both light and darkness will be mine. I'll be free." The look in her eyes was madness, but her voice became seductive again. "You should consider joining me, David."

The train on her side of the tracks was pulling into the station now, the engine rumbling loudly, vibrations shaking the concrete under David's sensitive feet. Suddenly Michel bit into Ariel's wrist. She gasped. Her lips snapped back in fury, exposing sharp teeth. Spontaneously she shoved him away from her. In that split second Michel jumped out in front of the westbound train and just missed being crushed to death. Then he was in the middle of the eastbound track. Whistles blasted.

"Hurry, Michel!" David yelled. He reached down and grabbed the boy, pulling him up onto the platform inches from the Halifax-bound engine.

David and Michel raced down the crowded platform, out of the station, and into a cab. Through the rear window David watched three from Ariel's group jump into the blue van.

"I'll double the fare if you can lose the van that's following us," David gasped. "The blue one."

The driver stared at David's scarred face with a mixture of pity and revulsion, then located the van in his rearview. He said in thickly accented English, "They are not police?"

David touched Michel on the knee, signaling for him to be quiet. "It's custody. The boy's mother wants him. So do I."

"Entendu!" The driver nodded, increasing the speed. Within a dozen blocks the van was no longer in sight.

"Stop here!" As the driver turned for the money, David caught his eye. "Do you have a pencil and paper?"

As if mesmerized, the man handed both over the backseat. David held his eyes a moment longer, then wrote two sentences on the paper: *You have Kathy, I have Michel. Think about it.*

He folded the note, wrote *Ariel* on the outside, then handed it and one hundred dollars to the driver.

"Drive to the airport farthest from the city. When you're asked about us, say you dropped us there. I told you to give this note to whoever inquires. You will remember nothing that occurred before."

As soon as they were on the sidewalk, the driver pulled away.

"How come you said that?" Michel wanted to know.

"Because Ariel can track me through the blood, but it takes time. They'll know soon enough we didn't go to the airport, but perhaps the driver can be saved. Her troops are too new to this life to get past the suggestions I embedded in his subconscious, but they may kill him anyway. The note is to keep her from harming Kathy further. Come along."

He led Michel to a car rental office across the street.

"What's the fastest way to drive to New York?" he asked, signing the rental forms, handing over a large deposit, and then waiting for the papers to be finalized.

"I thought you were headed to Chicago," the clerk said, rechecking the form. He looked up.

"I want to go by way of New York." David casually glanced at a map on the wall.

"Well, you can cross Quay Richelieu, you'll end up further east, or south from Lacolle, goes into Champlain, New York. There's points at Hemmingford, Trout River . . . And you can always sneak in." The man laughed.

David looked back at him. "Is that done?"

"Sure is. There's all kinds of small roads between border checkpoints. Of course, the Americans have them fenced off and cops patrolling the roads, because of all the illegal immigrants that visit Canada and then try to get to the States. And the drug smuggling."

David grinned. "Amazing what some people will do."

"Sure is." The clerk smiled, handing over the keys and papers. "If I were you, I'd drive to Toronto, then Windsor, and then across at Detroit. Gas is cheaper in the States, but the speed limit's higher up here. Saves time."

"Sounds super. I think that's what we'll do," David said, leading Michel outside. They got in the car and David drove half a dozen blocks. He stopped at a pay phone.

Almost as soon as Michel punched in his phone number for David, André answered. He sounded frantic.

"André, listen to me. Are all four of you there?"

"Yes. Why didn't you stay here, David? Have you heard anything about Michel?"

"Just listen. There isn't time. Get everyone out of the house immediately. You're in danger, all of you. Write this number down." He gave the number of the pay phone. "Call me from a phone booth in three minutes." And he hung up.

David looked around. "Keep your eyes peeled, Michel. Can you recognize our kind?"

"Yeah," the boy said, scanning the four streets.

A long three minutes later the phone rang and David snatched it up.

"What's going on, David? Where are you?"

"I've got Michel."

There was a huge sigh of relief over the line. "Let me talk to him."

"All right, but please be brief."

"Dad? Yeah. I'm okay. Yeah. We're at—"

But David blocked the mouthpiece with his hand.

The boy looked up at him with a new fear in his eyes, then said, "We're both okay. Hi, Mom."

While Michel spoke, David formed a plan. He took back the receiver. "André?"

"Just a minute." Carol handed the phone to André.

"Where are you, David? We'll come right there."

"It's not safe."

"Why? What's happening?"

"Ariel is tracking me, and I can't leave Michel for you to find. She's not alone. There are at least eight of them, and she indicated more. They've still got Kathy. I think they'll be at your house any minute."

"Hold on a second."

When André came back on the line, he sounded shocked. "Gerlinde drove home to get some cash she'd left in a wall safe. She saw five of them and hung back. They set the house on fire."

There was a pause. Finally David said, "André, you're in danger. We're all in danger. I think you should get out of the city—leave in twos, go to Julien's, and take an indirect route."

"But what about Michel?"

"I'm going to keep moving until I can hide him where he'll be safe, then I'll get him to you. As I said, they're tracking me even now."

"But let's arrange to get Michel right away?"

"André, it's Michel they want. They've wanted him all along and used me as the connection." Finally David said, "Trust me."

"That goes without saying, *mon ami*. It's Ariel I've never trusted."

When the arrangements were concluded, David hurried Michel into the car. Pulling away from the curb, he felt the electrical charges in the air increase just as the boy shouted, "There's the van!"

Chapter 24

THE TIRES SHRIEKED AS THE CAR SKIDDED THE CORNER. David tore up a narrow side street, ignored a stop sign and turned again. No sign of the van. "They may not have seen us," he told Michel. "But they'll find us. Soon."

"Where we goin'?" The boy was terrified, and David reached over to ruffle his hair, thinking, He's incredible. So much like André. A feeling of happiness hit that completely surprised him, especially given their present circumstance.

"Michel, before I arrived, did your father ever talk with you about me?"

"Sure. Lots. Can I put the radio on?"

"Go ahead."

As Michel fiddled with the dial, David said, "Then you understand we're very good friends. I wouldn't do anything to harm André or you."

"I know," Michel said, not looking at him, fine-tuning a rock song.

"Michel, did Ariel take your blood?"

The boy shook his head.

"You're going to have to trust me."

Michel didn't respond, just looked out the window, then

214

suddenly said, "That Ariel. Was she gonna burn me like you?"

David pulled onto the highway headed south. He checked his watch and the speedometer. In about an hour they should be at the border. "I'm afraid she had something else in mind. But I won't let her have you. I'm going to take you to a place where you'll be safe. And then I'm going for Kathy."

"How you gonna get her?"

David wondered the same thing. "I can track her," he said.

But that wasn't the problem. The problem was that there were so many of them. And that they might kill her to stop him from finding them. *Unless she's been with them since the start.* The thought came into his head and he crushed it. He was betting on Ariel keeping her alive, believing he would exchange Michel for Kathy.

As they drove through southern Québec, the land became less urban, more farms and small towns. The buildings were wood or gray fieldstone, quaintly French, very provincial. Maple trees dropped red, orange, and yellow leaves at an alarming rate. David saw the riot of colors with his night vision but was too preoccupied to enjoy the spectacle. He was in physical pain and would need blood soon. And plenty of it.

They passed Saint-Jean-sur-Richelieu, the last city, and after that it was little towns, Saint-Blaise, Saint-Paul-de-I'Ile-aux-Noix, and then west toward Hemmingford.

As they drove, David asked, "What happened in the park?"

"Ariel came up to Kathy and told her you were hurt and we should go with her. Then Ariel said my dad was hurt too. There was a fire at the house and we'd better come quick 'cause you might not live."

"Did Kathy know Ariel?"

"I don't know."

Ariel may have been lying in saying that she'd taken Kathy's blood, but he didn't think so. More likely she had, but Kathy had been unaware of it. At least he hoped Kathy's involvement was against her will.

"Then what happened?"

"When we got in the truck, Kathy started to say something. I think she knew the guy driving. There were other guys in the back, and one of 'em hit her and she fell over, but she was okay. After that she didn't say anything till we saw you."

Michel was frightened, and David said, "Why don't you sit over here." The boy moved close, and David put his arm around the small shoulders. "We'll be in the United States soon."

"We goin' to Chicago?"

"No. I wanted the man at the Hertz office to think that and pass it on. Ariel will track us anyway, but it might confuse her a bit."

After Hemmingford they turned south again onto a dirt road. Within half an hour they reached a bushy area and David tried several dirt trails leading south. Most were dead ends. Eventually he found one that stopped short at a chain-link fence nearly obscured by dense foliage. Barbed wire was strung across the top.

"How come we're sneakin' in?" Michel asked.

"Because you don't have any identification. And my face is distorted, which will make mortals suspicious. And also, I think Ariel will be watching the airports in Montreal and probably the main border crossing points."

Along the way David had stopped to purchase a couple of things he thought he might need. The wire cutters came in handy, and the large carving knife. First he hacked at the thick bushes. Then he snipped enough of the chain links so he could push the fence back and drive through. Seconds after he entered the American side, an enclosed light green Jeep with a United States Department of Justice, Border Patrol, symbol on the door pulled up. As he had anticipated, radar sensors were the real border protection.

Two officers in dark green uniforms, one wearing a matching green cap and the other a Smokey the Bear hat, got out. A bright spotlight bathed the scene in stark light.

"Hands up in the air," the shorter one in the hat said stiffly, his gun already drawn.

"Do as he says," David told Michel, who raised his arms above his head.

The tall, heavyset officer in the cap opened the back of the Jeep and a large German shepherd jumped out. He hooked a leash to the dog's collar and walked him to the car. When he opened the door on the driver's side, the dog hopped into the car, sniffing his way over the front seat.

The short, leaner one pulled a set of handcuffs from his belt. "What's your story? Trying to smuggle you or the kid or something else in?"

David caught his eye and concentrated. "If you'll put aside your weapon, Officer, I'm certain I can provide a satisfactory explanation."

The slender man, his eyes glued to David's, lowered his revolver.

"Doesn't look like drugs," the taller cop said, slamming the trunk of David's car. He and the dog turned to his partner.

"Bill? You okay?"

"Officer?" David said calmly. "If I can have your attention for a moment?" The dog snarled and the policeman took a firing stance and aimed his weapon.

Soon David had both of them calmed, relaxed, the gun back in the holster, the dog lying on the ground. He instructed the one named Bill to radio his headquarters and report that it looked as if a large animal had attacked the fence and somehow must have been picked up on the scanner. The area was secure and they did not need backup.

Before leaving, David took blood from each, and the dog as well. He needed more, much more, but this was neither the time nor place.

They left the officers in their Jeep listening to music, the shepherd in the back napping. In fifteen minutes they would regain consciousness and drive away, forgetting that this encounter had ever taken place.

Back on the road David checked the sky, although he had no need to. It was near sunrise, and he felt the heat from that fire as surely as he felt the beat of his heart. If anything, he was more sensitive than before. "We need to find a place to sleep immediately. If you see a motel or even a sign, let me know."

Eventually they came to The Sheltering Pines, a small motel off the side of the highway. He rented a room for two nights so they could sleep through the day, and requested that any cleaning be done after they checked out. Their room was in the middle of seven, all comprising one long pink-and-green clapboard structure that reminded him of old army barracks. The inside was dull, painted in shades of pasty green and yellow. Faded nature scenes in knotty-pine frames attempted to hide wall cracks. The closet was not large enough to hold even Michel.

David closed the drapes and covered the window with a blanket. He hung the Do Not Disturb sign out, bolted the door, and then created a barricade around the double bed using the mattress, and the dresser and night table, both turned on their sides. A second blanket protected the last open area. They crawled under the box spring.

"They're not gonna find us, are they?" Michel asked once they were settled.

"We should be safe here." But he could not be certain. He was not really sure of anything much, except that he wanted Kathy. And, for an entirely different reason, he wanted Ariel.

Chapter 25

THE FOLLOWING NIGHT, JUST AFTER SUNSET, DAVID TOOK nourishment from the middle-aged couple who ran the motel. Their blood was old, laced with impurities and pending illnesses, but he would have taken more if he hadn't been afraid of killing them. A pint from each sustained him. Temporarily. To recover fully he needed a constant infusion. And the hunger, now inextricably tied to revenge, raged. He would be feeding again, if not twice, before sunrise.

They drove about fifty miles and pulled off the highway to a Howard Johnson restaurant. While Michel devoured steak—rare—and eggs, David placed a call to Austria and spoke with Julien. "Have you heard from André?" he asked.

"Yes. All four are on their way here. They will arrive shortly. Are you bringing Michel to us?"

"Not immediately. It's too dangerous. I think they're only minutes behind me, and I can't risk putting him on a plane for Europe. I think she'll cover that possibility."

"I agree. But is there a safe place for the boy?"

"I hope so. I'm going to fly to different cities, just to make a complicated trail for Ariel, since she's the only one who can track me. She hates flying, so she'll need to be in constant communication with the others, instructing them where to go. It should be enough of a delay. The first thing I'll do is leave Michel in the care of a friend. It's the best I can think of."

"I see your plan. When Michel is safe? You cannot dodge them forever."

"I'm going to get Kathy."

Julien paused. "David, they number too many. They may kill her to keep you from tracking them through her."

"I don't think so. I'm leaving messages for Ariel along the way that I'll exchange Michel for Kathy. As long as Michel doesn't leave the country, they'll believe he's with me and a trade is still possible. That should keep Kathy alive." At least I hope so, David thought, wondering if it would work, if anyone as conniving as Ariel could be fooled.

"David, you must realize that Kathy may have been helping Ariel all along. Obviously she's under her power."

"I've thought of that," David said, not daring to express just how many doubts had crowded the corners of his awareness, including the knowledge that the two were related. "But I don't think so."

Julien said, "We are eight, including you."

He hesitated. The offer was a formality; they could not really help him, and Julien knew this as well as David. "They'd spot so many of us right away, and I don't know how many of them there are. I can move faster alone. I think this is best, for now." He hesitated. "I need to do this alone."

Julien paused again. "Yes. I understand. But should something happen to you . . ." He left it open.

"My friend will have instructions to phone within the week and let you know where Michel is. If I haven't found Kathy by then, it either means I probably won't find her, she's dead, or I am."

Both were silent.

"All right," Julien finally said. "I'll inform the others. Call when you are able. But David, do not be stubborn and foolish, traits which seem to solidify with the change. We will help you to the extent we can, given our restrictions. You have only to ask."

"Thank you." David felt pressure in his chest. He wondered why, in all his years, other than with André and Karl, he had felt so alone. It was clear to him now that more contact was possible than he had allowed himself. But what a painful means of discovery, he thought.

They drove west to Syracuse. "They'll think we're headed to Chicago," David explained to Michel. There they handed in the car and caught a taxi to the airport. David purchased tickets to New York. Their flight left within the hour, and within the next they arrived at Kennedy. A quick glance told David there were no unnatural lights weaving among the throngs of mortal travelers.

At a pay phone he placed a call.

"Mae's Fine Foods," came a familiar voice.

"Mae, it's David."

"David! How ya doin'? Kathy with ya?"

Pain stabbed at him. "Not at the moment, but yes, we're together. Mae, I need a favor."

"Just ask."

"Do you know Frankie? He stands around outside the Alexander."

"Yeah." Her voice lowered and he could picture a scowl crossing her aging features. "What about 'im?"

"It's crucial that I get in touch with him immediately. It's a question of life or death, and I'm not exaggerating. Can you have him phone me at this number?"

"I guess. That kid ain't exactly trustworthy, you know. Takes drugs, no job—"

"Mae, please. Have him call as soon as possible. This is a pay phone, and I'll be near it for the next half hour only. And don't tell anyone but Frankie I've phoned."

"Mum's the word."

David and Michel stood off in a corner, partly concealed by an advertising board. But the phone was in constant use, forcing David to join the line again. When he reached the front, he picked up the receiver and discreetly depressed the button, talking into the dial tone. Barely a minute elapsed

221

before grumblings emanated from behind him. He sent a meek smile back through the line.

"Shit!" the man next up for the phone said.

The phone rang and David released the button.

"Hey Dave, my man. Frankie here, what's your game plan?"

"Frankie, thanks for phoning. I need help. Big help."

"A favor with flavor to savor, right?"

"Something like that. Listen, will you take a taxi to Kennedy Airport? I'll meet you outside the departures' entrance of the TWA terminal and pay the fare. Come alone and do not tell anyone where you're going or that you've talked with me, understand? Tell no one!"

"The mystery, ain't history. You'll find me in a hack, Jack!"

As David got off the phone he turned in time to see a blazing form of light glide across the room. They could sense each other. Both turned. David had no idea if this was one of Ariel's group or just a stray of his kind taking a flight somewhere. He pulled Michel back behind him until he was hidden from view, although that would make little difference. Soon the light vanished through a security check-in and David breathed a sigh of relief.

He checked his watch, knowing that Frankie probably would not arrive before eleven. At 10:45 he led Michel to the TWA main entrance. He handed him a wad of money and hid the boy between two newspaper boxes with his back to a wall. He could be seen only from the front. "Listen carefully, Michel. You'll have to remember Julien's number."

"I already know it."

"Do you know how to make a long distance call?"

"Yeah."

"Good. One less thing to worry about. Michel, I'm going to stand out at the curb waiting for Frankie. He's about eighteen years old, has dark skin, tall, wears a scarf like a headband, red and blue. If anything happens to me, get in the cab with Frankie and tell him to take you to Mae's as quickly as he can. From there telephone Julien right away, collect. He'll tell you what to do."

"What's gonna happen to you?" Michel looked frightened.

"Nothing, I hope. But there is some danger. If anything does go wrong, if you see any of our kind approach me, stay back. When it's safe, get in the cab with Frankie and tell him to go. Immediately. Is that clear?"

The boy nodded. "How come I'm not going to my mom and dad?"

"It's too dangerous to fly out of New York by yourself, and I can't go with you to protect you because I add to the danger—Ariel is tracking me even as we speak. And right now I don't know if any airport is safe. She can't track you, so as long as we're not together, you should be safe." What he didn't tell Michel was that the boy was insurance. If he sent Michel to Vienna, even if Michel did manage to get there safely—and that seemed like a long shot—Ariel would probably have the airports watched. The minute she found out she'd lost Michel, Kathy would be killed.

David waited nervously on the curb, continually glancing in all directions. At twelve-forty a yellow cab pulled up and Frankie hopped out. The driver yelled out the window, "Hey, kid, where the hell you think you're goin'? My fare first, then you take off into the wild blue yonder."

"Wait, please," David told him. "You'll be paid."

The cabbie shook his head and pulled a Lucky from a pack.

"Hey, my man, you ain't lookin' good." Frankie brushed a hand over David's short hair and his eyes glided over the fragile new layer of facial skin.

David grabbed his upper arm. "Frankie, what took you so long? I told you I need help!"

"I had a little business. Anyways, relax. Help's the reason I'm present and accounted for. So what's the score?"

David pulled him out of earshot of the driver. "I need a child, a boy, hidden for a week, perhaps less."

"Yeah?" Frankie grinned. "How come?"

"I can't tell you because I don't want to endanger you.

There are people after him. Big people. Far more powerful than the Snake Priest, and twice as deadly."

Frankie popped a stick of gum into his mouth and grinned. "I'm shakin'. That all you need?"

"The boy must be kept in a safe place. No one but you may know where he is, and I mean no one. It should be completely dark, devoid of sunlight. He is not to go out at any time, and only you are to go in. He'll need a washroom. Take him two meals a day. Large pieces of steak, uncooked, very bloody. Leave the blood in, just give him the package and plenty of fresh water."

Frankie raised an eyebrow. "You're shittin' me, right?"

"I'm very serious. Will you do it? I've tried to arrange this so there's no danger to you, but I can't guarantee anything. That's why I didn't go into the city. They can track me."

"Well, can't they track you here, man?"

"Yes, but they won't know about you. If I went to the Alexander, they'd show up there."

David knew that without a detailed explanation this wouldn't make sense to Frankie, who said, "You ain't goin' paranoid, are ya, Floyd?"

"Trust me."

Frankie looked skeptical but hardly missed a beat. "Sure, Dave. Whatever you say. So where's this kid?"

"I'll bring him in a moment. First take this." David handed over five thousand dollars.

"Hey, Jack, that's a lotta energy."

"You'll need money for the cab, for food, a room. And I want you to buy a fake passport for the boy tonight, if possible. Give the passport to him. Hold on to the rest of the money, at least for seven days. If I don't come back for him, one week from tonight let Michel make a phone call to Austria. He knows the number. And one other thing. If there's any apparent danger, should you sense anyone strange hovering around, I want you to promise me you'll leave the city quickly. Just give Michel food and water for a week, access to a phone, and go. Will you do that?"

"You're serious."

"Deadly. And Frankie, I'm counting on you."

Frankie shifted his weight to his other leg and then sighed. Suddenly he slapped David's palm. "You got it."

David glanced around. It appeared to be safe. He gestured for Michel, who ran out from between the boxes. "Get in the taxi and duck down," he told the boy. "Remember, Michel, any trouble, phone Julien immediately. And give Frankie the number. Is that clear?"

The boy nodded. Frankie got in beside him and David closed the door.

"Be careful," he told them both.

"You too, Homes," Frankie called out the window as the cab pulled away.

As soon as they were gone, David purchased two tickets, one adult and one child, on the red-eye to Los Angeles. After L.A., he planned to avoid the larger cities as much as possible, at least initially, since those would be the spots Ariel would check first. But he'd change the pattern every now and then. There couldn't be that many on her side. On the other hand, if she'd been making them indiscriminately, like Reesone . . .

Just before boarding the flight, he bought a box of stationery. He jotted a brief note, stuffed it into an envelope, then wrote *Ariel Moon* on the outside. The note read:

> *Have you still got Kathy? If you don't, you'll never see Michel again.*

He left it at the information desk with instructions to page Ariel throughout the night. Eventually one of them would pick up the message.

Before takeoff he took a walk from the front to the back of the cabin. There were no glimmering lights on board. He sat back, breathing a sigh of relief, his first in the last two nights. But the relief did not last long. Doubts and worries nagged at him. How long could he outrun Ariel? What if Frankie didn't come through? Or Michel was discovered?

And, what he dreaded most: Had Kathy knowingly been part of this sinister plot from the beginning?

As the aircraft flew thirty thousand feet above the ground through the dark and silent night sky, he closed his eyes to loneliness and found Lord Byron's words drifting through his mind.

> A lovely bird, with azure wings,
> And song that said a thousand things,
> And seem'd to say them all for me!
> I never saw its like before,
> I ne'er shall see its likeness more:
> It seem'd like me to want a mate,
> But was not half so desolate,
> And it was come to love me when
> None lived to love me so again,
> And cheering from my dungeon's brink,
> Had brought me back to feel and think.
> I know not if it late were free,
> Or broke its cage to perch on mine,
> But knowing well captivity,
> Sweet bird! I could not wish for thine!

Chapter 26

"BASTARD!" ARIEL SHRIEKED. ZERO WATCHED THE VAMpiress's pale otherworldly eyes glint white sparks. Her full lips parted and pulled back into a snarl, fangs large, wet, and glittering like icy stalactites. She tossed her saffron hair behind her shoulders angrily. Reesone and the two other males in the room stayed very quiet. Zero cowered back into the corner where she sat on the floor, hoping no one would notice her.

Ariel shredded the note. It was the second, from Kennedy Airport. A cryptic smile spread across her sensual features, which frightened Zero even more. "He's smarter than I thought. I'll give him that. But not nearly as clever as he imagines himself."

Then Ariel began laughing; a low humorless laugh, to Zero's ears. "But David understands how I love a game, especially one I intend winning."

She looked down and Zero tried to keep her body from trembling. "I'll keep her alive. For now." She turned and walked to the French window. Her shin-length leather A-line skirt clung seductively to her hips as she moved. Zero glanced at the males. Their eyes were soldered to Ariel's body.

"Why don't we just kill her?" Reesone said. "You're not going to make any deals with him anyway." The actor clawed the air so quickly that Zero almost missed the movement. He caught the white butterfly that had been fluttering around the room, trapped indoors at the end of its life cycle. Reesone squeezed his fist tightly, then flicked the destroyed creature away with his index finger.

Zero felt almost relieved that it had been Reesone who made the suggestion. She'd noticed in the last two nights that anything he suggested, Ariel vetoed. The vampiress turned to him.

"Donald, you amaze me." Ariel's voice was light, airy, as though she were about to bestow a compliment, and Reesone smiled smugly. "You're reputed to be a clever man, a man who understand complex roles, and yet your solutions seem so—how can I put it?" She waved a hand in the air. "Simplistic?"

The other two males laughed, and Reesone looked like a little boy who had been punished in front of his friends. Ariel walked to the corner where Zero huddled like a trapped animal. They hadn't bothered to tie her up; she couldn't escape. Ariel stared, her strange pale eyes swirling like colorless tornadoes, spiraling inward. Zero looked away while she still could, thinking, Now I know how David got hooked. At the same time another, more horrible thought occurred: Maybe she made me fall in love with him.

"Of course," Ariel said, "having a not-quite rival to my beauty on hand, but certainly no threat to my personality or intellect, well, it's not my first choice, familial ties considered. However, Donald," and here she turned, "David is not nearly as naive as you imagine him. He has existed over a hundred years, which says something. It says he's strong. A survivor."

"He's stupid. Look how easily he let himself be trapped. And I was still mortal then." Reesone's voice faltered just a touch, but Zero heard it. She had the impression that he had not changed willingly and that it might even have come as a surprise.

"Yes, Donald, you were mortal." Ariel laughed. "And

David was a fool. And still is, no doubt. I suspect the idea of a trade is merely a bluff on his part, although I can't be certain. And I'm curious. He can track her, but he'll likely want to speak with her, or possibly see her, to be sure she's well. You are well, my dear, are you not?"

Ariel looked at her again, and Zero couldn't help but spit out a "Fuck you!" Reesone raced across the room and smacked Zero hard across the face. Her head reeled from the force of the blow.

Ariel threw back her head, laughing. "How chivalrous you are, Donald. Protecting my honor."

The door opened and a short man who looked about forty with straight black hair came in. His skin was craggy, weather-beaten, like a sailor who has spent most of his life at sea; a rugged masculine look, but oddly pale like rice paper. Zero felt an energy he exuded that was not only powerful, but commanding. He dominated the room. And as she watched him she had a feeling of déjà vu, and wondered where she had seen him before.

The man walked to Ariel, and Zero was surprised by the look of adoration the sensual vampiress gave him. As if he had been in the room all along, Ariel asked, "What do you think, Tony?"

The man named Tony turned and eyed the three males with disgust. Ariel giggled. "I think," Tony said, "she remains alive, for the present. So far your secondary plan works well enough, my love. You three! Take her to the house on the West Coast. Hire two bodyguards also and secure the premises during daylight. The others are in Vienna now, David's alone, with just the boy. Or do you feel that three of you are inadequate to stop him?" There was a sneer on his face.

Ariel laughed again. She walked over and patted the cheek of one of the males. He looked like a dog whose mistress had finally paid him some attention. "I think they'll do," she said.

Zero felt miserable, but she still had hope. They wouldn't kill her yet. And David had found her before; he'd find her again. At least he was still looking, he still believed she loved him. She just worried that they'd catch up with him.

"What about you?" Reesone asked Ariel. His voice was laced with unmistakable longing. Ariel moved to him slowly, her voluptuous body undulating. Reesone looked mesmerized. She slid a hand around the back of his neck, pulling him close as if to kiss him. Suddenly, violently, she clamped her lips to his throat. A look of painful ecstasy embedded itself in his features. But the moment he tried to embrace her, she moved away. Reesone's face was ravaged, his neck streaked with red gore.

"Fly out there tonight." Ariel turned her back on him. She licked her lips, her tongue flicking like a snake's, as she made her way into Tony's arms.

Tony kissed her, greedily sucking the sticky blood from her mouth. Then he held her at arm's length, looking into her eyes, while he said to the others about Zero, "Fuck her, of course. And take some blood. That's your right. But I want her alive, do you understand me?" His eyes left Ariel's briefly and locked on to the three males, one at a time. Each looked terrified, and it was as though Zero could see something inside them give way. Each nodded his understanding. She saw obedience replace terror in their eyes, and the violence in Tony's as he looked down at her.

His eyes, pools of dead dark earth, sucked at her will. She felt engulfed, suffocated, sliding downward into a muddy grave.

"Yes," Tony said. "By all means, take her." He laughed, and in Zero's ears it was unearthly, the cackle of a demon who had just cast a powerful, irrevocable spell. She felt stripped of a future, the victim of a perverse fate.

One of the males yanked her to her feet. The last thing she saw before being dragged out of the room was Ariel trapped by Tony's powerful arms. He pinned her wrists behind her back and fastened his teeth to her throat. Ariel's face reflected a look of painful yet orgasmic longing, similar to the look she had created in Reesone.

David left messages in every airport he disembarked in over the next three nights—St. Louis, Savannah, Milwaukee,

Phoenix, Wilmington, Green Bay, Lexington, and half a dozen other places.

He had spotted his kind, but because he had taken precautions, they had not seen or sensed him; he counted another eight strange faces. They stood out in the crowds of dull mortals like fireflies in the country on a moonless night. It let him know that Ariel had her recent recruits in strategic spots, and forced him to purchase extra tickets and catch off flights crisscrossing the country. Twice he had taken trains, from Minneapolis to Boulder and from Portland to Seattle, making himself harder to locate.

He placed calls to several airport information desks; Ariel had his messages. His notes changed. It was time to set up an appointment.

Just after landing in El Paso, he phoned the information desk at the Seattle airport.

"My name's David Hardwick. Are there messages for me?"

"Hold on," a young girl said. She came back on the line right away. "Yes, Mr. Hardwick. There's one message."

"Read it, please."

He heard paper being ripped and then an embarrassed voice read:

"A rendezvous? How romantic you still are. Midnight tomorrow, Gare Centrale. You realize I'm expecting your child. And you, my love? You may expect zero."

As soon as David hung up, he placed another call. In Vienna, André answered. "Is Michel all right?"

"Yes. They're still following me. They haven't figured out that I've dropped him off. I'll be sending him to you soon."

There was a sigh of relief. "Are *you* okay?"

"I'm tired," David admitted. "I've been drinking several times each night. It's barely enough."

"You're still recovering."

"I suppose. André, put Julien on, but get Karl and the others and stay near the phone. I need information and suggestions."

When Julien was on the line, David explained his plan. "I've tracked Kathy. She's been at the house on Vancouver Island for the last three nights. I'm going to get her."

"Unless she is one of them, they will be guarding her," Julien said.

"I know. Hopefully you can provide vital information. When I was with Ariel, she seemed able to withstand the onslaught of sunrise. If not the light itself, at least the lethargy. How much daylight can she tolerate?"

"I am able to remain awake after sunrise, although I do not function well, and, of course, only indoors; she would function less well," Julien said. "My strength is greatly diminished during daylight hours. And so far I have been incapable of obtaining sustenance."

"Can she track me during the day?"

"I cannot. Since I am older than she, I assume she does not possess this ability."

"Good. I've arranged to meet Ariel tomorrow evening in Montreal. I know she'll be there. If I can travel tomorrow, in the daytime, I can be on Vancouver Island before sunset. She'll know where I am after dark but won't be able to get there, or send anyone immediately. That lag time may be enough. I'll make certain to sever the phone line."

"It sounds like an excellent plan, David, although I am curious as to how you will travel in the day."

"That's the main purpose for this call. Have you or any of the others heard of any of our kind who have been out in daylight?"

Julien got off the phone for half a minute. While he waited, David's eyes darted down the sterile corridor. The phone was at the dead end of it and he felt boxed in. His nerves were on edge.

"None of us know of such a thing," Julien said when he returned. "You will either develop some tolerance to the pressures of the daylight hours eventually, as I have, or not. But to walk in daylight ..." He paused. "I do not know that it is possible. I have long believed that it is the ultraviolet light that affects us, as well as the earth's gravity, which increases during daylight, pulling us down and bringing on the exhaustion. I can think of no way unless you hide and have yourself shipped there, but that, undoubtedly, will take time. And you are crossing a border and are likely to be detected."

"Yes," David agreed, and they both were silent.

Finally Julien said, "David, there may be a way, although for one in your weakened condition, it is not without risk. Chloe has experimented. She wishes to speak with you."

André's aunt came on the line. David could still picture her in his mind—a warm but firm woman looking sixty, with white hair and piercing blue eyes the color of lapis lazuli. Her voice was soft, feminine, holding just the hint of a French accent. And, like all of the females of his kind, she was utterly mesmerizing.

"David, I've been so worried about you. Are you all right?"

"Yes, Chloe. Thank you for your concern." He sighed, realizing again how much he'd missed contact with his own. "Chloe, has Julien told you what I need?"

"I understand," she said. Then, "I've developed a natural remedy for our allergic condition. It's similar to the sunscreen mortals wear, more like zinc oxide, but geared to our chemistry. So far I'm the only one who's tested it, and then it was just after sunrise and before sunset." He jotted down the ingredients she listed and how to mix them.

"Once they're blended," Chloe continued, "apply a thick coat to your skin. You must cover every inch of yourself and keep the covering thick, which means you'll need to make a large quantity so it can be reapplied at regular intervals. And it must be chilled to keep the ingredients active. Because it's natural, your skin will be able to breathe. The aloe will cool too, and heal the burning that has already taken place. I'd advise wearing cool clothing, light colors. No polyester. That material's not porous and air doesn't penetrate. And it's too hot—like wearing a green garbage bag. Wear natural fibers, or a high percentage, although those pose a danger of letting in too much light through the weave. But David, you must test all this in full sunlight, provided you can remain awake. Even in our mortal state, each of us had a different skin type and a different resistance to UV rays. And your skin has been severely damaged. Think what would happen if you get caught and this does not work."

Karl came on the line, saying, "I'm not sure this will help, but there's a fabric I've read about. It was developed as part of the experiments used during space flights. They designed it for travel to cold planets but it works as an insulator, both hot and cold, like a thermos. I've often thought that since our bodies are cooler during the day, if we had clothing made from it, and wore wraparound sunglasses to block ultraviolet light and infrared radiation . . . but of course I don't know if it would work. And I don't know how you'd protect your face and neck. You'd look very strange, wearing a foil suit. Just a minute."

Carol took the phone. "David, if you could do that, maybe even use it like bandages to wrap yourself in, you could buy a latex face and neck mask from a theatrical supply store. I used to work in theater. If you put Chloe's cream underneath and makeup on top of the plastic, you might pass. It's worth a try."

"Thanks, Carol. Put Karl back on, please."

"The big problem is the bulk," Karl said immediately, "although I understand that the material comes as thin as gold leaf."

"Where can I buy it?"

"That's the thing." Karl sighed. "Outside NASA, I don't know where you can find the thinner material. It would take you time to locate the source, and you'd probably have to steal it anyway, since it's still experimental. It's too bad, because they've already got it on the market, but it's too thick and makes a crinkling sound when it's moved."

"What is it called?"

"Space blankets. You can buy them at camping stores. It's what you had in the truck."

David almost laughed. Of course. What Kathy used to shield him from the sun. Kathy and her survival instincts. She couldn't be part of this, he knew it now. A sudden love for her shot through him. He was choking back the emotion as he said, "It just might work. I'm going to try."

"And if it doesn't work?"

"Then I'll try something else."

"David, are you sure? You're risking your life. If a mortal gets hold of you in the daytime and drags you to a hospital . . ." Karl paused. Then he said, "She tricked you. Lied. Why . . . ?"

"I'm going to get her!" He heard Karl sigh. "One more thing," David said. "I've seen another eight—that makes sixteen including Ariel, so far. I don't doubt there are more."

"She really does have an army!"

"I think you'd best be in touch with any others we know. Something tells me no matter what occurs on Vancouver Island, you might need the safety of numbers. I've a feeling this is shaping into a war."

Chapter 27

DAVID STAYED IN EL PASO TO PREPARE. ARIEL MUST HAVE realized by now that it was almost impossible to outguess him; the others, showing up after the fact, were always too late. She would trap him in Montreal herself. That was more her style.

He spent the early part of the evening feeding, then gathering the supplies he needed. He found the space blankets easily and a seamstress who fashioned socks, gloves, and a very rough suit—pants and shirt with elastic wrists and cuffs. He also purchased two suits several sizes too big. Luck was with him; he found a theatrical supply store open.

As for Chloe's mixture, some of the ingredients were easy to locate—coconut oil, cocoa butter, and sesame seed oil. He also bought thirty large aloe vera plants, and, just before blending the ingredients, slit the hard leaves to scrape out the clear mucuslike gel inside. For the rest of the ingredients he'd had to travel to the Mexican part of town, gathering jojoba oil and osha root and oddly named ingredients he had never heard of. Once he had collected everything, he rented a hotel room and mixed the formula in a blender, as Chloe instructed, a little at a time, adding a few drops of oil of chamomile to cut the powerful smell. He stored the cream in glass jars in an insulated suitcase which he would carry onto the plane.

An hour before sunrise he coated himself head to toe in the cool, soothing, greenish cream. Then he attached the mask he had created earlier. It became a lineless, lifeless version of his own face. He applied natural-looking makeup to the latex then added a blond wig, false eyebrows, and a full moustache and beard, creating a less artificial effect. The whiskers also provided some protection for his nose and mouth.

Despite Chloe's instructions, he'd purchased polyester suits and donned one, plus plastic high boots and vinyl gloves, hat, and special matte-red wraparound sunglasses. His skin might not "breathe," but he did not trust porous fabric to protect him from the sun. He didn't know if the polyester would work, and hoped he was not making a fatal mistake—he had visions of himself suffocating to death.

He picked up the thermal case and the plastic bag containing the other polyester suit and turned to examine himself in a full-length mirror. The image was bizarre—an eccentric man, bulky, with unnaturally smooth and glossy skin, who looked as if he were hiding something. But there was nothing else he could do, so at the last possible minute he headed out to the airport for the eight A.M. departure to Seattle, praying that when the sun hit, he would not be writhing in pain in a public place.

To get to the boarding lounge he had to walk through the metal detector. He closed his creamed eyelids and took off the glasses. He sent the case and bag through the hand-luggage X-ray.

Fortunately no alarm went off, although it would have been simple enough to pull the metallic suit out and show the guards. Once he was safely in the boarding lounge, he ducked into the washroom and hid in a stall. He applied more gel, slipped on the cool socks and gloves and the shiny silver suit, then the white polyester one over it.

While he waited in safety, he could feel the pressure of sunrise pressing on him. Sheer willpower kept him awake when normally he would have succumbed by now to the pull downward toward sleep.

At the last call for boarding, he stepped out into the lounge area. And stopped dead in his tracks. Light blazed all around him, light that pulsed with white-hot energy. This was the first daylight he had seen in over one hundred years; he did not count the room on Vancouver Island. He had forgotten the directness of this brilliant power that contrasted so sharply with gentle, indirect moonlight. Even through the dark glasses he could not keep his eyes open. The heat, the pressure on his body, the *penetration* he felt terrified him. This was not the light he stored in his memory, and he no longer found it appealing, although a hint of nearly forgotten wonder nudged at him. Still, that wonder was obliterated by an overwhelming sense of discomfort. And terror.

He felt as though he were dreaming a weighted dream. A nightmare. And despite all the precautions, the burning rays reached through the polyester, past the metal fibers, embedded themselves in the cream, and danced across his sensitive skin, causing it to prickle. He retreated to the men's washroom again, stripped a little at a time, and applied another coat of the mixture.

As much as the tingling was uncomfortable and the fear that he would suffocate nearly irrepressible, lethargy was equally a problem. He felt pressured down by an extra thousand pounds and sinking, as if the floor beneath his feet were quicksand drawing him into the earth. It took effort to stay awake and coherent, let alone move.

He knew from the way people stared and avoided coming near that he resembled the corpse of a rock star and walked like a zombie. Still, he managed to board the plane. He spent as much time as he could in the washroom, where he opened the suit for air and smashed the light so it would be completely dark.

When he arrived in Seattle, the sun was high in the sky. He did not dare face it directly, but hurried as quickly as his sluggish body would permit to the men's room to apply another coat of gel. His flight to Vancouver left at one, and from Vancouver he was able to hire a helicopter to take him to Tofino, paying the pilot to wait twenty-four hours.

Of this day's experiences, the helicopter ride was the worst. During the brief moments his thoughts cleared through the pain, David could only thank whatever gods might be sympathetic for the overcast sky.

In Tofino he rented a car with tinted windows and drove a short distance along the Pacific Ocean north to Clayoquot Sound, hardly aware of what he was doing. Just after three-thirty he passed the dirt road and pulled off onto another, not half a mile beyond it. Then he hurried through the dense coastal rain forest, his outer suit quickly shredded by sharp cypress branches and pine needles. The shrublike salal and stinging nettles tore at his feet and tripped him but eventually he came to the lodge.

Two men in lawn chairs sat on the front porch playing cards—the two who had been with Reesone and trapped David in the sun room. Two cars were parked in the driveway. His senses were not a tenth as sharp as at night, and he wasn't sure if there were more mortals around. His kind, he knew, would be sleeping. He had a vague awareness of Kathy inside.

He also knew that his strength was diminished, as was his speed. Even one of these mortals would be stronger now than he, but he had an idea.

He tossed pebbles into the brush a few feet away, near the edge of the clearing. Apparently it was annoying enough; one of the men got up to check. He had a gun but left it holstered. David hid behind a ten-foot-wide Douglas fir. When the guard was within range, David struck the man on the back of the skull repeatedly with a large rock until he fell. Realizing that he moved too stiffly to approach unnoticed, he waited for the second man, gun drawn, to come looking for the first. David knocked him out as well. He found rope in the garage and tied and gagged both; he had to keep them alive because the ones inside, even if they were new to the world of night, could sense whether a mortal was living or not. But David kept the men alive for another reason; at sunset, when he would again be able to drink, he would need their blood—most of it. And time would be of the essence.

After severing the phone wires, he hid in an abandoned log shack down the road, near where he'd parked, catching a couple of hours' sleep in the not-quite-dark-enough structure. By sunset he felt almost refreshed, his skin hardly the worse for wear, but he was starving. Before he could do anything else, he needed blood.

He approached the lodge cautiously, pausing just long enough to drink. The first mortal only whet his appetite. The second half filled him. It was less than he needed, enough for them to pass out without serious damage to their vital signs.

The blood cleared his senses. Inside, there were three of his kind and Kathy. She radiated waves of fear—he smelled it on the air like the stench of mildew clinging to long-damp clothing.

He found an axe in the toolshed and moved quickly because he knew they probably sensed him too. He circled to the side of the building and entered through the back door. They were just above, their energy apparent. They were not weak. Catching them off guard was what he aimed for.

He took the stairs silently but quickly, three at a time.

Surely they would have tuned into him by now. He felt them, at the end of the hall, all in the sun room, and he hesitated. Terror seized him—not the fear of the fight, but the horror of that room and the unspeakable agony he had suffered there.

But Kathy groaned, and that jolted him away from panic. When he peered around the door, he was startled by what he saw; it explained why they had not come for him. They did not sense him because they were preoccupied.

She was on her hands and knees whimpering, her petite body painted with bruises and bite marks, some still seeping blood.

One of the males had mounted her, taking her anally, while another had her orally. And Reesone was lying under her, his penis inside her vagina, his teeth clamped to one breast. As she moved, like a robot, automatically, back onto Reesone, the other one behind thrust into her. When she moved forward, the one in front shoved himself into her mouth.

The ugly, disjointed rhythm mesmerized David momentarily, and then something in his brain seemed to snap, like a steel door clanking shut. He saw through a red filter, barely associating himself with his actions. He felt he moved in slow motion. A sound roared from his gut, the cry of a frenzied warrior. He swung the axe through the air. The head of the one behind Kathy flew in an arc across the room. Then the one in front was decapitated before he could react. But Reesone was quicker, out from under her in seconds, gripping her by the throat.

"Move and she's gone," he said, tilting her head at an angle that looked excruciating. Her face was ravaged by pain and fear.

She looked completely out of it, not seeing David. Blood dribbled from Reesone's mouth, and the sight of it enraged David.

"Put it down and step back," Reesone ordered. David dropped the axe. Reesone smiled. "Ariel was wrong about you. You're just a stupid shit." He backed toward the door dragging Kathy with him, grabbing the axe on the way.

No! a voice inside David screamed. Terror rose like a river flooding when the dam bursts. Pain stabbed at his memory. He knew beyond a doubt that this time he would die in this room. That terror propelled him forward.

"One more step and she's dead."

"Afraid to fight, Reesone? Is this the only way you can kill? Passively?"

Reesone stopped, but then smiled. "Sorry. Old tricks, new dog." He backed farther away.

"Ariel's had hundreds like you," David taunted. "Little boys with no balls and small brains, ready to jump as she yanks the strings."

"Won't work, sucker." But David could see that the bait had hooked something.

"Did she order you not to fight me? Tell you she wanted me for herself?"

Reesone was silent.

"She doesn't trust you, Donald. Doesn't think you can take me. You're weak, and she sees that. It looks like she's right."

Reesone was quiet, and David said softly, beckoning with his fingertips, "Fight me, Donald. If you don't, you don't deserve Ariel. All three of us know that."

Reesone shoved Kathy aside. She landed on the floor with a thud and lay quiet. He took a prizefighter stance, bunching his hands into fists—an actor playing the role of a fighter—and David laughed. "You're no longer mortal. This won't be a fair fight."

"But it will be to the death!" Reesone said dramatically.

David's nails became murderous claws. Muscles tensed. Sharp teeth bared, ready to rend his victim to shreds. Power built as the blood haze darkened. Reesone looked startled by the transformation, but only for a moment, because David was at his throat. He ripped away a large chunk of flesh, careful not to crack the spinal cord or slice into the esophagus.

His victim cried out and backed away. David went at him again. But Reesone had recovered his wits and took a defensive stance. As David neared, a hand swung out, catching his face and tearing away skin and muscle, exposing the hinge of the jawbone.

But Reesone had no time to admire his work. David bit into his chest, gouged the tender flesh of his stomach, and at the same time, twisted an arm to dislocate his shoulder. Reesone howled in pain; David couldn't hear it. His adrenal glands pumped overtime, transmitting surges of power and energy that kept him attacking again and again, almost mindlessly, rabid for revenge.

But even in his blood frenzy he was careful to keep the actor alive. In the back of his mind he had other plans for Mr. Reesone.

When David's fury was spent, he stood back shaking, breathing hard. The body before him was ragged and bloody. He did not feel the slightest trace of remorse, which he was lucid enough to recognize as being odd for him. But he no longer cared. Reesone breathed shallowly. He was alive. Left in this condition, he could heal during the night, and he could hear.

David picked up the axe and chopped the actor's arms off at the elbows, then his legs at the knees. Blood spurted from the wounds as the arteries pumped hard. A rumbling sound came from low in Reesone's throat.

"I have no direct experience," David gasped, "but it's rumored we regenerate limbs, maybe even a severed head and broken spinal cord, given time. But you won't have the luxury of time."

He scattered Reesone's blood-soaked body parts and the remains of the other two throughout the room, with enough distance to ensure that they remained apart. Then he searched the house for Kathy's things.

He dressed her in men's pants, running shoes, and a hunting jacket he'd found and gathered her up in his arms. She was hot, too hot. White lips, closed eyes; she seemed unaware of him. Her fever was dangerously high.

"Believe it or not, Reesone, I could feel sorry for you."

There was no reply.

"You actually deluded yourself that Ariel cared. And you probably expect even now she'll come out here and rescue you. She won't come. And if she does, it will only be to leave you here, a mouse caught in a trap. She despises weakness, as much as she's attracted to it." David laughed bitterly.

"You're young to this life, which means you're fortunate. You'll expire in one day. It would have taken me far longer. But still, suffering tends to obliterate time. I should know." The limbless form on the floor twitched slightly but still made no reply.

David took Kathy from the room. He slid the six heavy bars in place, not that Reesone could get to the door anyway. Outside he stopped briefly to drain dry the two guards; he was seriously weak and needed the blood.

From Tofino they flew by helicopter to Vancouver Airport, Kathy comatose the entire time. Her skin was on fire, her body bruised and bleeding. Before the flight, he cleaned her up, but he still couldn't get her to respond. There were no direct flights to New York until morning, and he didn't want to wait that long.

He booked them on the late plane to Seattle. She revived enough to walk onto the plane, for which he felt grateful. In Seattle not even a private plane was available, and they were forced to lay over until the following morning.

Ariel would have had someone check the house by now. *By sunrise she'll know where we are,* he thought, *but she's the only one who could possibly get here during the day, and he didn't think she could do it.*

Despite the risk, he decided to spend the night and part of the day in a hotel room near the Seattle airport. Both he and Kathy needed rest.

During the remainder of the night he put through a dozen calls to Frankie at the number he'd been given. A cranky woman answered in Spanish and kept hanging up on him. And David was worried. *What if Frankie was stoned? Or had been followed from the airport? Or abandoned Michel? And if Michel had been found?*

Finally, at nine A.M. New York time, Frankie answered. "Is everything all right?" David asked.

"Couldn't be better, 'cept for the weather. It's fuckin' pissin' from the sky here." The familiar voice had a ring of sanity to David's ears, rooting him to the earth for the first time in a week.

"Frankie, I hope you have the passport. I've counted on you."

"You bet! No sweat. Scared I'd letcha down, Homes? You ain't the first."

David felt ashamed that the thought had crossed his mind. He told Frankie, "Phone the airlines and order three tickets to Vienna from Kennedy Airport. I'll pay for them when I pick them up."

"Where?"

"Vienna. In Austria. For David Hardwick, Kathleen Stevens, and the name on Michel's passport. Kathy and I will be flying in about eight tonight, your time. Meet me at the airport, same spot, hide Michel the same way. And Frankie, be careful."

"Always am."

David tucked Kathy into bed just before sunrise. As bad a shape as he was in, she was worse. She had drifted in and out of consciousness all night.

"Kathy?" He wiped her face with a cool cloth. She opened her eyes, the blue now a flat extinguished shade, closed them, and then opened them again.

"David!" she whispered. "I knew you'd come." She seemed so pale and weak to him.

"Did they take your blood?" he said, caressing her hair, now reduced to a greasy, stringy tangle.

She nodded.

"Did you take theirs?"

"Yeah. Reesone. And those two guys. And Ariel. They made me." Her voice trailed off.

He knew it was not just the torture they had subjected her to, but the many exchanges of blood taking a toll on her system.

But with the two dead and Reesone close, only he and Ariel were left to influence her, battling it out for dominance. If Kathy died now, she would change. And she would be bonded to both.

Just before eight at night they landed at Kennedy. The first thing he saw was three moving forms of light, and he recognized the faces. They had been at the train station with Ariel.

Chapter 28

DAVID FOUND FRANKIE AT THEIR PREARRANGED MEETING place outside the terminal and pulled him aside. "There! Those three. We've got to avoid them." He hung back with Kathy and Michel and pointed through the glass at the figures.

Frankie grinned. He jimmied open one of the paper boxes and ripped a cardboard ad from the inside. "Wait here," he said.

David watched him approach a pretty clerk at the information desk. Within seconds she was laughing and handing over a pen and two pieces of Scotch tape. The boy wrote something on the cardboard and disappeared.

When he returned, he led David, Kathy, and Michel to a men's room not far from the entrance. An Out of Order sign had been taped to the door. "Make yourselves comfy right in here and I'll tell ya when the bad guys disappear," Frankie said.

David could sense the three, as, no doubt, they sensed him. They would know he was somewhere in the terminal, but not exactly where, because their abilities were not yet refined. The sun had just set when the flight from Seattle arrived, and he suspected they most probably had slept near the airport. He hoped they had not yet fed; the blood would accentuate their perceptions. If he could keep them at bay until the plane for Vienna left ...

About twenty minutes later Frankie poked his head in. "They vanished, Homes. Like that." He snapped his fingers.

David checked; he did not see them anywhere in the terminal, but the feeling of them was still strong.

"I need to leave Kathy and Michel in here while I purchase the tickets. Will you watch the door?"

Frankie nodded.

"Michel, I'll need your passport."

He made his way through the dense crowd to the ticket counter. He paid for the tickets quickly and returned. He had just reached the washroom when he saw the three blaze around a corner. Frankie noticed them too.

"Stay cool, my man. They can't see your face from here."

"It's not my face I have to worry about them seeing."

"Yeah, I noticed," Frankie said, scanning the bizarre sunglasses and plastic features.

As David checked his watch, he heard the boarding announcement.

"Come on, ace," Frankie said. "I'll getcha there. There's only three of 'em. And the place's tight with the man." David hesitated. "I can't risk it. It's not possible to fully explain right now, but they can see me through this disguise, even from the far end of the terminal, just as I can see them. Together they're as strong as a dozen men. You'll have to believe me."

Frankie looked at him quietly for a few seconds. "Homes, you're strange. I think I know what's goin' on, though."

David said nothing.

"Yeah, man. It hit me. You, so skinny and good at a fight. And I never seen you in the day, just at night. And the kid, eatin' raw meat and all. I finally figured it out. The old brain nearly broke from the strain."

David stared at the boy.

"You're an alien, right? Mars, Pluto, that kinda shit. Like, outta the sky one dark and fateful night."

Under the mask David's skin moved toward a smile that was thwarted by the plastic even before it got under way.

"And those dudes are from space. Another race?"

"It's a long story, Frankie. I'll try to tell you about it sometime, if you're still interested."

"I'm all ears." He grinned, shuffling across the floor a few feet, checking out a pretty girl wearing a miniskirt who passed in front of him.

"Frankie, I've thought of something that might work, provided you'll help."

"Cut the deck."

"Will you permit me to hypnotize you? It won't take long nor will you be harmed."

Frankie looked skeptical and a large smirk spread across his features. "Yeah, a brain drain. 'Cept I'm insane. That I can't feign."

Inside the washroom David relaxed him, fed the information, and then fed on a small quantity of the boy's blood; Frankie would not miss it. David and Michel left the building so the three would perceive an energy shift, and watched through the glass.

Frankie headed to the airline check-in counter near where one of the three was headed. When he got to the desk, he said loudly, "Hey, babe, I got a couple tickets, and to me they're trash. I wanna trade 'em for some green and white cash." He was getting some attention, including from the glowing form nearby.

"I'm sorry, sir," the woman said, looking him over. "You'll have to call our office. We don't give refunds here."

"Listen." He leaned over the counter and into her face, dropping his voice only a decibel, exerting all the charm he was capable of. He was still loud enough to be heard. "Dude lays these three tickets on me, says he can't use 'em." He looked down and read, " 'David Hardwick.' Yeah. Anyways, he says trade 'em. I'm gonna stash the cash for my birthday bash, *comprender?*"

The light moved on him, signaling the other two, and David held his breath.

"Look, I'm sorry—" But the clerk never finished.

"Who gave you the tickets?" The one closest grabbed Frankie's upper arm and spun the boy around.

"What's it to ya, Stan? You don't look like the man."

"I asked who gave you those tickets, kid." He squeezed the arm and Frankie yelled.

As the other two approached, one of them took charge. He pushed the aggressive one back because they were drawing a crowd.

"Just tell us where we can find the man who gave you the tickets. We won't hurt you."

"Hurt? I'm alert. Some dude just shoves 'em into my hand and says, 'Cash 'em in.' "

"Where is he?"

"Don't know, Homes. Saw him and his lady and kid hop into a yellow. That door. Heard him tell the driver, Newark."

The one who asked the questions, who looked more hungry than the others, looked into Frankie's eyes. The boy's face grew relaxed, dreamy. If they tried to take Frankie with them, David would be forced to intervene. "He's telling the truth," that one told the others.

"Let's go."

"Maybe one of us should stay here, just in case this is a trick."

"It's no trick. He spotted us and got out fast. He's not in the building, I can feel it. We can beat him to Jersey."

They left Frankie standing with a peaceful smile on his face. David watched them head for the exit opposite the one he was at. The second they exited, he and Michel entered the terminal. He sent Michel into the washroom, then headed to Frankie's side, bringing the boy back to reality.

"Homes, you gotta bottle that, put it inna pill. We gonna make a kill."

Back in the men's room, Michel looked frightened. Kathy lay on the floor in a limp heap, and David splashed cold water on her face to revive her enough to board. He heard the last call for their flight.

"Frankie, you'll never know how grateful I am. You saved all of us from a dire fate."

Frankie grinned like a soldier who had just been given the Purple Heart—a little bit of humility and a lot of pride.

"Yeah, Homes, guess I did that. But now it's old news. You gonna keep in touch?"

"Definitely. I'll be back when this is over," he said, wanting to embrace the boy but fearing the gesture would be misunderstood. Instead he just squeezed his shoulder. "Get a taxi and leave here as soon as you can. And stay away from the airport for a while, all right? If you ever see any of those men on the street, run. Into a crowd."

"Hey, I'm crazy 'bout crowds. Bubble city."

"One more thing. Michel gave you a phone number in Austria. Call from a pay phone downtown, collect. Ask for Julien and tell him we'll arrive at two A.M., his time. Do you still have money?"

"Lots."

"Good. This might be an excellent time for a vacation. And should you ever need help, Frankie, you can reach me through that number. Understand?"

"It's on hard disk," he said, knocking the top of his head with his knuckles.

"I count you as a friend," David said.

Frankie nodded and said, "Same here, man. Same here."

David got Kathy and Michel onto the plane. None of his kind were on board. The second the seat-belt sign went off, he made a trip to the washroom and, with a great deal of relief, removed all the paraphernalia. He was hungry, starving, and could barely tolerate the scent of living flesh and blood surrounding him.

In Vienna, as they approached customs, he saw five forms of light waiting just on the other side of the barrier. They were not friendly faces. The five watched him, and he hung back, stalling for time. Within seconds more luminous forms materialized: André, Karl, Julien, Gerlinde, Carol, Chloe, and several others he didn't know. The five saw them too and, realizing they were outnumbered two to one, backed off. Once David, Kathy, and Michel came through the exit, they were surrounded.

"Fortunately I anticipated the need for numbers," Julien said.

Carol and André grabbed Michel, hugging and kissing him. Gerlinde, Chloe, and a tall, elegant woman with white-gold hair and eyes the color of the Caribbean sea took charge of Kathy. David leaned into Karl, suddenly exhausted, aware of his wounds, the old burns and the new, the bites, tears, and rips to his flesh. And the emotional ones as well.

Julien said, "Our private plane awaits. There is nourishment for you." He glanced at Kathy, who had collapsed and was being held up by the strong arms of the women. Julien was silent, and David wondered what he was thinking. But when Julien turned, his piercing black eyes became so soothing that they backed David to the brink of unconsciousness.

André and Karl each took one of his arms as Julien said, "Come, my friend. You need rest."

Part 4

Everything goes, everything returns;
eternity rolls the wheel of being . . .
Crooked is the path of eternity.
                              —Nietzsche

Chapter 29

"Kathy's dying," Chloe said. "It might be humane to take her."

David looked at André's aunt, a white-haired woman with strong, kind blue eyes. He knew she meant well. "But she's connected to both Ariel and me."

"The last to drink should secure the connection," Karl said.

"I want time to make sure the balance has shifted, to ensure I'm the stronger influence."

"You may not have that time, *mon ami*," André said gently.

David glanced around the room. There were not quite two dozen, including Michel, Julien's two teenagers, and another child who looked Michel's age but clearly had existed at least a century. That boy was with a couple from India.

Kathy lay prone on a Victorian chaise longue in the corner. Julien's wife, Jeanette, the tall, exquisitely beautiful woman with the milky-green eyes he'd seen at the airport, cooled Kathy's head with wet cloths.

Michel had been the only true miracle. All the rest, including the other children, had been altered from human to whatever they had all become. And, David knew, most in this room had been transformed as he had been, against their will. He didn't want to inflict this on Kathy.

She lay motionless. Her fever had not lessened. If anything, it was on the verge of rising. Since arriving in Vienna, she had experienced fewer and fewer coherent periods. David ran a hand through his hair. He knew everyone felt sympathy for him, but that did not help him. "Damn Ariel!" he said, but it was too late for bitterness.

He walked to the corner. Kathy's skin was a sickly color, her lips dry and chalky. Her forehead should have been beaded with perspiration, but it was not. He picked up one of her hands; it was hot and limp. Her lungs barely filled. "Is there a place outdoors?" he asked quietly.

Julien lay a hand on his shoulder. "Behind, there are woods. You will be undisturbed."

He picked Kathy up and carried her outside. The land was rough. The medieval Spanish-designed castle embedded into the side of this snowcapped mountain had existed long before hordes of warring human beings had fought over the soil and then, finding the acquired terrain inhospitable, left it isolated again. He eased between the dull green bushes and shrubs and trees bared for the fast-approaching winter, working his way higher up the slope until he came to a rocky plateau that also served as a clearing in the dense uncharted brush. There he sat against the gray rock ledge under the clear night sky and positioned Kathy between his legs. He held her propped against one knee.

Her face was worn, aged. Pain sliced his heart. She had suffered, and he had been unable to alter her fate. He had wanted to make the change pleasant for her. He'd planned to bring up her father and Bobby first, clear that away. He longed for her to experience the stars and the ocean, to feel surrounded by his love during this pivotal moment in her existence. But he could provide none of that.

"Kathy. Can you hear me?"

She stirred but didn't open her eyes.

"You'll be with me now," he told her, stroking her dry hair back from her forehead. But the only response was a slight sigh, and he wasn't even sure that hadn't been the wind. The night was chilly, and he pulled her close, opening the collar on the hunting jacket she wore, exposing her throat and the faint pulsing.

Despite his love for her and his desire to bring her over gently and with compassion, his body reacted to that pulsing. The ravenous animal that he constantly battled bullied civilized parts of him into retreat.

His lips found her artery, but a feeling of horror overwhelmed him; he couldn't bear the thought of taking her that quickly. He moved to the vein instead. He pierced it slowly, the least painful way. Drops of the crimson life stream wet his lips. It was as though a switch had been turned on. He felt animated, energized. Famished.

Her eyes were slits of feverish pain laced with fear. "Ariel," she murmured.

Anger surged. Immediately he pressed two fingers hard against the wounds and Kathy moaned. "It's me. David. Don't be afraid, little one."

The sight of her forced a groan from him. Those droplets of simmering blood had expanded him even as they contracted her. He stared at her emaciated face, kissed her pale dry lips. How could he do this? He had sworn to himself that he would not take her without her awareness and consent. No matter how much her condition itself might justify his action, in his heart he knew that to suck the life from her body when she was unconscious was not love, but rape.

Her eyelids dropped and he had to bend his ear to her lips to hear her whisper, " 'How do I love thee . . .' "

" 'I love thee to the depth and breadth and height my soul can reach . . .' " he said immediately. The silver moon cut across the ebony sky, and the sky turned slate and then smoke, causing the moon to fade, and still he battled the demon within.

He held her heavy body close, rocking her, kissing her hot lips, letting the blood-tinged tears that had gathered in him wash her pale face. If it was her destiny to die, then so be it. Whether or not he took her made little difference in one regard: she would still transform. There was no way to know whether her allegiance would be equally divided between him and Ariel or if one of them would dominate. He could not control that now. He could control very little. But one decision he could make might bind him to the last vestiges of humanity still desperately clinging to his soul. He would keep the promises he had made to her, and to himself. Because if he could not, what he had become was far less than human, less than a microorganism. The tiniest particles in the universe were affected by other particles, and contrary to much he had seen and experienced since altering to this unique state, he would not believe that he and those like him were alienated from the complex fabric of life on this planet.

The blood had long ago clotted beneath his fingers. The wounds were so vulnerable to being reopened. But it would not be by him.

When he could speak, he clutched her to him and swore as Elizabeth Barrett Browning had sworn to her husband so long ago, " '. . . and, if God choose, I shall but love thee better after death.' "

Chapter 30

"AM I DEAD YET?" KATHY ASKED.

Gerlinde laughed. "Not quite, kiddo, but you were pushing the envelope."

Kathy felt impossibly weak. Turning her head required heroic effort. "How long ... ?"

Carol, sitting on the other side of the bed, leaned over and wiped a cool wet cloth over her face. "You've been out of it for the week you've been here. We weren't sure your fever would break. Thirsty?"

"Yeah."

They lifted her a bit so she could sip from a glass of water, the best drink she ever remembered having. But that movement too was exhausting, as if the energy had been drained from every muscle in her body, which had then collapsed. "Where's David?"

"I'm here."

She looked to the corner where his voice came from and felt relieved.

A woman with white hair standing next to him said, "You were right to follow your instincts."

He moved toward the bed and gratitude washed over Kathy. She was alive. And safe. And with David. His firm, delicious lips pressed onto hers. He gathered her up in his arms as if they would never be parted again.

Days went by while she collected strength, but when David felt she had recovered sufficiently, he took her to meet the others in a large room that at one time had obviously served as the banquet hall of this immense castle. Relics from the past adorned solid wooden shelves. Banners and stamped leather hangings cluttered the vaulted ceiling. Intricate and textured tapestries depicting the tale of Vulcan adorned two walls. One suit of armor looked to David as if it dated from the Crusades. At the center of the space stood a dark, solid table fifteen feet long, made of a heavy exotic wood with grapevines hand-carved into its thick round legs. The scarred top must have been used for countless feasts over the centuries. This room gave the effect of a time warp.

Kathy was suitably impressed. She stared in disbelief around the room, fingering the polished wood and worn petit-point embroidery on the seat of the enormous chair on which she sat. Her innocence still delighted him to the roots of his being.

"I want all of you to know I'm grateful for your help," David said to the others in the room.

"And we're grateful to you too," André told him. "Ariel's tenacious. She wanted Michel and would have found him eventually. Now that we know, we can protect him." André bent over his son, who sat on the floor with a teenage girl, playing chess, and ruffled his hair.

"I want to leave Kathy here, where she'll be safe," David said. Her head jerked around in his direction. "I'm going after Ariel."

"No!" Kathy jumped to her feet. "She'll kill you. I don't wanna lose you."

He pulled her close and kissed her hair, but then he looked over her head at the others. "I know Ariel as well, I suppose, as anyone can. She won't capitulate. She'll attempt to kidnap Michel again. And she can track both Kathy and me. If nothing else, revenge will drive her." He looked at Kathy. "And you're connected to her, as connected as you are to me."

She shook her head. "It's not true, David. It's you I love—"

"I know your feelings for me," he interrupted. "But Ariel is as powerful an influence as I. It's the nature of the blood exchange. She can manipulate both of us, and has. I can't exist this way, Kathy, and before you ask, I won't change you until you're free of her."

Her eyes had filled with horror. Before she could protest further, he said, "Should anything happen to me, the house in Manchester is yours. There's money. You'll find it. André? Karl?" He looked at his friends. "I want to be assured you'll look after her." They both agreed.

Kathy pulled away from him. "No! You can't do this. It's crazy. She's got lotsa help and she'll kill you. I don't want you to go. If you love me you won't."

"It's because of my deep feelings for you that I must."

"But how're you gonna find her? You don't even know where she is."

David hesitated. This was the part he hadn't figured out yet. "Perhaps you can track her, because you've shared the blood."

It didn't surprise him when Julien interrupted. "Kathleen will not be able to track until the change, and even then her powers will be unreliable." David knew that was true. He also felt Julien was inferring that she was unreliable for a reason other than that she would be a neophyte.

"I'll begin in Montreal, then."

"She's not there," a small voice said. "She's gone."

Everyone looked at Michel.

"How do you know, Michel?" André asked.

" 'Cause I bit her and swallowed some blood and I just know."

"He can track her!" David said, astonished. "Michel, will you help me? If we teach you how to track, will you let me know where Ariel is? And you can take some of my blood; that way you can track both of us."

"Sure," the boy said, and then grinned and yelled "Check!" at his opponent.

David turned to André, who turned to Carol. They looked at each other momentarily, communicating telepathically. "All right," André said. And then, "I'll go with you, at least part of the way, if you'd like."

Karl added, "Me too."

"I'm going!" Kathy said.

"No," David said, knowing how hard it was for Karl and André to offer. "I'm grateful, but this is between Ariel and me. I can see now that it always has been."

"David, I'm concerned about you," Chloe said.

"And I," added Morianna, a tall stately woman with Eurasian features, whom David had just met. Splitting the widow's peak in her white-quartz hair was a wide black streak. Her violet Oriental eyes were old, very old, and her voice penetrating.

"I appreciate that," he told the women. "But my body has healed. I can take care of myself."

"It is not your body that concerns us," Morianna said. She moved toward him. Her regal presence reduced him to silence. "It is your soul."

He shook his head in confusion.

"The hatred," Chloe added.

"You feel I have no right to despise her? After what she's done to me, to Kathy, what she tried to do to Michel and the others?" He felt indignant.

Morianna placed a finger in front of her lips, then said calmly, "It is not for me or any other to judge. I am merely concerned that the hatred might blind you. To kill another of our kind—well, it is serious."

"Don't you think I know that? I extinguished three on Vancouver Island. But do you expect me to live in fear?"

"Trust her, *mon ami*," André said. David looked at him. *"Faites-la attention! Elle est la sorcière."*

"David," Morianna continued, "your soul is enormous and your heart clear, that is obvious. But a dark worm has recently settled there, and I suspect it was once a larva you nurtured."

Something about those words or perhaps the way they were delivered reached him.

"To kill is nothing. We all understand this," she went on. "But to destroy our own, particularly an ancient one, well, the chain will be affected."

He exhaled loudly, frustrated and angry, but Morianna just continued to study him, her face cryptic. Most of his kind he could read. But the old ones were like layers of granite, impenetrable.

Morianna pulled something from her pocket, two disk-shaped pieces of brass, each two inches in diameter, attached by a gold cord. "May I?" she asked. He had no clue what she wanted, but found himself nodding.

She motioned. He released Kathy and took a step toward this strange female. Morianna's fingers touched his eyelids, which closed automatically, as if he'd fallen into sleep. A current passed between him and this ancient one; the rush of a dream. He exhaled, exhausted.

The room was silent and minutes seemed to pass. Suddenly a sound originated near his chest. It was a bell, but unlike any he had ever heard. The reverberation pierced his heart and then rippled outward, through his chest and into the room. But the rippling seemed to go on forever, stretching into infinity, and he found himself smiling and then laughing, the vibrations stirring up so much joy that he could not contain the happiness.

When he opened his eyes, Morianna was still before him. She held the cord above each piece of brass, and he understood that she had touched the disks together. Her eyes shone as she said, "It is always better to kill with love, especially the Medusa, whose eyes, if the hero were to meet them with hatred, will turn him to stone; they reflect only his own heart. The kindest death blow is that which refuses to hesitate. A ragged edge inflicts pain. A sure and true hand severs cleanly. This is important for both the victor and the vanquished."

He noticed the Asian male in a corner who'd been introduced as Wing nodding. He was short, nearly bald, and, as well, old.

The others gathered around David, offering suggestions and advice. "You must remember that your reality is different than hers," Chloe told him. "You understand the language of poetry, metaphor, the food of the soul."

"And Ariel?" he asked.

"Also metaphor," Julien answered. "But poisonous. Be on guard and do not be charmed by charming words."

"Don't meet her eyes," Kaellie, an East Indian female, suggested. "It's the fastest way to lose yourself."

When the initial excitement evened out, David found himself alone in a corner talking with Julien's wife. Up close Jeanette was even more elegant, her white-gold hair swept gracefully off her face so that large, inquisitive, aventurine eyes sparkled warmly at him. She emanated the sensuous allure of the females of his kind, and David fought to keep from being mesmerized by her beauty. Around her throat she wore a tiny silver chain-metal pouch. Inside was a pink stone onto which a symbol had been carved.

As they spoke, she took the stone out of the pouch and put it into a magenta velvet drawstring bag. She shook the bag and the contents rattled together. Then she said to David, "Why don't you pick three, one at a time. Let them find your hand."

He reached into the bag and felt cool clay rectangles. He selected one. The rough bisqueware had a mark etched into one side. She motioned for him to lay it facedown onto a small gold cloth she had placed on the edge of the table. He picked two more and, as she indicated, lay them to the left, then left again, in a row. "What are they?" he asked.

"They're called Runes, which means the Mystery. Shamans have used them as a divination tool since before the New Testament was written. The last widescale use was probably the Vikings in Iceland during the Middle Ages." She turned the one on the right over. A symbol was carved into the porous pink clay. In David's mind the closest connection he could make was the Greek letter sigma. But that wasn't it really. It was like no written-language letter he had ever seen.

"This glyph is Perth and relates to your situation."

"What does it mean?"

"It talks about initiation, subjecting ourselves to fate, what is beyond our frail manipulative powers. It's the Phoenix, the mystical bird consumed by fire that rises from his own ashes. The eagle who lifts himself above the endless ebb and flow of ordinary time and space to accomplish something extraordinary."

He felt befuddled and Jeanette must have noticed. "The Runic script is ancient. Each glyph possesses a meaningful name as well as a significant sound. They never were a formal or even spoken language, but more a kind of sound poetry." This made sense to him.

She turned the second Rune over. On the rectangle was a straight line. "This is Isa, your challenge, what can stop you. It speaks of standing still, holding on, avoiding emotional depth and therefore being out of touch with the natural currents. A chill wind that reaches you over the ice floes of old, outmoded habits. The secret is in letting go."

She turned the third over, an arrow pointing down. David caught the flash of a frown on her face.

"What is it? The outcome?"

She nodded. "Tiewaz symbolizes the warrior."

"That must be good."

"Normally, yes. But this is reversed. The arrow should be pointing up."

They were both silent, staring at the three strange symbols.

Then Jeanette said, "The warrior is the sun, masculine energy. Expressing the will through direct action. Cutting away what's extraneous, or what's dead."

"And when it's reversed?" David asked, feeling a dread settle over him.

"When it's reversed it signifies danger. Energy has leached away. Trust and confidence are issues."

He hesitated. "Does this predict I'll fail?"

"Not necessarily. It means you need to examine your motives. What is your attachment to the outcome of your quest, and the process by which you move toward that end? Unconsciously you may be trying to dominate or punish, and that's not your task. You'll find guidance inside yourself."

She reached into the pocket of her dress and placed something into his palm. It was a clear crystal skull, only as big as a thimble, yet every detail perfect. "Take this with you," she said. "It will draw you to the foundation of your existence, leading you to your deepest needs and most profound resources."

Throughout the long night Kathy had sat in the large chair, watching and listening, looking stunned and hurt. Before sunrise David gave Michel a little of his blood, then he, Julien, and André instructed the boy in the art of tracking. When that was finished, David led Kathy to a small room close by, filled with textured pieces of furniture made of old ivory.

He pulled her close. The feeling of her skin sliding against his, almost liquid electricity, charged through his body.

They played like cubs, nipping and clawing each other, laughing, falling onto the wide bed, and wrestling until he pressed her down, containing her with his strength.

She arched her back as he kissed the hollow of her throat, a spot he knew she now experienced as erotic. Their mating became fierce and passionate, ferocious, the copulation of wild creatures. She was hot inside when he entered her, making him hot too. Each thrust felt like a match striking flint, each strike searing both surfaces and creating yellow-hot sparks. She clutched his back, digging into him. He propped himself up with one arm and gathered her against him, his other arm around her waist. As he thrust into her, tension zinged from inside out. Suddenly the sparks ignited, setting off a reaction, like dynamite in a chain exploding. She cried out from her soul, and in his ears it was the sound of their connection sent out into the universe.

As they lay together damp and exhausted, she said, "I'm going with you!" Her voice was soft but stubborn.

He shook his head.

"Yeah! Every time we been apart, awful things happen. When we're together, it's better."

"It's too dangerous."

"But I'm stronger now."

"Not nearly as strong as Ariel."

"Then it's too dangerous for you too."

He pulled her close, caught off guard by her cascading beauty. Her hair glittered like ancient gold, her eyes reflected the blue of a rainbow. He inhaled scents, the sweet fragrant rose-milk soap she had used, the musky odor seeping from below, juices—a mixture of both of them—the pungent smell of fear and worry. The salty-sweet minerals in her blood.

He felt his energy collecting. "We'll talk about it tomorrow night, shall we?"

She looked at him for a few seconds then nodded.

He could see that she was tired and sleep would take her soon, but she struggled to stay with him. His entire being reached out to her again, and she put her fears aside.

Just as she drifted off, Kathy said, "We're gonna talk about it tomorrow, promise?"

"Yes. I promise." It was the first time he had lied to her.

Chapter 31

"DAVID?" KATHY FELT THE EMPTINESS. SHE LOOKED AROUND the bedroom and spotted the note.

Kathy, my heart, my soul, my eternal dream,

Believe me when I say that you give my existence meaning. I've gone after Ariel because I must. My love for you leaves me no choice. Always remember that for me you are the mystery of the universe, and my love for you as expansive.

There's money, as I said, and the house. André, Karl, and the others will be there for you. If I cannot, I want you to help Frankie. I don't wish to sound as if I'll not return, but nothing can be certain; nature is impassive to the desires of both mortals and immortals.

Kathy, sweet Kathy, innocent child, passionate female, creature of azure fire, like a blue diamond with infinite facets. You've led a tortured life. I've been unable to keep the pain from you, and I want to do that. But I think I can leave you a legacy of freedom. If I cease to exist, I'm going to take Ariel with me.

You will be released from her spell. She will no longer track you and harm you. You'll be safe. This is what I want for you, and perhaps all I am capable of offering.

Love,
David

She burst into tears and ran from the room, along the long hallway and down the three levels of marble steps. She threw open the door of the banquet room. The others turned as she rushed in.

"Where's David?" she screamed, her eyes streaming, body trembling.

Gerlinde took off her jacket and wrapped it around Kathy's naked body. "Take it easy, kiddo."

"Where is he?"

"He left two hours ago," the redhead said.

She shook her head. "No! He said we'd talk about it! Where'd he go?"

No one answered.

"Tell me!"

"He asked us not to tell you," André said. "He's afraid you'll follow him."

"Yeah, I'm going. He can't do it alone. She'll trick him."

Karl said, "Kathy, Ariel's blood is in you and yours in her. She's as strong an influence as David is. It's how she made you do things you might not have otherwise done. If you follow, you could hinder him. Not because you want to, but because of her power."

"I'd never do that. I never did nothing to hurt him."

"You tried to kill him," André reminded her. "And you've lied."

She started to cry. "That was the junk. And I lied because I wanted you guys to trust me. Please, you gotta let me go. If David dies, I don't wanna live."

Gerlinde and Carol held her. Someone handed her a cup of mineral water which she drank, but it did nothing to soothe her.

She turned to Gerlinde, looking for something in her eyes. "If it was Karl, would you go?"

Gerlinde thought for barely a second. Her lighthearted tone belied the emotion in her eyes, which became like hard-packed earth. "A pack of werewolves couldn't keep me away."

Kathy turned to Carol. "If it was André?"

"Yes. Of course."

She went across the room to Julien's wife, Jeanette.

"What if it was Julien?"

Jeanette nodded without hesitation.

Kathy walked up to Kaellie, who was sitting next to Gertig. The Indian woman's eyes, dark seductive almonds, held Kathy longer than she wanted to be held. "Nothing would hinder me."

She had confronted those who seemed most like her, or at least somehow less solidified into this unnatural state. Now she turned to the others in the room. "Please let me go. I gotta help him."

There was silence for a few seconds until Gerlinde said, "I say let her go. How can it hurt anything?"

"I agree," Carol added.

Kaellie was silent, as was Jeanette.

"Don't be ridiculous." André crossed his arms over his chest. "We must respect David's wishes."

"What about Kathy's wishes?" Carol asked.

"She'll be in the way. And she'll probably help Ariel."

"Some of us can go along to make sure that doesn't happen," Gerlinde said.

"You didn't hear André," Karl argued with her. "David doesn't want help. He needs to fight this dragon alone."

"He's obsessed! He won't even get to Ariel. She's got too many guards."

"David's not weak."

"Karl, could you fight off a dozen bloodsuckers, even if they are still teething?" Gerlinde asked. "Come on, he needs help."

André said, "He'll do better alone. This is both a question of honor for him, and one of an ancient code of ethics none of us dare interfere with. We can't help him even if we wanted to, and you all know that."

"What code?" Kathy asked.

Carol tried to explain it. "There are certain rules, if you like, we must obey. They're embedded in our genetic make-up. We can't interfere with one another."

Kathy crossed her arms over her chest. "You guys can't help David, but Ariel can get help. Right!"

"Ariel is breaking all the rules," André said.

"Fuck the rules. If she can break them, so can you!"

Gerlinde shook her head. "Kiddo, you don't know the half of it. The only reason she can get those babies to help her is they're so young to the life, they're a cinch to control. They can't feed easily, so they're as dependent on her for food as a newborn is on a human mother. They either fall in line or starve. I don't know how to break it to you, but it's not in our nature to cooperate."

"But you and Karl get along okay. And you and André," Kathy said to Carol, avoiding looking at André. The males, in general, felt more dangerous to her. She found the women easier to talk to, as if they had a grip on their urges. But still, Kathy felt the pressure of those urges directed toward her—she was the only being in this room with warm blood flowing through her veins.

"And it isn't easy," Carol was saying. "Some of it has to do with the intimacy that develops between the one who brings over and the one who is brought over. André and I shared the blood, and that sacrifice goes a long way toward establishing a bond. But it doesn't always have that effect."

Gerlinde tried to get her to understand. "Our natural inclination is each to him- or herself. We're hunters, competitors for the same meal. Don't think of us as dogs or cats, or even wolves. Maybe more like spiders. It's in our cells to be isolated, and we have to work at it for anything more to happen."

Kathy shook her head. "I don't buy this. I think you guys are chickenshits. You're scared of Ariel."

"Hardly." André's voice was dangerous. When Kathy looked at him, his face had changed. It no longer held the beautiful transfixing quality all these vampires exuded; now he resembled a ferocious animal, and one that might be rabid. The black hairs streaked with gray on his head seemed fuller, bushier, his eyes intense and wild. His face had thinned and the skin looked translucent, the tone paler. She saw his lips pull back and his large eyeteeth flash; her heart jumped a beat.

"Look." Gerlinde grabbed her shoulders with chilly fingers, forcing Kathy to turn away from the horrific sight. "Nobody here is afraid of a one-on-one with Ariel."

"We'd like to help him," Karl added, "but the reality is, even if we managed to get there, we might not be impelled to act."

Kathy, still exhausted from the fever, fell back into the same chair as on that night after she'd come back from the brink of death, the night she'd first met most of these creatures. And that's the way she thought of them now. The ones in this room had far more in common with Ariel than they did with her. They weren't like people at all. They weren't like anything she knew or understood. It suddenly occurred to her that she was on the verge of becoming one of them. Terror snaked up the back of her legs. When she died, she would become like them. That was crystal clear. For the first time she questioned just what they were, and what she would be.

Discussions erupted about David and Ariel, and Kathy listened. She felt removed, isolated, frightened—for herself and for David. She was not like them, not yet, but some part of her had altered enough that she could not resent them completely. It was almost as if she understood where they were coming from.

"I say if some of us have the desire to help David, we'll function well enough," Carol said.

André pressed his lips together. He looked angry. "Don't you find it strange that only you and Gerlinde feel this way? Why, is obvious."

"Not to me it isn't."

André shook his head. "With the exception of Jeanette,

you two were the most recent ones brought over. You still have ties to human morality."

Carol looked at Jeanette. "Do you feel the way I do?"

"I'm of two minds," Jeanette said.

From another corner of the room Kathy heard a different argument.

"Ariel is exceptional," Karl said.

"Why?" Gerlinde wanted to know. "Because she's old?"

"She is strong," Chloe said.

"I think it's because she's female," Kaellie added. "You don't fuck with the female of most species."

Gerlinde groaned. "I can't believe I'm hearing this. What is she, some supernatural being? The reincarnated Elizabeth Bathory?" She paused. "I mean, we're *all* supernatural beings to mortals, so what are we arguing about, anyway?"

The room was in a general uproar. Kathy didn't know how to turn the tide. They were losing valuable time.

"André, you are wrong!" Kaellie, annoyed, had jumped into the other discussion. "Our kind have been known to band together in a mutual defense. We fought side by side at the time the Pyramid of Cheops was built, when mortals disturbed our sleep and tried to extinguish us, digging us out of our resting places, exposing us to sunlight and the stake—"

"Yes, I've heard the legends too, and that was millennia ago!" he interrupted. "If we had to band together to fight mortals, fine. That makes sense to me. I'm sure we could manage that. But our own? Where's the incentive to turn on them? And don't forget, they're far stronger than mortals. You all know that. We could be outnumbered."

"David will be outnumbered too. All the more reason we should help him," Gerlinde said. "Ariel's fang gang is brand new. We already have an edge. I'm going."

"Then you're forcing me to go as well," Karl said, obviously very frustrated. "The thought of any of them attacking you ..." He spoke to Gerlinde. "We'll probably both end up injured, if not worse!"

"This is getting out of hand," André interrupted. "David wants to do it alone. I refuse to act against his wishes."

273

"I'm going," Carol said.

André was utterly silent. Everyone in the room felt the change and stopped talking. André and Carol stared at each other. Kathy sensed volcanic pressure build between them, which threatened to erupt, and she had a feeling this would not do her cause any good.

"There's one thing everybody forgot," she said into the tense silence. "This ain't just between David and Ariel. She's out to get Mikey. And she's trying to take over the world. She can do it too. And if you guys think there'll be room for any of you when she's in charge, you're really out to lunch."

André sighed, thoroughly annoyed, but easing down from the emotional pitch he was riding. "I think we need a vote on this. We're going against a long tradition here"—he turned to Kaellie—"at least the tradition within our own experience. Not to mention instincts that can't be programmed at will. The children, including Julien's, will not vote. Those in favor of helping David, hands."

Carol and Gerlinde raised their hands.

"Against?" André and Karl raised their hands.

"Abstain," Kaellie said, as did most of the rest of the group. Julien, Morianna, and Wing were the only ones who did not participate.

André threw up his hands. "Well, I don't know what to say. Julien, Morianna, Wing, you three are the eldest. None of you have said a word. You haven't voted. You haven't even abstained from voting."

Julien, tall and slender, stood. To Kathy's eyes he was a strong and intimidating father, a patriarch, a man who by his presence alone commanded respect and attention. He glanced around the room. His eyes were the darkest shade of black she had ever seen. They reminded her of an insect's eyes, otherworldly. His face was tight, his lips downturned, as though existence had been particularly hard for him. And long. But there was something about him that offset that, and she couldn't put her finger on it. What she did know instinctively was that this one held David's life in his hands, and by extension, her own. And that knowledge made her run to him shamelessly, tossing out all rules of fair play.

"Please! I'm begging you. I love David so much it hurts me. If you ever loved anybody that much, you'll understand. He'd risk his life for you if you were where he is now, I know it. And this is bigger. It's about everything. Please, think about it."

A look of surprised amusement flashed in his coal eyes before they became inscrutable again. He patted her head, as if she were a little girl, or a puppy, and a high-voltage charge rocked her.

Julien locked eyes first with Morianna, who nodded, then with Wing, who bowed his head, both signaling permission to him to speak to the others on their behalf.

"I well understand the isolation each of you has suffered," Julien began. "The agony and horror of being apart from what I had formerly been, the fury and jealousy that kept me segregated from those such as myself while at the same time being inextricably linked. You all know I had not aligned with any until recently, and this bond has not been directed against either mortal or my own kind."

He looked around the room. "We have all been transformed through death in a way that human beings cannot comprehend. At best we can do nothing but accept our state and try to view it as a gift rather than a curse. But that death was only the beginning; each of you has experienced many 'little deaths' since that time. I myself have experienced the unimaginable during my five hundred years of existence. I see changes in our species. Many have mated, a union unknown to the old ones."

Kathy watched Morianna nod slightly, but she couldn't read any emotion in those amethyst eyes.

"You are all so young as compared to we three, you cannot see with our eyes, you cannot know what these changes signify. You can tolerate one another, reside under one roof. For you, what has been difficult has verged on the impossible for those who have existed many centuries. And yet we too have managed. I would not have believed it possible, but I too am different."

He turned to his wife and held out a hand. She joined him. She was almost as tall as he, so he couldn't kiss the top of her head, but he kissed her neck and held her around the waist. Kathy wondered at their relationship, what they were like alone, together, in their most private moments. She couldn't imagine.

"You are not mortal and are far from weak. Physically you are not afraid, and, of course, that emotion should not concern any of you. But as strength, even in battle, is not always physical, so too fear assumes a myriad of forms. To kill our own severs a vital connection. You fear this on a cellular level. On a spiritual level.

"But among us as with mortals, evolution has accelerated, I believe by necessity. The global village human beings speak of must relate to us as well. We are called to change: cooperate or perish. Had I not altered myself, I would have no hope that collectively we could overcome the primal terrors that cling to our very essence."

He paused to look at Kathy. "I too believe that David needs help. He feels our limitations and strengths as keenly as any in this room. He could not ask for help in this way partly because of his code of honor, which everyone here understands, but mainly because he knows we may be unable to respond. But you in your humanness are correct in reminding us of one thing: Ariel will not be easily stopped. If she defeats David—and without our help I see no other outcome—she will try to take us down one at a time, out of vengeance, if not today, tomorrow. Or a hundred years from now. Our chain will be severed again and again. She is old. I understand only too well her thinking; I know the barbarous time that spawned her. She will not be dissuaded, and she will fight to the death."

He looked at Kathy. "I cannot say if your heart is more with David or with Ariel, but if you are against him, it is best he learn this now. I release you."

He looked around the room. "It is not safe for any to remain behind. Those who have the need to depart may do so with no loss of face. As for the rest, we must form an army if we are to do battle."

André sighed and ran a hand through his hair. He looked at Julien silently for several moments, his eyes almost pleading. Finally he turned to his wife. She held out a hand. He took it and brought it to his lips but did not look happy. "I hope we're doing the right thing."

"All of us," Julien said, "share your hope."

The group flew by private plane to London. From there they caught a late flight on the Concorde to New York. Michel had used a globe to track Ariel, and could follow David's movements too. By the time they hired a boat and reached Fire Island, it was four in the morning. The island, because the season was long over, was nearly deserted. A dense aura of tension hung in the air, making it feel heavy against the skin. Gerlinde explained to Kathy that because she was so close to the change, she was able to pick up on the vibrations of their kind.

The group kept off the boards, silently moved past the dunes, through withering cattails standing in pools of stagnant water closer to the shore, toward the eastern lands where there were holly, sassafras, oak, red maple trees, and then the pines.

It was as though the lesser creatures felt the same thing Kathy did. Raccoons and shrews scurried through the trees, frantic to find safety. Overhead, bats intermittently blocked the moon's glow. Kathy was worried, and at the same time couldn't help but be in awe of the beauty surrounding her. She discovered that when she wanted to, she could even see the microscopic organisms crowding the air. But as they emerged from the thicket of trees, all her attention was sucked in one direction.

Near the water, at a clearing ahead, it was as bright as an amusement park, there were so many phosphorescent forms illuminated by a large fire.

"Ah," Julien breathed softly, the sound of a ghostly wind rustling the reeds. "Would that our numbers were greater."

Chapter 32

DAVID HAD HIRED A BOAT AND ARRIVED ON FIRE ISLAND JUST after midnight. The density of the air and the scent on the currents, the energy, the tense re-formation of negative ions, all convinced him that he was far from alone. He knew she had been tracking him, so hiding was pointless; he would simply get close enough then to do what he had come to do.

Even before he reached the house, five of them approached. It amused him that she felt he was dangerous enough to send so many. They looked frightened; they must have found Reesone.

Without touching him, they escorted David farther east through the trees and then north. Across the water he could see Long Island.

Ariel waited in a clearing. The crisp fall breeze blew her loose-fitting clothing around her body. She stood with hands on hips, the ocean behind her billowing. To her right was the last likeness she had sculpted of David decades before, the only one she finished. She smiled at him, and he stopped a yard in front of her, the five keeping a healthy distance from him.

"David!" she said softly. And then with a change of tone, like a mother reprimanding a child, "You *are* foolish. You could have stayed safely in Austria with the little mistress I gave you, fucking her brains out, which wouldn't take long. And yet, here you are. I'll never understand you."

"I hadn't noticed that you ever tried." Behind him, he sensed others join the ones who had brought him here.

She smiled to one side of her face and dropped a hand to her thigh, then took a few steps toward him, moving sensuously, her hips swaying one way, her breasts the other. She reached out to stroke his scarred cheek but he pulled back.

"I came here to extinguish you, Ariel."

She laughed. "How dramatic poets are. Of course you did. But the night is still young, or at least not old yet. There's plenty of time to decide who extinguishes whom. Sit. Relax." She dropped to the sand and sat cross-legged. Ghost crabs scuttled away.

Immediately he was surrounded. He looked at the males briefly. There were too many and he'd have to wait for the best opportunity; he sensed he would get only one chance. He sat and they moved back a little.

"Where's Reesone?"

She smiled. "You and I are a lot alike, David. We're not typical predators. We have no interest in taking the weak, only the strong. The challenge."

"You found him, didn't you? And left him there."

She shrugged. "You've always been too sensitive. It's survival of the fittest, in our world or any other. You were fitter than Donald, you deserved to survive. He didn't."

"A neat philosophy you've developed. Not hampered by loyalty, kindness, compassion, or humor. It must be a simple world to you, using mortals and immortals alike to suit your whims. Doesn't it ever get lonely?"

She pulled at a thread on her skirt, bending forward a little so that the swell of smooth, full breasts was visible.

Then she looked up at him through pale lashes, those lighter-than-light eyes, colorless as quartz. "Yes, I get lonely," she sighed softly, tilting her head seductively, the saffron hair curling and sparking against one shoulder the same way Kathy's did, and David was amazed. "I've missed you," she said, her voice like wind chimes.

Now it was David's turn to laugh. "How can you miss what you've never had?"

She jerked up angrily. But then she smiled suddenly. "Remember this?" She gestured at the plaster sculpture.

He examined his likeness, shocked to realize that the genitalia were missing. Had it always been like that? Were all the forms she had made of him emasculated?

"Many primitive cultures believe that a photograph steals the soul. The ancient Greeks thought that when a sculpture is made, the model's essence is captured within. What do you think?"

"Were you always like this, Ariel? Was I blind?"

"Not blind, David, in love. Remember our love? I still love you."

He shook his head. "When you say love, you mean power."

"Power and love are intertwined. Look around. These and many others, all loyal to me, all in love with me, as is your little mistress. You haven't brought her over yet, have you? You've been worried—can she love you as much as she loves me? I can give you more than she's capable of. And I know you still want me. We're like Arctic wolves, mated for eternity. That's really why you're here, isn't it?"

He was furious. Arctic wolves? More like a black widow who devours her mate. Well, he was tired of being devoured by Ariel. He didn't want to put up with any more of her games.

Inside his boot was the silver rapier Julien had given him; he would dart behind her as he pulled it out.

But before he could even get to his feet, as if reading his thoughts, Ariel shouted, "Take him!"

It was a brief struggle; he was acutely aware of being outnumbered. Even though they were novices, they soon had him sprawled on his back, locked to the earth.

One minute he was staring at the clear sky streaked with stars, and the next, Ariel's face hovered above. She smiled her inscrutable smile. "Keep his head still," she ordered. "Pry his mouth open. Hold his nose."

He struggled again, but within seconds she had opened her wrist. Cool blood trickled into his mouth. He choked, struggling not to swallow it. But he had to swallow, or suffocate. And as always, blood was its own reward.

"There," she said moments later, caressing his face like a mother feeding a child. "You've always longed for that, haven't you, my pet?" She looked insane to him, and he wondered why he had never seen that before. "The last step. Now the three of us are bound to one another. But we still have time before she arrives."

She? He hoped the reference was not to Kathy. But even as he wondered, he tuned in and knew that she was no longer in Austria.

Ariel undressed first him, and then herself, slowly, sensually. He closed his eyes but that did not stop her from touching him. The touch was a distant memory that grew more immediate. His body reacted against his will, and he hated himself for responding.

She worked her mouth over him, and when he firmed, slid on top, pulling, squeezing, tightening her muscles around him until he gasped for air. "You love me, David, only me," she chanted again and again, the sound becoming like water rushing over rocks downriver, to merge with the sea. And he was terrified, wondering what kind of monster she had become.

She seemed to yank the fluid from his body, forcing him to cry out. And in that split second when he was most vulnerable, when his hatred for her blazed, he made an irreversible mistake.

He looked into Ariel's eyes.

White gusts of snow swirled inward, dragging him out of himself. Sucking him down into a frigid, colorless sea of frozen corpses.

"David!" Kathy screamed. She started toward him, but Julien grabbed her arm.

"Wait," he told her. To the others he spoke quickly, like

a military leader commanding troops. "Wing, Morianna, André, Karl, Gertig, Kaellie, block the strongest. Two each. When they are in position," he told the others, "block the rest."

Sixteen of Ariel's group had formed into a circle, and Kathy watched the six Julien had dispatched move inside, positioning themselves so that they were stationed at two, four, six, eight, ten, and twelve o'clock. Then Gerlinde, Carol, Jeanette, and Chloe went inside the circle too and stood before the remaining four. Even though they were outnumbered, Kathy could see that Julien's strategy evened things out a bit.

"Follow me closely and bring the children," Julien instructed his daughter. Immediately the girl, who looked frightened, and Julien's son took hold of the two boys and led them into the circle behind Julien.

Kathy followed.

Ariel stood in the center with her arms folded across her chest, as still as the statue next to her. David sat on the ground, naked, head bent in a submissive gesture.

Between the two of them a bonfire blazed; black smoke curled up into the night air like dark phantoms. Kathy stared at David. He seemed to have had all the wind knocked out of him. He looked deflated, shrunken.

"David!" Kathy yelled again, and this time Julien let her go. She fell on her knees in front of him, gripping his shoulders in her hands. His face was pale, his eyes vacant. He didn't seem to recognize her. "What'd you do to him?" she demanded, but Ariel laughed.

"Nothing that he did not thoroughly enjoy, believe me." The vampiress looked at Julien, as if reading his thoughts. "No longer one chain, but two—good and evil? Which chain will prove to have the stronger links, I wonder. Who will gain power and who lose it?"

"It is you who have selected this game of power," Julien replied. "However, the rules are our prerogative, and we choose not to play by yours."

She laughed. "But you are. All of you." Ariel spun in a circle, arms stretched wide like a girl showing off a new dress. Abruptly she stopped and looked down at David and Kathy. "How pathetic."

"And you're a bitch!" Kathy went for Ariel, but the vampiress was far faster. And clever. Kathy stopped suddenly a foot from Ariel. It was as if she had slammed into a stone wall. A brittle voice inside her head silenced her. And then her body collapsed and fell limply to the ground. She slammed her head on a large rock, nearly losing consciousness.

Ariel turned back to Julien. "Between him and me. One wins, one loses. One chain is strengthened, one weakened." She glanced at Michel, who sat with the other children. "And to the victor the spoils. Or do you find your warrior wanting?"

Both André and Carol, from their positions inside the circle, turned abruptly. Their faces showed fear. Julien motioned slightly and they turned back.

Then he looked at David for a long time. Kathy was afraid to hear what Julien would say. David looked awful. He didn't seem to know what was going on. As she crawled to him she heard Julien answer, "As you wish." Ariel laughed again, the sound like glass shattering.

Kathy took David's face in her hands, searching his eyes, but he was so far away, too far to reach. She glanced around at the luminous figures, white lights with slivers of primary colors spliced in, positioned like the stones of an ancient religious monument. Michel, the other boy, and the two older children sat contained within, Julien protecting them. Now just the four were in the center—Ariel, Kathy, David, and the sexless effigy.

Suddenly from between the trees a strong light emerged. Kathy watched him stalk confidently into the circle and right up to Julien. It was the one named Tony, who had been with Ariel in Montreal. There was something about him; he glowed as brightly and as severely as Julien, yet Kathy felt that besides being powerful and old, he was also very sinister.

The balance had shifted, and she felt despair. Somehow Tony being here made her feel as though they would lose.

"David!" Ariel called softly. He looked up at her like a pet automatically responding to its master's voice. "You have a weapon. Show us."

Mechanically he reached under his legs and pulled out the short, narrow sword. The honed metal glinted from the light of the flames. He held it out to her in both hands, like an offering.

Ariel got behind him, so that Kathy was looking at both of them. "You can tell him now," Ariel said. Kathy wondered, Tell him what? But Ariel's eyes had become white whirling disks that seemed to be transmitting important messages, and suddenly Kathy found herself giggling insanely.

"Yeah, I tried to kill you, remember, David? I was having a lotta fun without you, fucking around, doing dynamite dope. But you just can't believe that, can you, because you think you know everything. Didya know I fucked my old man? And that he was a better lay than you ever were? And Bobby was *my* kid?"

Her body jerked. She was startled at what she had said, and wondered what made her say such things. But there was a stark reality to the words that she felt in her bones. If Ariel controlled what she said, maybe Ariel could control what she was thinking too. But Kathy knew that couldn't be or she wouldn't be wondering how Ariel was controlling David. But there has to be something she's doing, Kathy thought. We're from the same family, so I oughta be able to figure her out. Maybe . . . But she never finished the thought.

David stared at her, looking wounded, and she opened her mouth, struggling to say, This's crazy. She's making me say this stuff. But what came out was, "I lied, David. Right from the start. I never loved you. It's Ariel I love. I hate you. I just want you dead."

He looked crushed. She searched his dull hazel eyes, silently pleading for him to understand, to recognize the truth.

But even as she did, she felt herself reaching out for the sword. David's hand tightened on the handle. And then something drifted through the air, a haunting sound like the cry of a solitary loon on a dark night. It caused the hairs on her neck to prickle.

"Daaa-viid. Killlll hheerrr!"

Kathy watched in horror as he raised the sword. His face was a mask, etched with confusion and impotent fury.

Before she could move to defend herself, he grabbed her by the hair and Ariel moved behind, pinning her arms back.

The throat was slender and white, so exposed. He held the glinting, magical silver in a line with the hollow, a spot he had a vague memory of worshiping with his lips. Now he just wanted to obliterate all trace of it. Except for the blood.

"Kill her," the wind howled.

A voice in his head screamed, but his body seemed no longer under his command. I'm lost, he thought. Confused about something. I should wait, until I'm certain. But the rapier moved forward, the tip destined for the glowing skin. He could see the artery pulsing. The putrid stench of terror reached his nostrils, but it was as though his mind was clogged by something thick, like quicksand, and the thoughts struggling to work their way through never materialized in action. Only the sound, a command from the elements, got through, a direct link that he had no hope of circumventing.

The face before him was tortured. He could see it, feel it, but he could not make the emotional connection. Behind was another face, and he was shocked by the resemblance: twin goddesses, one affirming, one devouring, with no way to tell them apart. He felt hysteria welling, and battling it down absorbed all his strength. The one behind sparkled, the face of a victor radiating confidence and power. And the other? Yes, he thought, I'll compare them. But even as the thought reached his awareness, he was distracted, mesmerized by the colors. One had blue eyes, but were they the blue of a summer's sky or the bottomless ocean that was drowning him? And the other's eyes, they were white, airy, like clouds, dreams. Or a snowstorm intent on burying him in a coldly silent grave. Their eyes meant nothing to him, although he knew he should remember which color belonged to whom. But . . .

He heard a sound and glanced around the circle. His gaze drifted to Michel, who stared back, trusting but frightened.

All of his friends were here. They had come to help, but how could that be? In some way they were counting on him, and if he failed, it would affect them all. It would affect everything. But he had no idea what he was expected to do.

Julien was the only one whose face David managed to linger on. The old one's features were strong, tense, set. And then David saw the one opposite Julien. Malignant energy. The demon who had forced the change on him. Raped him in an alley and left him struggling to survive. David trembled remembering his helplessness, the brutality. This can't be happening, he thought. All of us here? I must be dreaming.

"I said, Kill her!"

His attention catapulted back to the two females. The voice, and he now understood that it was a voice, focused him again. In horror he watched his hand move forward, the blade just piercing the skin. A thin line of red fire trickled down the white alabaster and he wanted to scream. Instead, fascinated, he watched the color being absorbed by the fabric of the raven dress. The scent of copper and honey swirled up his nostrils, filling him with lust. The idea of restraint never occurred to him.

He snatched her by the throat and yanked her to him. Her wound opened wide to his lips. As he sucked at the fire, the anticoagulant in his saliva kept the hot blood flowing. He gulped down what was rightfully his.

She was warm, trembling, the salty taste of her making him greedy for more, and he pulled harder, struggling to get the liquid in faster. But the pulsing soon weakened and the flow became unbearably sluggish. Only an artery would give him the intensity he craved.

Reluctantly he pulled away to reposition her. Movement caught his eye. Her lips were parted yet no sound emerged. Where had he seen that before? But something else was happening. Hot liquid sprang from the blue pools. A primal memory surfaced; these silent tears had touched him once. Drops splashed onto his arm, one, two, burning his skin, scorching the muscle beneath it. He felt the wet penetrate his bone. The fragility of such pain startled him, ripping away some of the thick barrier between predator and prey.

"Cut off her head, or I will!"

The voice grated, jarring him. The screech of a vulture. The wail of hopelessness. He felt driven to silence it.

The blade bypassed one throat. He watched the sword lunge toward the other's. For a moment she looked shocked. Her hands clamped around his wrist to prevent him from slicing across her esophagus and severing her spine.

He shoved the one in front aside and grabbed the one behind by the hair. An elemental moan seemed to come from the earth itself. Fear stripped him to the bone, the fear of isolation. Of disconnection.

The pale eyes opened wide, round white balls of crystal-line snow. "You can't do it, David. You love me. Only me." She released his arm to caress his face. "You'd die with-out me."

He hesitated. Her fingertips sent strong promises of nexus that he could not ignore.

She seemed to sense the crippling effect she was having on him and laughed. "You don't have the balls, my love. You never did."

He felt himself slipping away again. He fought to hold on to a fragile, rapidly disintegrating reality.

Suddenly there was a crash. Something contacted hard-packed sand. He heard a scream.

Words reverberated through him. "Yes he does!" He glanced right and saw Kathy, her clothing blood-soaked, pounding the effigy with a rock. Her flesh was ghost-white; she was near death, yet somehow managed to knock the head off and was now trying to split the statue up the mid-dle. With each blow he felt his will vibrate.

Ariel leaped for her. Kathy spun around, terror creasing her pale face. Ariel sank her teeth in deep, tearing away flesh, and sucked hard. He saw Kathy's chest convulse—her weakened heart could pump no more blood.

Ariel's lifeless, colorless eyes swirled to infinity. Finally he understood. And with the understanding came the clarity to act.

As Ariel grabbed Kathy's head in one hand and her shoulder in another, about to rip her head from her body, David sprang. Ariel's face reflected a chilling horror: the pity and the love that, in those moments, he felt for her. A love strong enough to free all of them.

He yanked back Ariel's head and dragged the blade across her throat, cutting into the windpipe. She struggled, floundered, a bird caught in a whirlpool, gasping for air. Her eyes were wild. And then one snowy-pink tear appeared at the corner of one eye. It stopped him from finishing what he knew he had to do. Mesmerized, he watched the drop trickle down her fine cheek, and secretly he prayed the Fates could be persuaded to alter this path. The water landed on his skin, near the spot the other tears had touched him. But Ariel released dry ice and it froze him to the marrow.

With a quick, decisive movement David sliced cleanly through, decapitating her.

A cry pierced the air, which chilled him—it came from his own lips. The sound of a piece of his heart being torn away forever.

Chapter 33

THE NEXT MOMENTS WERE CONFUSING. MANY WHO HAD BEEN loyal to Ariel fled. Six remained, looking defeated yet relieved of a burden.

David gathered Kathy's heavy body into his arms. At the same time he was cut by the loss of Ariel and cried uncontrollably. André and Karl got to him first.

"Finish her, *mon ami*. You have got to do it now!"

David bent to Kathy's throat. Her wound tasted of Ariel and he sobbed.

"Do it or you'll lose her," Karl said.

David knew it was true. If Ariel was the last to drink, his connection with Kathy would always be tainted. He repierced the wound and pulled in all the remaining blood. He felt the life begin to leave her body and then stop, as though it had met a wall of resistance.

He held her inert body close, rocking her. Knowing she would revive was all that kept him glued together at this moment.

An argument had developed. Wing and Morianna had joined Julien. They faced the one who had taken David, Karl, Chloe, and perhaps others. Perhaps Ariel.

"What's he saying?" Carol asked André.

"I'm not sure. The French is archaic, from the Middle Ages, or earlier. Chloe, you're better at translating from that period. Julien knows him. Called him Antoine."

"Tony!" David said. He looked at Karl and Chloe. Both wore shocked expressions.

"He says Ariel deserved to die," Chloe managed. "Because she was weak. Now he's insulting us. Calling us his bastard children, timid, deformed. He's ranting, claiming he made a mistake, honoring us with the change. He should have destroyed us outright. Not one is worthy."

"He must have loved Ariel," David commented. He stared at this being who was responsible for his existence. The night he'd been taken, David had seen this one as impossibly strong, ferocious, invincible. Now he looked old, worn-out, insane. And weighted by a powerful loneliness that David realized, by comparison, he had only briefly tasted.

"He wants her body," Chloe continued.

"Does he think we're stupid?" David lay Kathy carefully on the ground and grabbed the rapier. With energetic chops he began severing Ariel's corpse. Karl and André threw the limbs onto the fire, then the torso. A horrible stench of burning flesh filled the air, but they did not stop until all of her was ablaze.

Antoine, blocked by three as old and strong as he, could do nothing. He seemed locked in helpless fury. But suddenly he focused on the group near the fire. His face distorted into that of a menacing gargoyle. He screamed something then vanished into the night, becoming one with the shifting shadows.

"What did he say?" David asked.

"It's an old French curse," Chloe said, her hands trembling. "The essence is, beware of your shadow. He's threatening all of us. This is not over."

Julien, Morianna, and Wing joined the others, and suddenly everyone fell silent. "It is an important moment," Morianna said softly. "The death of one so old must be felt by all."

David found himself overcome with grief and at the same

time released, as if a weight had been lifted from his shoulders, a deadly worm plucked from his heart. While the flames reduced her body to ashes, he could almost hear Ariel's spirit sighing, departing, as his own soul returned to earth and took root again in his body. He held Kathy, feeling her close to him in so many ways.

He knew that if it hadn't been for Ariel, he and Kathy would not have met. And he would not have been reunited with his friends. But it was more than that. Within him he felt the dark and light merge. Suddenly he understood that both he and Kathy owed Ariel something. In the mysterious predawn, when all living things resort to primitive instincts and humble themselves before the awesome powers of the unknown, he let Byron speak:

> "And she was lost—and yet I breathed,
> But not the breath of human life:
> A serpent round my heart was wreathed,
> And stung my every thought to strife.
>
> . . .
>
> "I loved her, Friar! nay, adored—
> But these are words that all can use—
> I proved it more in deed than word;
> There's blood upon that dinted sword,
> A stain its steel can never lose . . .
>
> ". . . Love indeed is light from heaven;
> A spark of that immortal fire
> With angels shared, by Alla given,
> To lift from earth our low desire. . . ."

Chapter 34

"OHMAGOD!" KATHY SCREAMED. HER BODY JACKKNIFED and she puked again. Gerlinde steadied her on one side and Carol on the other. "I thought vampires never get sick," she gasped.

Gerlinde laughed. "Yeah, well, this is the part they leave out of the manual."

David stuck his head in the bathroom. "How is she doing?"

"Not bad," Carol said. "She's near the end of it."

Kathy looked at him through the tears that leaked over the rims of her eyes. He was a shimmering, blurred light. She attempted a smile but never quite made it.

"I'm okay," she managed.

Carol handed her a glass of water to rinse out her mouth, and Gerlinde turned on the shower, adjusting the knobs and rechecking until she was satisfied with the temperature.

"Hop in, kiddo. It'll feel great."

She stepped under the warm spray and pulled the curtain. To her intensified senses, the water was the roar of a waterfall, a million tiny, blunt needles jabbing into her pores. She closed her eyes and leaned her head back, letting the water slide down each strand of hair, feeling each liquid molecule cool and refresh her. She inhaled metal and earth. It was as though she could see through her eyelids.

Two hours ago David had woken her to a new life. She had been disoriented, confused, frightened. But quickly pain intruded, spiking through her body so that she thought she was dying all over again. He reassured her, as did the others, that it would pass. But she hadn't been convinced. Until she stopped throwing up. Now, finally, she was coming out the other end—it was worse than bad dope.

And she did not feel dead—far from it. The major changes so far were heightened sensations and longer incisors. She could handle that.

After the shower, the women helped her into a dress of Gerlinde's, black new-wavish with asymmetrical splashes of brilliant red, yellow, and blue fabric paint forming no distinguishable pattern. She was handed a silver goblet. Inside, liquid rubies sparkled. She looked up. "It ain't blood?"

"O positive," the redhead joked. At least Kathy hoped it was a joke.

"Is it from an animal?" she also hoped.

"Don't worry, kiddo. I brought a snack from home. We own a pharmaceutical lab and buy stuff from blood banks, supposedly for research. We get a deal every once in a while when some bank decides to ditch stock that's contaminated, like with the HIV virus or hepatitis."

Kathy stared at the goblet. "You mean this stuff's got germs in it and you want me to drink it?" But even as she said that, making a face to emphasize her disgust, the mineral-rich scent wafted a path through the air, up her nostrils and down her throat; her stomach contracted violently, but this time with hunger.

"We're immune to both bacterial infections and viral invasions," Carol told her.

It wasn't the information, but almost uncontrollable lust that convinced her to sip the thick, slightly salty contents. She was surprised by the rich taste. Up until tonight, meat had to be almost burnt before she'd touch it. Now she just wanted the blood.

The crimson meal passed smoothly over her tongue and

down her throat and quieted a need she had been unaware of. And as her hunger became sated, energy surged.

Besides Carol and Gerlinde, and David just outside the door, she could see André, Karl, and the one named Julien in the next room, all of them what she would have so recently called vampires. Each blazed like an animated form of shimmering light, almost translucent, yet solid, so that they had shape and vivid color. Their eyes were so alive, like entities of dancing movement. Every gesture she saw thrilled her; they reminded her of a ballet she'd seen on TV, but better—exquisite, breathtaking, graceful. Magical.

David turned to speak to Chloe, whose white hair was blinding. Kathy caught her breath watching them. All that she loved about David crystallized. He was the most magnificent being she'd ever seen, like a wild stallion from a mythical realm, a glittering golden angel. When he turned again and glided toward the bathroom, even before he reached her she hurled herself into his arms, feeling his firm yet vaporous lips pressing onto, almost melding with, hers. His strong arms enveloped her with warmth and love and light, and she sighed, then sighed again.

"Welcome." He smiled, and that smile almost choked her up with its joy and brilliance.

He led her to a small room close by. This was Ariel's house. How she knew that, she wasn't certain. Yet when she focused, she realized that everything here was as David had described it. Nothing had changed in decades. And now, with Ariel gone, it would be this way forever.

"You still feel her inside, don't you?" he said.

"Some. Not a lot."

"Come here." He opened his arms.

They lay entwined on the bed where he and Ariel had once slept and loved, and watched through the narrowly opened slats of the shutters as the night sky gave way to the encroaching dawn. She squeezed her eyes shut against the gray light. Her body felt heavy and exhausted, and her skin uncomfortably warm and sensitive. She wondered how long it would take to get used to this.

"We never get used to it," he said, as if reading her thought. "Time helps, though."

"Can you read my mind?"

"I feel what you feel."

She lay her head on his shoulder, terrified as a deathlike lethargy sank into her pores and pressed her down toward the earth. It was a death she knew she would feel every morning. But he would be here. With her. Every night. When the sun set.

"Yes," he said. "I will be with you."

But Ariel would not.

She sighed and thought of Bobby. If she could let him go, she could let Ariel go, but it would be hard. She hated Ariel as much as she loved David. But that made them both a part of her, as if they lived inside. Emotions so deep couldn't be ignored, but then, she didn't need to ignore painful things anymore.

She snuggled close to David and let this little death enfold her in its cool dark embrace.

About the Author

Nancy Kilpatrick has published two erotic horror novels (under a pseudonym). Her 60 published short stories have appeared in the anthologies *Deathsport, Freak Show, Northern Frights,* and several *Year's Best Horror* collections. She has been a finalist for a Bram Stoker Award and an Aurora Award, and last year won the Arthur Ellis Award for best mystery short story. She is considered an expert on vampires, and has one of the world's largest collections of books on the subject. She lives in Toronto and loves to hear from her readers.